PRAISE FOR
DESERT
CREATURES

"Existing at the sweet spot where *A Canticle for Leibowitz* and *Blood Meridian* meet, Chronister's *Desert Creatures* is a vivid investigation of faith, perseverance, and human violence as they exist at the end of the world. A scintillating first novel."

—**Brian Evenson**, winner of the World Fantasy and Shirley Jackson Awards

"Kay Chronister has crafted an incredible setting, pushing the wild weirdness of the Sonoran Desert toward the furthest extremes of possibility. I will never forget this uncanny world, nor brave Magdala's quest across it, contending with holy saints and hellish killers in a landscape whose every inch and inhabitant is as dangerous as they are in dire need of healing."

—**Matt Bell**, author of the *New York Times* Notable Book *Appleseed*

"If *The Canterbury Tales* was set in future Sonoran and Mojave deserts, it might look a little like this. . . . [A] strange and frightening vision."

—**Publishers Weekly**

"This genre-bending story ... culminates in a new and original species of post-apocalyptic fiction where attempts at recreating civilization are anything but civilized. Ultimately, this is a harrowing coming-of-age tale of a girl growing up in a world where not many things are allowed to grow tall and strong."

—Library Journal

"Chronister's futuristic, dog-eat-dog Sonoran and Mojave deserts are as devastating as they are inventive. ... Chronister cleverly deploys and subverts horror, dystopian, and western genres alike in this razor-sharp novel."

—Shelf Awareness, starred review

"Genre-shredding ... A story of both creation and apocalypse, where characters struggle with both belief and heresy."

—Tor.com

"Heartbreaking."

—Foreword Reviews

"[*Desert Creatures*] does for the Southwest desert what Jeff VanderMeer did for Florida's swamps and Algernon Blackwood did for the Danube. ... Unlike most post-apocalyptic works, the narrative never revels in the downfall of modernity, but scavenges in the remnants of what was and calls forth the twinned opulences of medieval Catholicism and Las Vegas as its guideposts. ... This is the book of monsters our liminal year deserves."

—Ancillary Review of Books

DESERT CREATURES

KAY CHRONISTER

Erewhon Books

an imprint of Kensington Publishing Corp.

www.erewhonbooks.com

EREWHON BOOKS are published by:

Kensington Publishing Corp.
119 West 40th Street
New York, NY 10018
www.erewhonbooks.com

Copyright © 2022 by Kay Chronister

First published in North America, Canada, and Other Territories by Erewhon Books, an imprint of Kensington Publishing Corp., in 2022.

ISBN 978-1-64566-083-5 (trade paperback)

First Erewhon trade paperback printing: November 2023

10 9 8 7 6 5 4 3 2 1

Printed in the United States of America

Library of Congress Control Number: 2022942290

Electronic edition: ISBN 978-1-64566-05405

Edited by Sarah T. Guan
Cover design by Dana Li
Interior design by Cassandra Farrin and Jenna Schwartz
Illuminated letters designed by Viengsamai Fetters
Desert mariposa lily illustration by Shutterstock / Ksenia Meteleva
Author photograph by Caroline King

DESERT CREATURES

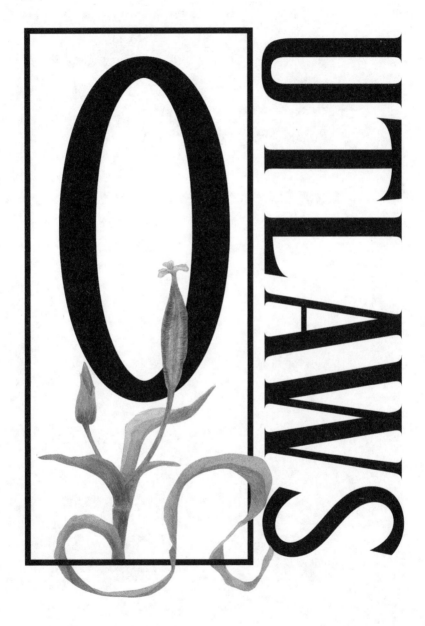

THE FIRE CAME AT NIGHT, a flash of gasoline scent and shattered glass, then a column of flame that swept across the floor. As the room burned, Magdala followed her father, Xavier, out the window. When she was still a few feet from the ground, she crumpled into his arms. Xavier steadied her on her feet, looped her arm around his back and set her clubbed right foot atop his left one. And then they were gone. They ran for hours, for miles. From a distance, they might have been one two-headed creature.

When the light on the cliffs became soft and blue-yellow, he stopped them at a thicket of creosote bush. "Rest your feet a little," he said. Magdala laid down in the shadow of the brush, then rolled onto her side to face her father. He sat with his gun propped between his knees, his back stiff, facing the horizon.

"Papa," she said to him. "Where will we go?"

He wouldn't look at her. "We'll find somewhere. We're not troublesome people. Someone will take us in," he said. Her gaze stayed on him as he stared ahead, his eyes shutting then snapping open, then shutting again. She fell asleep counting his breaths.

When she woke, the sun was high, and the cactus blooms had closed their faces. "Best be moving on," said Xavier. "We'll find water in the hills," he added, seeing her tongue fumble to coat her cracked lips.

Magdala's eyes followed his pointing finger to the cluster of rock that rose in the distance. "How far?" she asked.

Her father crouched low and motioned for her to climb onto his back. Magdala wrapped her arms around his neck and swung her feet awkwardly at his sides, brushing the barrel of his gun. With the slow, resigned gait of a pack mule, he carried her across the desert. Above them, the sun whitened with noon.

The hills yielded no clear water; the pool they found on a shelf of rock was lush and green and rank, too full of life for human consumption, even in desperate times. Xavier counted back the days since he'd last heard thunder and guessed more than a month had elapsed since it had rained.

Midafternoon, when their mouths were stuck shut and their hopes running thin, they came suddenly to a forest of cactus arms wrapped around each other: thin and sinewy and curling from the trunk of a limbless human form in a dust-crusted denim shirt. Rising from the arms were red flowers with wide yellow stamens. Some were young and thin, but others looked mature, even near-rotting, and from these hung heavy, knuckle-shaped fruits.

Even from a distance, the smell of the vegetation was bright, rusty, palpable. Magdala's mouth tried to water; half-consciously, she strained closer. Someone or something had already torn one fruit loose from the cactus, then tried to eat another straight from the vine and left it unfinished, pulpy white-green tendrils hanging from the dense wadded ball of the fruit's center.

Xavier crossed himself, regarded the human form in the center of the vegetation with revulsion. "Never seen one still rooted," he murmured.

"What is it?" said Magdala.

"Used to be a man. He died and the desert got inside him."

She was silent, considering this. Then she whispered, "Can I have some?"

Xavier was almost horrified. "Be like cannibalism," he said. "Wouldn't it?" He seemed not to know the answer.

Magdala fidgeted away from the question. "I'm so thirsty," she said, her eyes on the fruit.

"Listen, we can dig for water here. He's blooming, there might be moisture underground," said Xavier. But his digging yielded nothing; the earth was parched. At sunset, he relented and they gorged themselves. The scent and taste of the fruit made Magdala gag, but she ate until her belly swelled. Afterwards, Xavier insisted that they walk away backwards.

In the dark of night, she woke trembling and sick, her stomach reeling and her vision blurred. In spite of her shivering and weakness, she wanted to walk, to walk and walk and never cease. Unsteadily she rose to her feet. Xavier was still sleeping, his gun beside him. The full moon throbbed before her eyes as she climbed the hillside, the track of her rubber sandal distinct beside the long divot left when she dragged her clubfoot.

She walked through the night without direction or purpose, borne on by a kind of hunger which she felt not in her stomach but in the heartbeat that galloped beneath her ribs. When her father caught her, she saw him as if through a veil. He was distant, hardly real. She could hear him saying her name, but somehow his cries did not really reach her. She woke only when he slapped her cheek, and then the hunger faded but somewhere down deep, she could feel the sickness stayed.

"Should never have let you eat that," Xavier said, crouching before her. Her stomach twisted as she tried to focus her gaze on him. His eyes were wet. Magdala wrapped her arms around his neck and buried her head in his shoulder, as much to console him as to console herself. She thought she had never seen tears in her father's eyes before.

"I'm sorry," she whispered, and he drew back.

"It's not your fault," he said. "None of it. Understand?"

But it *was* her fault: not only the sleepwalking but the rest, the fire from underneath the door and the flight into the desert and the desperate, stupefying thirst. He didn't know.

They had gone two days in the desert when they saw from afar the glistening mass of the town, a low, flat sea of glass and brick and corrugated tin. "Could be uninhabited," Xavier warned. But neither of them could resist hope. Magdala was still sickly, and afraid to close her eyes in the desert for fear that the hunger to walk would come back. As they made for the road, they passed another of the many-tendriled creatures that was once-man-but-now-cactus, and Xavier refused even to slow his pace.

Late at night, he killed a gopher snake. They cooked the animal in the coals of their fire and shared it, sucking the moisture thirstily from the charred meat. Magdala knew as she ate that the snake meat would not stay down, that her stomach was hungry for something else now, but she held her breath and held her belly until her father fell asleep, and only then surrendered her meal back into the buffel grass, retching until she was breathless and weak.

In the end, she had to be carried the rest of the way to the barbed wire barrier that surrounded the cluster of flat buildings. There Xavier stopped, set Magdala on her feet and paced the fence line with the restlessness of a caged predator. Through heavy-lidded eyes, Magdala saw a man wearing leather chaps and a Stetson approach them from the other side. She did not see the gun he was carrying before he lifted it to his shoulder and aimed at her father.

"Weapons down and hands up," the man said. "You and your girl."

The words broke faintly through her confusion, and she understood their meaning but not what they demanded of her. Only when she saw Xavier's hands lifted, his gun lying on the dirt beside him, did she lift her own palms to the wind.

"My daughter's sick," her father said. "We've been traveling. Looking for shelter. If you could just let us in for a single night—"

"She eat raw desert fruit?" the man said abruptly.

"We both did."

The man nodded. "Not everyone gets sick," he said. "And you can cure it. But we're not some pilgrim stopover. We don't take visitors."

Xavier's eyes moved from her to the man and back again. "What do we have to do to get inside?" he asked.

The man's chaps rustled like they were a living thing as he shifted. "I guess I can bring you to Oscar," he said. "He'll tell you if you're fit. Come around, now. We've got a gate; we're civilized people."

Xavier crouched so Magdala could climb onto his shoulders, and they trudged the half mile to the gate, an assemblage of garage doors on pulleys the man yanked to admit them. As they got closer to him, passing through the shade of the elaborate structure, Magdala could see the outline of a wolf stenciled faintly on his pale neck.

"This is Caput Lupinum," the man said as he led them down the gentle slope into town. "Was a ghost town for a long while before we settled in. Infested with everything nasty you can imagine. We've been making progress with it."

Magdala regarded their surroundings with dizzied wonder. The tenement where they'd lived before stuck out of the desert like a single finger of civilization, every man-made thing around it long since collapsed, and she had never seen so many buildings so close together. Enthralled by the *Savings & Loans* sign in unlit neon lettering, the buffet chili pepper mascot still grinning beatifically from a window, Magdala half-forgot her sickness. She squirmed and twisted on her father's back to see as much as she could.

Down the road a ways, the man held open the glass door of a long, flat building marked *LARDER* in spray paint. Inside, hanging aisle markers still promised the impossible: produce, eggs, meat and fish. Someone had propped the back door open with a rock, admitting a thin slice of sunlight and a heavy black cord running to an industrial fridge.

"Stay here," their escort said, disappearing through the door.

Once they were alone, Xavier set Magdala down and paced the length of the room, surveying the sacks of mesquite flour spilling over and crates of the dried desert fruits stacked like imports from another country, like things that hadn't sprouted from dead bodies. Magdala felt a hum inside her head, low and insistent, when she saw that fruit; the taste of it returned to her as real and full as if she were chewing still. But her father was more interested in the fridge. He approached it cautiously, then at once opened the door and shut his eyes and let the cold waft out in a full thick blast that tore Magdala loose from her desert-fruit pining.

"Never seen one that still works," he said.

Magdala edged up close to him, and they stood a moment bathing in the chill together. They both startled when the man came back in the door. "I should warn you, brother," he said to Xavier, "that's not exactly the sort of thing that makes Oscar likely to smile on you."

"How'd you get power out here?" her father wondered.

The man only laughed. "How long you been wandering out there?"

Xavier didn't reply. The man clucked at them like he was cueing a horse, and they stepped through the back door, sidestepping the generator that rumbled contentedly on the brickwork. Inside a cloud of smoke sat a lean man, his skin the same copper-brown as her father's, his hair shaggy beneath his white Stetson. A hand-rolled cigarette hung from one side of his mouth, and a revolver sat in his lap.

"Oscar," their escort said by way of introduction. "He's the one in charge here." He disappeared back into the larder.

"So you're the trespassers," Oscar said, smiling around his cigarette. "Come on, pull up a chair." He nodded to the stack of folding lawn chairs in the corner. "For the girl, too."

They were all like men from a campfire story, Magdala thought. Their hats and their chaps and their dusty, drawling way of speaking. They could have been actors in one of the theater troupes that had come occasionally past the tenement and performed spectacular dramas full of fake gunfire and weeping, golden-haired women. Her head still cloudy, her stare lingered long on the man, and he regarded her with something between disgust and amusement.

"How'd you end up here?" he asked Xavier. "Someone tell you about us on the road? Give you direction?"

"No one told us. We just saw you from a distance. First settlement in miles," Xavier said. "Didn't know anything of you, just hoping for someplace with a well and a roof."

"We aren't looking to be a roadside motel," said Oscar. "You're miserable-looking enough that I can't but believe you were hard up and desperate. Still." He exhaled a puff of smoke, shifted his revolver in his lap. "You taking the girl to kiss Saint Elkhanah's feet?"

"Elkhanah?" Xavier shook his head. "Never heard of it."

"You're not pilgrims?"

"Just travelers."

"Excuse the assumption. With the girl's deformity, I just figured—well, that's one mark in your favor, not caught up in the Holy Church circus. Seems like half the people who wash up here are hungering after some long-dead holy man's hair or tonsils or clavicles to cure what ails them, and not a one has the strength to even get all the way there to get grifted. But I'm straying from my purpose. What brought you out to this stretch of the Sonoran?"

Xavier glanced at Magdala. "Got evicted," he said. "I guess that's what you could call it."

"What for?"

"The neighbors were telling stories. Food gets scarce and folk get jealous, suspicious. You understand." He shrugged his shoulders. "It was time to be moving on. But we weren't expecting so many miles of nothing ahead of us."

"Nothing is all you ever oughta expect," Oscar said, laughing. "Well, we don't mind evictions here. Nor banishments, marks of Cain. You know what Caput Lupinum means?"

Xavier shook his head.

"Wolf's Head, if you want to be literal. But really, it means outlaw. All of us here got exiled from somewhere. Ran afoul of other men's laws. Here, we just have a few simple ones. And if you follow them, we don't infringe upon your freedoms. One, you gotta take out less resources than you put in. That includes you *and* your women or children." He jerked his chin at Magdala. "You're gonna have to pull her weight and your own here. You prepared to do that?"

"I didn't say we're staying," Xavier said.

"'Course you didn't," he said. "But we're not a charity. You want protection, food, you need to throw in your lot with ours. And I'll tell you now, you're not gonna find a better deal anywhere in the Remainder. I didn't tell you rule number two. So long as you're not interfering with someone else's property, no man can tell you your business. I've been around long enough to see a thousand communities spring up and then go to rot. Always, they're plagued by folk not pulling their own weight, or one man interfering in another man's business. Sift through any pile of ash between here and Vegas, and you'll see it."

"You're so well-off, what do you need me for?" Xavier asked.

"We got plenty of use for good, strong men without too many compunctions," said Oscar. "We prefer when they don't come with dependents hanging off them, but like I said, it's no trouble so long as you're prepared to feed and keep her."

"I'm not making a promise to stay here," Xavier said. "But I'll work, for some time, if that's what you require. I understand there's a debt, what with her curing."

"A canny man," Oscar said. "What do you think, girl? You want the antidote to your desert sickness?"

From the thick haze of her illness, Magdala managed to nod.

Oscar got to his feet and shook her father's hand. "You're a man of your word," he said to Xavier, and it was not a question.

Magdala's father carried her as Oscar led them to an old bank. The lobby was empty except for an enormous hole in the middle of the floor where a ladder had been propped, leading them down into a darkened vault. Magdala buried her face in her father's chest as he carried her down, her nausea rising and subsiding with the motions of his descent. When they reached the bottom, Oscar told Xavier to lay her out on one of the mattresses. "Any will do," he said. Then he called, "Alma! We got a child, desert sick. You think you can manage?"

Magdala emerged from the clammy shelter of her father's arms to find a woman standing above her with an infant strapped to her chest. The woman crouched; she pulled on Magdala's eyelids, then pressed the back of her hand to Magdala's cheek.

"She just needs to purge her system," she said to Xavier. "How much did she have?"

"Too much," Xavier confessed. "I shouldn't ever have let her."

"I understand what thirst can make you do." She left Magdala's side and returned a second later with a sweating glass of water. She lifted Magdala by the armpits onto a wad of blanket and poured a thin stream of water through her cracked lips and down her throat. "This isn't enough by itself," she said as Magdala drank. "But it'll help. You have to sleep a while."

"What's the cure for it?" Xavier asked.

"There's no cure," Alma said. "Just water, rest, and staying inside. That's it."

"That's not what Oscar said."

Alma made a sound that was like a laugh but was not one. "So I suppose he left out the part where it will always come back," she said. "Well, the rest of her life, it'll keep coming back. There's no getting rid of it. Only keeping it at bay."

When Magdala woke, her father was gone, but she was surrounded by women wearing loose, sack-like, colorless dresses, all with brands on their necks. As they crossed the room, washing their faces and gathering their hair into plaits, Magdala silently read their marks to herself: *Mateo, Robert, Oscar*.

"She's awake," whispered one woman to another, and a few of them crowded closely around her as if she were an object of wonder.

"You feeling all right, honey?" someone asked.

Magdala pushed herself up onto her elbows. "I'm better," she replied. When she got to her feet, at once two of the women moved to steady her. Their eyes fell to her club-foot, absorbed the fact of it, then moved elsewhere.

"She's just a child," sighed one of the women, as if this by itself was tragic.

"Are there other children here?" Magdala asked.

"Only Alma's baby."

"I'm the only girl?"

"Dulcinea's just fifteen," Alma said, and nodded to the youngest of the women, who was still halfway a girl with coltish limbs and eyes deep-set in her round face. She had two brands on her neck, one still distinct and the other faded so it was almost invisible on her brown skin.

"Where's my papa gone?" Magdala said.

"With the other men, eating dinner, I think." She looked to Dulcinea. "Will you take her to him?"

The girl bristled. "Why me?"

"You know why."

"It doesn't matter if I got Oscar's brand." Her voice rose, getting louder, getting higher, sounding younger with every syllable. "They don't treat me any different."

"I can go by myself," Magdala offered.

The women were silent for a minute. "I'll take you," Dulcinea said, firmly now, as if the idea had been her own.

The sun was setting when they emerged from the permanent twilight of the bank vault; Dulcinea led Magdala down the road to the larder. Outside, a long wooden table had been set and men sat crowded on a motley assemblage of chairs and benches. When Magdala saw her father, she quickened her pace and stumbled the distance to him, heedless of the eyes that followed her.

"I got better," she said to him, and his embrace was unhesitant, encompassing.

"You look better," he said, drawing back to examine her. "They take good care of you?"

Her father was filthy, she saw then. His arms and face were paled by the dust that stuck to every inch of him, his eyes stark and wild-looking in his face, his hair stiff and sheened over. And he had a raised welt on his neck, bright and angry-looking, in the shape of a wolf.

"Papa, why do you have that?" she asked, reaching out to brush the brand with her fingertips.

Xavier glanced at the other men, then back to her. "Part of the deal," he said. He swallowed hard, with forced lightness said, "You get one too."

"Do I have to?"

"Seems that way."

"Why?"

Her father lifted her into his lap. When he spoke, his voice was low and tender. "You remember when you were just six years old and you got that gash all down your leg from playing in the junkyard?"

"I remember."

"And you remember how it started to get infected, and every day I made you wash it with alcohol, in spite of how you cried and how it hurt, to keep it from making you sicker?"

She nodded.

"It's gonna be almost like that. Pain, but it'll protect you."

"Why will it protect me?"

"Because it tells people that you're my child, and that you're under my protection, so I don't have to watch you every moment while we're here."

Magdala narrowed her eyes, watching his face. "I don't want it to hurt," she said. She felt the swelling in her throat that presaged tears and remembered suddenly the strangers all around them. Embarrassed, almost angry, she buried her head in Xavier's chest and inhaled her father's familiar odor, laced now with the foreign smell of jimson smoke.

"It'll be all right," Xavier said to her. He didn't say that she wouldn't have to do it. As the sky darkened, he pushed his chair back from the long table, leaving his food half-eaten. They trudged down the road together until they came to a sagging pink bungalow, where her father held the screen door open and Magdala stepped inside to find herself in a filthy kitchen lit by a pair of kerosene lanterns. Across from them, a hulking man knelt low before a gas oven, contemplating the heat that flared low in its belly. Seeing them, he reached for an iron from the stovetop. Magdala shrank away.

"Hold my hand," Xavier said. "It's X-A-V-I-E-R," he informed the man at the oven.

"She's gotta get on the floor," the man said, without looking at them.

"No need for that. I didn't," Xavier said.

"Don't trust her not to squirm. All the women do."

Xavier looked down at her. "Magdala, can you do what the man says?"

Slowly, Magdala lowered herself to her belly. A lizard skittered across the room and into a hole in the wall, and her eyes followed the creature as the man with the branding iron approached her. When he came close, she flinched.

"Hold her down," the man said to Xavier. "If she moves, it'll be worse."

"Magdala, hold still for the man, all right?" Her father's hand moved hesitantly to the small of her back and Magdala startled, hunching up her shoulders as if to hide her neck from the brand's hot, hungry reach.

"Get her to stick her neck out," the man said.

Obligingly her father pressed harder, his other hand grasping the back of her head. Magdala, determined, shut her eyes and clenched her teeth and ground her face into the rotting vinyl floor. The branding iron was lowered, singed through dirt and flesh and hair, did its work and then was lifted.

"Not so bad, was it?" Xavier said.

Magdala saw the hopefulness on his face and made herself nod her head, swallow the lump in her throat.

"You did good," her father told her.

She nodded again.

As they left the pink house, he explained that they had a rule in Caput Lupinum. "You have to bed with the women," he said. "But you'll be all right. Have a nicer time with them than you'd have with me."

"I want to stay with you," said Magdala.

"It's for a few days," Xavier said. "Only a few days. I just gotta work off the debt we owe them and then we're out of here."

She wanted to believe him, but she was afraid he didn't mean it. In the tenement, he was always saying he'd be gone for a few minutes, a few hours. "Things'll change in a few weeks," he'd say. It was a way of not saying anything. "If it's only a few days, then how come I had to get branded?" she asked.

"Magdala, listen to me." Her father crouched low so his face was level with her shoulders. "We will find a better home. We will not stay here. It's just what we gotta do for now. That man, Oscar, he showed me a map. There's nothing for miles around here. We didn't make it two days in the desert. Not twenty miles. If we wanted to make for the pilgrim highway he mentioned, the main road, the big one, the one where we'd have any hopes of finding a scrap of civilization, we'd have to make it almost fifty. Now, you and I aren't ready to do that. Are we?"

Looking him in the eye, she thought she could see that he was afraid. "No," she said reluctantly.

"So we need to stay here a little while. Shore up our strength. Make our plans. All right?"

She understood that he was not really asking her. "Yes," she said, just the same.

"Tell me you'll be brave," he said.

"I'll be brave," she repeated, and she meant it. She did not want to be troublesome to him. She did not want to see fear in his eyes again.

But when she descended into the bank vault and saw the bed that had been made up for her, she thought inescapably of her old bed in the tenement: of the ragged scrap of blanket that she'd held close to her face as she slept since she was too young to remember; of the blue dress she used to cover herself, which her father said had belonged to the mother she'd never met. And she thought how those things probably had all burnt now, and how stupid she had been to believe the tenement was worse than anywhere else they might end up. She stood at the bottom of the ladder and cried silently, angrily, until Alma handed her baby to one of the other women and came and collected her.

"The pain will fade," she said with her arms around Magdala. "Come here, sit down. I want to show you something."

Magdala climbed up into Alma's hammock and sat wiping the tears from her eyes as Alma took up Rosy and handed the baby into Magdala's lap. The baby's eyes were wide and dark and alert. She reached toward the fresh brand on Magdala's neck with her small brown fist, and when her fingers brushed it, the pain dissipated.

"Is that her?" Magdala said, taken aback.

"It is."

"How is she doing it?" As long as the baby's hand stayed on her, the pain of the brand was muted, almost vanished.

"She's saint-touched."

Magdala shook her head uncomprehendingly.

"Haven't you ever met anyone born saint-touched?"

"No."

"Well," said Alma, "the Church doesn't *officially* recognize it. But ask anyone in the Remainder and they'll have a story of their cousin who was canny about the weather or their neighbor who could always hit a mark. That's the saints, interceding for us all through their chosen ones."

"Oh," said Magdala, reappraising Rosy's puffy cheeks, her spit up–stained nightgown.

"When Rosy was in the womb, I prayed every night to Saint Rosalinda the Comforter. I never imagined she'd answer me like this. Of course, you never can expect it, or wish for it, or they won't give it to you."

"Is she nice?" Magdala said. "Saint Rosalinda, I mean."

Alma looked amused by the question. "Lie down with Rosy," she said. "I'll tell you her story."

Magdala looked back toward the ladder. Then, slowly, she laid down in the hammock with her forehead pressed to the baby's back, Rosy's fingers still curled around Magdala's thumb. Alma settled into the hammock beside them, the arch of her legs forming a wall between the girls and the world.

"Saint Rosalinda," she said, "was a child when she performed her first miracle. One of her father's goats was birthing a two-headed kid. It was terribly painful, and the goat cried and cried all night long until Rosalinda, feeling such pity, such compassion for the creature, left her bed and laid comforting hands on it. At once the goat's cries softened, she rested her head in Rosalinda's lap, and her kid slid out as easily as anything. Two-headed, but otherwise healthy. That was Rosalinda's first humble miracle."

"Why didn't she heal the two-headedness?" a soft voice asked. Magdala lifted her head and saw Dulcinea standing in the back of the room, a blanket draped around her narrow shoulders.

"It's in the name," someone else chided, and Magdala realized all the women were listening from their beds to Alma's story. "She's the *comforter*, not the *healer*."

"Couldn't she heal?" said Dulcinea. "If she wanted?" She gathered the blanket closer and sat down on her mattress, knees tucked to her chest.

"That is not what she was called for," said Alma.

"Unfortunately for the two-headed kid."

"Hush," Alma said. "This story's for Magdala. When Rosalinda was sixteen, her village was stormed by desperados. They had come to rob the bank, but finding that the village had almost no money to take, they killed and pillaged without mercy. Rosalinda survived by hiding in the rafters of her father's barn. When the desperados left, she tended to every hurt man, woman, and child still living, held their hands as the town surgeon plucked the bullets out of them."

"Can Rosy do that?" Magdala whispered.

"Perhaps she could, one day," said Alma, stroking the baby's downy cap of hair. "After that day, Rosalinda was called to leave her home village and become a wanderer. Before she was twenty-four, she had crossed all the most desolate lands in the Remainder. Everywhere she went, she brought comfort to sufferers."

"Don't tell of her death," someone said. "You're getting to her death."

"You have to tell of her death," Alma said. "It's part of the story."

"All saints die violently," Dulcinea said with loathing.

"Not all saints," said Alma. "But this one did," she admitted.

"One day, Rosalinda was riding through the mountains on her white donkey when she heard gunfire. She galloped toward the sound into the town of Durango, which *some* say is the place you must go if you want to see Rosalinda's true grave, although her shrine is in the holy city of Las Vegas with all the great worthies. She knew desperados were attacking this village just as they had attacked her own. And on that day, she met a true black hat, a man whose heart was so full of cruelty and wickedness that nothing gave him more pleasure than the idea of snuffing out a life devoted to comforting others. Rosalinda's reputation was already well-known then, for she had performed many miracles. When she came to comfort the survivors, the desperado strung her up and gave her a choice: She could join his band, pick up a revolver, and bring suffering to a hundred other villages, or she could be the last sacrifice they made in Durango. She chose the second. And even as he burnt her alive, the smoke that rose from the fire gave him a feeling of peace for the seconds he inhaled it, the one short moment of mercy he would experience thereafter."

"Why didn't she run away?" asked Magdala.

"She was a martyr," said Alma.

"They never run," said Dulcinea. "Not the lady saints. You're supposed to stay and suffer."

"Was she real?"

"She is as real as you or me or Rosy," Alma said. "If you go to the holy city of Las Vegas, even now, you can see her preserved left hand, a little charred but still recognizable. It has never rotted. Pilgrims go there to pray for intercession, and afterwards they have been reported to forget the pain of lifelong ailments."

"You ought to go for your itching," one of the women said to the other.

"Someday, I pray, we will all go there," said Alma solemnly. The vault fell silent as they all reckoned with the force of imagining it.

Magdala fell asleep that night with the faint ache of the brand throbbing in her neck, images of two-headed goats and virgin martyrdom and Las Vegas filling her dreams.

In the morning, the other women were sent beyond the barbed wire barrier to gather desert fruits for stewing and mashing and canning. Alma was allowed to stay back, on account of the baby, but when Rosy at last succumbed to a nap in the hottest hours of the day, so did she, and Magdala was left alone. She was sitting outside the bank tracing patterns in the dirt with a stick when a man passed, whistling a road ballad. He stopped for a second and looked at her from beneath the brim of his Stetson. He was a tall, narrow figure in faded blue jeans that ended above his ankles, hitched to his waist by a belt with an ostentatious golden buckle. As if he'd borrowed Oscar's clothes, Magdala thought.

"Do you know where my papa's gone?" she said to him.

"The newcomer? Probably digging trenches." He grinned. In the shadow of his hat, Magdala could only see his mouth and not his eyes. "Oscar won't be much pleased by an interruption of the work out there. Something you need?"

Magdala hesitated, glancing back at the bank. "No," she said reluctantly.

"That don't sound like a real sincere 'no' to me. They got you babysitting in there? Think you'll die of the tedium?"

"They're just napping."

"Even worse." He shook his head ruefully, then lowered his voice, drew a little closer. "Would you rather go hunting?"

She leapt at the idea; her father had said they should be stronger before they returned to the desert. If she could learn to find food, she thought, she would be useful to him all through the fifty miles to the pilgrim highway. "With my papa?" she asked hopefully.

"With me. I could use a partner. Just got to talk with Oscar a moment, and then we can be off. I'll have you back before your papa knows to look for you."

Magdala brushed her fingers across the brand on her neck. It was protection, she thought; that's what her father had said. And the man was not really a stranger, he was their neighbor.

"Can you teach me?"

"Teach you to hunt?" The man laughed. "'Course I can teach you. Only right for a little wolf to be lethal." He extended his hand for her to shake. "Name's Rawley."

Magdala let her palm be swallowed up in his as she told him her name.

She sat on the steps of Oscar's porch while Rawley went inside. The men's rumbling voices came faintly from the house, interspersed with the occasional peal of laughter. She sat impatiently until Dulcinea came by with a wheelbarrow. When she saw Magdala, she stopped short, nearly spilling her burden of fruit peels and pulp.

"What are you doing here?" she demanded.

"Waiting," said Magdala cautiously. No one had said she couldn't go with Rawley, although if Dulcinea told her father or Alma or one of the other women where she was going, she was certain she would be in trouble.

"Waiting for who?"

Magdala drew her knees up to her chest. "My father," she said, but her voice wavered.

Dulcinea worried her lip and stared past Magdala at the blue house. Magdala was afraid she would go inside to see if the story was true, but when the sound of laughter reverberated, she returned hastily to her wheelbarrow and left without looking back.

Rawley emerged a moment later with two revolvers and a small box of bullets, which he slid into the left pocket of Magdala's dress, patting her hip as if to seal the bullets inside her clothes. "You ready, girl?" he said, whooping at nothing in particular. Magdala nodded eagerly. She shadowed him to the big-bellied black truck that was parked behind Oscar's house and watched with fascination as he turned the key in the ignition and the car roared to life.

"Ever seen its like?" he called over the sound of the engine.

"I've never seen a car that worked," she confessed, clambering up into the passenger seat beside him. She was barely tall enough to see through the cracked windshield. "Doesn't it scare away all the animals?"

"You're a canny one," he said. "We just drive it out a few miles for the distance. Otherwise the walk's too long to be borne. We'll know to stop when we see hoofprints or watering holes; that's how we can tell there's been big day-dwelling animals around."

With a roar, he revved the engine and the car jolted to life, bumping through the pitted earth. Rawley showed her where they had cut a hole in the barbed wire for the car, said it was Caput Lupinum's only vulnerability. Beyond the fence line, they thudded across the desert at a breakneck pace. As scraggly clumps of vegetation passed in a blur, Rawley explained how to find water. "Willow's a thirsty one," he said. "Got desert willow, got water somewhere near. Now, paloverde, that can survive anywhere so it's no good indicator, but if you're desperate enough, you might be able to dig into the bark with a little blade and catch yourself a nice fat beetle." Seeing the disgust on her face, he laughed. "I said desperate. You won't ever need to do that as long as you live here."

Abruptly, he braked. Magdala was thrown against the seat back; Rawley fumbled in her pocket for the bullets and loaded the first of his revolvers, then settled the gun on his shoulder. "You see it?" he whispered.

Magdala leaned across the dashboard. Twenty yards away from them, a deer was moving through the sagebrush at a slow, painstaking pace. Its body was obscured almost to the waist, but she could see still the fleshy growths that bloomed from its chest and head and back. Rawley gestured for her to come closer, and she clambered halfway on his lap to peer through the driver's side window.

"How come it didn't run when we drove up?" she asked.

"Bet it can't hear us. Some of them are deaf that have tumors on their heads like that."

The deer moved slowly forward, its stride pained and deliberate, its head vanishing now and then into the sagebrush.

"Easy mark," Rawley said. "If this gun didn't have the kickback that it does, I'd let you give it a go."

"I don't wanna shoot it," Magdala said.

"Why not?"

"It's not fair," she said. "It can't hear us, so it's not fair."

"You ever been hungry before?"

"Yes," she said.

"I mean truly hungry. Starving hungry."

Magdala was quiet; she didn't know.

The animal lifted its head, fixing its dark eyes on them. Its ears tipped forward; it became very still. If not for the nakedness of the landscape it could almost have been mistaken for an assemblage of tree limbs, something deep-rooted and inanimate.

"Does it see us?" Magdala whispered, settling back into her seat.

"Maybe so," said Rawley. He looked grim. "There's something wrong with it. Apart from the tumors, I mean."

The deer began again to advance through the sagebrush, its motions clumsy and labored, but fast now, purposeful. Rawley let out a low whistle. "It's not hiding," he said. "It's hunting." The words were barely out of his mouth when a ground snake skimmed through the brush into the exposed soil. The moment it showed itself, the deer attacked, exploding clumsily forward and lunging open-mouthed at the snake. The snake struck back, missing its attackers' forelegs by a narrow margin. When the deer lunged again, it aimed true. The snake lashed frantically between its jaws as the deer tossed its head.

Rawley wedged his revolver out the window of the truck and fired. He struck the deer in the shoulder, then in the hindquarters, and it folded, collapsing down onto the heavy bundles of its tumor-riddled legs; the snake hit the ground and maneuvered itself back into the depths of the brush in ragged, desperate motions.

"You still sorry it had to be shot?" Rawley said.

"What's wrong with it?" said Magdala.

He shrugged his shoulders as he climbed down from the truck's cab to collect the deer's body. "One, the usual. Cancer of the skin. Two." He bent and examined the animal, then pointed at a wound on the flank, angry-red and weeping yellow around the edges. "Desert sick. As I thought. Means that this animal was done for no matter whether I landed a bullet in it."

"Desert sickness? Like what I had?"

"Like and not like." He lowered himself to a crouch and shouldered the deer, flinching back from contact with its bloody mouth. "Heard folk *say*, the kind of sick you get depends on how the desert gets inside you. Or what kind of creature you are. Sometimes you just wander. Other times you rave. And the raving ones are the ones that die fast-like. But eventually, it always ends the same. You die, and you end up stuffed."

Magdala watched as he heaved the deer carcass into the back of the truck. It landed with a heavy rattling thud, its legs spilling over. "Will we get sick from eating it?" she asked.

Rawley settled back into the driver's seat with a satisfied grunt. "You're already sick," he said, and his laughter was raucous, cruel, half-frantic as he gunned the engine and launched them back to Caput Lupinum.

At sunset, the rest of the men came back in throngs of five or six, sweat-soaked and dry-mouthed and snarling, tired of each other and the heat. Wearing a borrowed Stetson and a gun in a holster that was not his, Xavier was almost indistinguishable from the rest of them. From a distance, Magdala could recognize her father only by his stride, short and precise compared with the long, loping cowboy's walk of the others. When she ran out to meet him, he was speaking in low, confidential tones with another man, hanging back a little ways from the rest. "You just have to get used to it," the other man was saying, punctuating the sentence with a long swig from the bottle in his hand. "And get *her* used to it, that's the important thing."

"Papa," Magdala started saying, but the word died on her lips as her father swept her absently into a side embrace, his stride slowing only long enough so she could keep up with him.

"What does your wife think?" Xavier was saying to the other man.

"She's got her objections." He shrugged, looked at Magdala as if only now seeing her. "Is this little Magdala?"

"My daughter," Xavier agreed. "Magdala, this is Mateo. He's married to your friend Alma."

"Let's eat together tonight," Mateo said. "We'll all get to know each other. Couldn't be gladder to have another family man in Caput Lupinum."

At the larder, the women were serving stewed desert fruits, boiled pads of prickly pear and slim hunks of charred meat. "Same as the morning," Mateo murmured.

"No complaints from me," said Xavier.

"You'll complain when it's been a month of the same." They dodged the hard looks of the women serving them and found seats at the long table, Magdala sitting on the end between the two men. They were almost through eating before Alma emerged from the larder, a plate balanced precariously in one hand, the baby tucked into a sling on her chest.

"You met Xavier?" Mateo said to her.

"Yesterday," Alma said. She was not the same around Mateo, Magdala thought; it was as if she was tucked partway inside herself. "What do you think of Caput Lupinum?" she said, looking narrow-eyed at Xavier. "Meet your expectations?"

"It's shelter," said Xavier. Then, as if he had not said enough, "Seems like you folks have done well for yourselves."

"You don't gotta pretend with Alma," said Mateo. "She'll be the first to say we should've hitched our wagon elsewhere long ago."

"So you didn't come looking to be outlaws," Xavier said.

"Never been outlawed from anywhere, to tell the truth," said Mateo. "We just got lost looking for the pilgrim highway. Never did find it. Alma was pregnant at the time. We had three stillbirths before Rosy, and we were scared we'd have another. Alma was courting a blessing from Saint Rosalinda the Comforter, but as it happened, the only blessing we needed was Oscar's."

"Wouldn't go so far as to call it a blessing," Alma said.

"You were pilgrims before?" said Magdala.

"Almost," replied Mateo, laughing. "Does it count as a pilgrimage if it ends before you're even on the route? Suppose it should. We toiled. We suffered. Went nearly four days without a drop of liquor."

"It's brave of you folks," Xavier said. "I can't fathom taking the risk, going all that way for an uncertain thing."

"No certain thing in this world now," Alma said, stabbing a prickly pear pad with her fork. "Not even death."

They stayed in Caput Lupinum as the days unfurled and the desert craned its neck toward the depths of summer. While Xavier dug trenches and hammered fence posts, Magdala sat in Rawley's passenger seat and listened as he rattled off the name of every creature they could see, where to find them and whether they could be eaten.

Rawley was confusing: sometimes rough-affectionate, tugging Magdala onto his lap or under his arm, other times abruptly short-tempered and mean. But he never said no when she asked to come with him, and he never threatened to tell Alma or her father.

She did not ask why he kept her secret. She thought he must be as lonely or as restless as she was. Rawley never worked with the others. At night, when the rest of the men lingered on their porches smoking jimson cigarettes and sharing cups of the moonshine Oscar brewed in his bath-tub, Rawley was never among them. When she mentioned his name to her father in passing, Xavier didn't know who he was.

"You mean Oscar's lackey," he said, when she insisted.

"He drives the truck," she said.

Xavier shrugged.

In the evenings when the other men came back, Rawley pretended not to know her. On one occasion, she served dinner to him alongside Dulcinea, and he said not a word, only winked first at her and then at the older girl too. Dulcinea dropped her spoon and stormed inside the larder and would not be urged back out even when Oscar went in after her demanding to know why she'd gotten so temperamental. Magdala wondered, then, why Dulcinea had gotten so angry, if Dulcinea had once been Rawley's friend as Magdala was now, and why she wasn't his friend anymore. Later, in the bank vault, Dulcinea came and sat down beside her and said half-audibly, "You have to get out of here."

"My papa says he has to work a while first," Magdala said, although her father's insistences on the debt that he had to pay for her curing were by then coming less and less frequently, interspersed with suggestions that the desert was too dangerous; that anyway they had nowhere else to be; that they were safe and fed and sheltered, and wasn't that enough? She could feel with growing certainty that he didn't want to leave Caput Lupinum.

"They all say they'll only stay a little while," Dulcinea said. "And then they never leave. Unless you make them. Look at Mateo and Alma. They were only supposed to be here until the baby was born, and now Rosy's eight months old."

"We won't do that," Magdala said, although she didn't really believe what she was saying. "Papa knows I don't want to stay."

"If he stays here long enough, he won't care. Try it and see. They all forget they ever cared for anything. Soon he'll be like the rest. They're as stuffed as the ones walking un-rooted in the desert with cactuses for heads. Nothing but jimson and meanness and fear inside them."

Magdala dreamt that night that her father *was* stuffed, slender stalks erupting from his body with yellow, fat-bulbed flowers on their ends; to reach him, she had to hack and hack and hack at the green stalks. But when she cut them, they bled, and she saw at last that he had been overtaken by the thing growing out of him. She woke as weak and queasy as she had been when she'd had desert sickness. Her hands trembling, she climbed the ladder out of the bank vault and snuck through the moonlight toward the yellow house where her father stayed. She tried the door, found it locked, knocked hesitantly and then pounded with a desperate, wounded anger. At last she heard some-one insist, "Xavier, it's *your* cripple girl-child." The door opened; her father, looking groggy, somehow not like him-self, slipped outside.

"Not safe for you to be here, Magdala," he mumbled. "We got a house full of drunks and sleepwalkers. And who knows what kind of creatures roaming the streets at night."

She could smell moonshine on him. "I had a dream," she said. "I dreamed that you were dead. Or not dead, but one of them." She could see from his face that he didn't know what she meant. "Show me that you don't have plant parts," she said. "Show me that you still are who you are." Even now, through her tear-blurred vision, she thought she could see tendrils budding from his arms and his neck.

Her father raked his hands across his face. "Listen to me," he said. "It's gonna be all right. Go back to bed. You're just tired."

"I'm not," Magdala said. "You're not the same any-more." By the way her father glanced back at the house, she could tell he was afraid of the other men overhearing. "I want to leave here," she said. "At the beginning you said we were only going to stay a little bit. We were supposed to find a good home, but this is worse than the tenement."

"Safer here than the tenement," he said. "Neighbors won't string me up for a witch. Don't have to leave you locked in one room. And it's much safer than the desert. We wouldn't make it a day, not in high summer."

"I've been learning how to survive!" she said, and once the words were out, so was the secret. She wondered with a faint murmur of guilt if Rawley would be angry that she'd told.

But Xavier didn't even ask what she meant. "You can't even walk right," he said. "What makes you think you got the right to dictate what we do and where we go? You owe your life to me, and I don't wanna hear one more word about what you think I'm doing wrong."

They stared at each other for a second, each too angry to break the silence. Then Xavier turned and went inside and shut the door behind him.

Magdala stood unmoored for a long moment, hands at her sides, until she was certain her father was gone. She returned to the bank vault, dragging her clubfoot, feeling Xavier's gaze and the gazes of all the men inside the yellow house at her back as she made her slow, stumbling retreat.

When she got back, the women were all awake, although dawn was hours off yet. "We were afraid of where you'd gone to," Alma said. "Are you all right?"

She didn't know how to answer the question. "Can I sleep with Rosy?" she said, at last.

"Are you hurt?"

"No," Magdala admitted. Alma had said that Rosy could only comfort people who were sick in body, not in spirit, and so she knew that the baby would do no good if she was only sad. But it was almost a miracle just to cling to Rosy's tiny, clammy hand, to feel the baby's slow draw and release of breath. When the other women went back to bed, Alma sat at the foot of the hammock and combed her fingers through Magdala's hair and said, "It'll be all right," as she always did, though the words had a hollowness to them that Magdala noticed more and more; she did not mean it, she did not really believe it.

"Papa said we can't leave here because I'm clubfooted," she said to Alma.

"Because of the walking?"

"Yes."

Alma sighed. "I'm sorry."

"It means we can *never* leave. I'll *never* go un-clubfooted."

Alma said nothing for a moment. Then, "Magdala, did I tell you the story of Saint Elkhanah Fleetfoot?"

Magdala shook her head. On the listless nights when none of the women were wanted by their men, Alma often recounted for them stories that she pieced together from ballads and roadside sermons and handwritten pamphlets, some of them long and full and lush like Saint Rosalinda's and others only fragments. But Magdala did not remember this name.

"He was born like you," Alma said. "Only, he could not walk at all. He spent most of his childhood in bed. He performed his first miracle when his home village caught fire. The villagers tried but could not put out the blaze. There were not enough of them. As the fire burned, Elkhanah heard the voice of God tell him to stand on his feet. He ran and ran with impossible speed to the next village, and returned with help in time to put the fire out."

"Is that why he's called Fleetfoot?" Magdala said.

"Thereafter, he was the fastest man, on horseback or on foot, in the Remainder," Alma said. "When he fired a revolver, his bullets flew with the speed of God. The holy city of Las Vegas still loves him today for all his daring rescues and acts of vengeance. Outlaws would say to each other that if he was on your tail, there was no hope for you. The bones of his feet still rest now in a shrine in the holy city, and it is said that when the crippled kiss them with reverence, he intercedes on their behalf."

"Like me?" asked Magdala. Her heart was hammering inside her chest; Rosy turned restlessly in her sleep, as if she felt the motion of it. "Would he intercede for me? If I went there?"

"*Just* like you," Alma said. Then, softly, "I think he would."

It was only a few days later that Dulcinea pulled her into the scant shade of a mesquite and whispered, "I want you to help me get out of here. To make it so we can all get out of here."

Magdala didn't ask how or why. "I'll do it," she said, sticking out her hand for Dulcinea to shake as she had seen her father do with Oscar. Dulcinea shook with the same firmness.

She only had to do one thing: get inside Oscar's house when he was not there and pour desert fruit concentrate in his moonshine. "I've been saving it," Dulcinea said, withdrawing a baby food jar full of pale juice from her pocket.

"Why?" said Magdala.

"You know what it does when a man swallows down enough of it," she said. "He'll get desert sick. Go raving."

Magdala thought of the deer in the sagebrush, the frantic motions of the ground snake in its jaws. "I don't want to hurt him," she said.

Dulcinea made a face like she'd been struck. "You should," she said. She glanced both ways, then hitched up the skirt of her dress to show Magdala the dark bruises that climbed her legs, vanishing beneath the hem of her underwear. "He hurt me first. You stay here a few more years, I bet you he'll hurt you too."

Magdala looked aghast at the wounds. After Dulcinea lowered her skirt, she kept seeing them, mottled black and violet superimposed on the pale linen of her dress. "Why does he hurt you?" she asked.

"Never mind," said Dulcinea. "It doesn't matter for you. What matters for you is that you need Oscar out of the way if you don't wanna stay here for the rest of your life."

"Why?"

"Because as long as Oscar is king here, the men are all too busy digging trenches and hunting stuffed men to think of trouble. But they hate him. Even if they don't know it, they do. If they get a chance, they'll turn on him. And if he's raving, they'll have to."

"And then what?"

"And then, it won't be what your father calls safe here anymore."

Magdala thought of the firelight under the door of their room in the tenement, the shock on her father's face as they both woke to the sound of glass shattering and the sharp chemical-tinged scent of the smoke that poured under the door. It had been her fault they had to leave the tenement, and she thought if she made him leave Caput Lupinum too, he might realize that she had been the trouble all along. But if they could only reach the shrine of Saint Elkhanah, she would be healed, she would be made whole, she would not be a burden to him.

"How come it has to be me?" she said.

Dulcinea smiled sadly. "Because you're the only one they don't see."

She crept into Oscar's house on a day when he was gone hunting with Rawley. The door was unsecured; no one in Caput Lupinum, not even Oscar, had ever found keys to the houses they called their own, and so they had broken the locks. Across the threshold, with the door shut behind her, she squinted into the darkness. Oscar had nailed boards to the windows so the house was not only dim inside but almost black, illuminated by what daylight snuck stubbornly beneath the door and through a knot in one of the boards. As her eyes adjusted, Magdala could see the sagging armchair posed like a throne in the center of the room; the clumsy drawing of a wolf etched in chalk across the sun-faded floral wallpaper; the dresser in the corner with its drawers all hanging slightly open, like jagged teeth in a dark narrow mouth. A rosary hung from one drawer pull, a dreamcatcher from another. On top of the dresser, a long-necked glass bottle sat beside a car's side-view mirror with a long crack running through it. Magdala approached slowly, standing on tiptoe to reach, seeing herself bifurcated in the mirror.

She uncorked the bottle to the sharp and too-familiar smell of moonshine, then set it on the floor and leaned over and carefully dribbled the concentrate inside. The liquids swirled together, the concentrate vanishing into the liquor.

She was still screwing the lid back on the bottle when men's voices came faintly, then louder, from outside. Hurriedly, she set the bottle back on the dresser and concealed the empty jar of concentrate in her pocket. She couldn't hope to get out the front door in time, so she retreated to what had once been a bathroom, squatting across from a long-dry toilet through which a centipede crawled. It was only a few seconds before the door swung open and Oscar came inside with Rawley, the men bearing their hunting rifles and the sour stink of dissipated sweat on their skin.

"Starting to think that was a damn lie you told me," Oscar said to Rawley. She heard Oscar pry his boots from his feet, setting them aside with twin thuds. "When's the last time you seen a javelina that wasn't grafted to something vegetable, anyway? Of any size."

"I swear to you, cross my heart, I saw it," said Rawley. "It was full pig still, and healthy."

"Don't know what I'm arming you and filling that gas tank for, if you can't shoot things on sight," Oscar groused. The bottle uncorked and he made a sound of disgust. "Think it's gone off," he said.

Rawley tromped across the room to smell for himself. "Smells like liquor," he said, laughing and then getting quiet when Oscar didn't.

She was startled when she heard Oscar set out two glasses; he was going to let Rawley drink, she thought, and with a spike of terror she listened as the men clapped the cups together and drank. Rawley was not supposed to get sick; he was not part of the plan. The weight of what she had already done, what she was still doing, fell heavily on her all of a sudden. The men might end up as gone from their natural selves as the deer, she thought, or even worse: they might die all the way, and the desert would fill them up and make them stuffed, and Saint Elkhanah would never heal a murderer, and almost worse, her father would never forgive one.

"Don't drink it," she cried, and stepped out from the bathroom.

Oscar lowered his cup and scrambled to his feet from the armchair; Rawley, who had already been standing, spit a mouthful of liquor onto the floor and stared slack-jawed at her.

"What did you do to it?" Oscar demanded.

Magdala glanced from them to the door. She was afraid to answer. Before she could run, Oscar crossed the room in long strides and grabbed her by the throat. As she gasped and struggled beneath his grasp, he lifted her against the wall so their eyes were level.

"Did you put something in there?" he said.

Magdala clawed ineffectually at him. She could smell the moonshine on his breath. Over his shoulder, she saw Rawley standing with his arms folded, his mouth set in a grimace. He wouldn't meet her eyes. It was, she thought, as if he was still pretending they didn't know each other.

"Answer me," Oscar growled, setting her down, his fingers grasping the air in front of her as if he wanted to choke her again.

She stared at him, stricken. She could not lie to him, and she could not bear to say yes.

"Answer me!" he repeated, grabbing her by the shoulders now, shoving her back into the wallpaper so a plume of dust rose like a halo around her, and Magdala replied by screaming as loudly as she could until her throat hurt. She opened her eyes when Oscar dropped her. She thought perhaps he had gotten over his anger. But he was only retrieving his rifle from across the room.

"She's young," Rawley ventured as Oscar loaded it.

"Old enough for you to be talking to me about putting a second brand on her neck, old enough to face retribution," Oscar said. He propped the rifle on his shoulder and fixed his gaze on Magdala. "You tell me who put you up to this, and I'll consider aiming below the knee," he said. "The good foot, of course."

Magdala shook her head, thinking of the bruises on Dulcinea's legs. Whatever Oscar would do to her, she was certain he'd do worse to Dulcinea. "Please," she said. "Just tell my papa what I did and he'll punish me."

Oscar came closer. The barrel of the gun was like a hole in the room, like a single colorless eye staring at her; she could not see anything past it. She opened her mouth to scream again, and then the door burst open and her father was there, Mateo close behind him, Dulcinea following them both. Oscar turned, his rifle lifted. She heard a gun fire and shut her eyes tight, as if by not seeing it she could make it not real. When she opened her eyes, Oscar was on the floor and Rawley had his gun propped on his shoulder, a thin tail of smoke rising from the barrel.

"Is he dead?" she said into the terrible echoing silence. She couldn't see Oscar's face; she didn't know if he had drank the moonshine before she'd warned him not to, and she was afraid that when she looked at him now, she would not see the slack face of a dead man, but the vociferous one of a man possessed by the desert.

"He's dead," Rawley said, nudging Oscar in the ribs with his toe. Mateo crouched, checking Oscar's pulse by resting his thumb on the dead man's throat, and nodded to Xavier.

"This wasn't supposed to happen," Dulcinea said softly. "He was supposed to go raving."

"You had all better tell me what the hell is going on," said Xavier, his eyes moving between Magdala and Dulcinea.

"No time for that," said Rawley. "I hope you don't got any prized possessions you'd be sad to part with, 'cause I'm sure we got no more than an hour before someone figures out Oscar is missing."

"And then what?" Xavier said.

"Then they string us up. Or draw and quarter us, or tie us to a cactus and do some target practice. Whatever they want," said Rawley. "It's not called Caput Lupinum 'cause it's a town of saints, and we just killed the closest thing they got to a lawman."

"What are you proposing?" said Mateo. "I didn't sign up for this. I got no trouble with Oscar—had no trouble with him."

"That we drive the hell out of here," said Rawley. "You're a witness now. An accessory."

"And go where?" said Xavier.

"Anywhere. Not here."

"To Saint Elkhanah," said Magdala, but her voice came out soft and hoarse, and no one acknowledged her.

They stayed only long enough for Mateo to collect Alma and Rosy. Within an hour, all seven of them had crowded into the truck, Rawley in the driver's seat and the rest of them huddled in the truck bed. Xavier said it ought to be a woman who got the comfortable seat, but neither Alma nor Dulcinea were willing to sit in the cab with Rawley.

As they bumped past the barbed wire barrier surrounding Caput Lupinum, Magdala clung to the side of the truck bed, named silently for herself all the trees and grasses as they passed. It was almost like she was on another one of Rawley's hunting trips, except now they were driving faster than he ever had before, smashing down brush and coursing over rocks that flung them unsteadily up and down. And she was not kneeling on the passenger seat with her face pressed against the window, but sitting wedged between her father and Alma in the open air.

"I hope you can answer for what you did back there," Xavier said to Dulcinea, after they had driven on for a while. "Getting my daughter tangled up in your lovers' quarrel."

Dulcinea looked wounded; she averted her gaze to face the night thudding monotonously by. "Wasn't a lovers' quarrel," she said, still facing away from them. "It was an assassination."

"Even worse."

"Don't be angry at her. It was my choice," Magdala said. "I wanted to leave Caput Lupinum, and you said we never could go."

Her father's anger filled his body like water inflating a cowskin. She saw his fists clench, his entire body tighten. On the other side of her, Rosy's face crumpled as they bounced off a rock. The baby moaned, then broke into a long, open-mouthed wail.

"You've made us homeless," Xavier said over Rosy's cries, half-shouting to be heard. "Do you understand what you've done? Do either of you?" His eyes flashed between the two of them. "You're children. And now we have to take care of you."

"Alma said if I go to Las Vegas, I can go to the shrine of Saint Elkhanah, and I can be healed," Magdala said desperately. "If I can walk everywhere, I can do things by myself. Isn't that what you wanted?"

"You put this in her head?" Her father's eyes were on Alma now.

"It's the truth," Alma said firmly, cradling the baby close to her chest. "I only told her the truth."

"Sounds like Alma," said Mateo, uncorking the bottle of liquor he'd taken with him when they left. He threw his head back and took a long swallow. "Here, Xavier, get some inside you," he said, passing the bottle to Magdala's father. "Softens the blow a little."

They had gone only an hour when the truck sputtered and died, bumping weakly through the dry grass until the land sloped upward and the truck came to a halt.

"Out of fuel," Rawley called through the open windows of the cab.

"You don't have more?" asked Xavier.

"Wasn't expecting to drive getaway," Rawley responded, stepping out of the truck and stretching with an exaggerated, cat-like gesture. "Went far out into the hills with Oscar today. He's the one who metes it out. Doesn't give me more than he figures I need."

"Ought to make camp for the night anyway," added Mateo, squinting into the half-emptied bottle he held. "They won't chase us this far out. If they get to chasing at all."

"You think if they decide they want vengeance they won't come out this far?" said Xavier. "Land this flat, they could see us from miles off, especially if we make a fire."

"No other cars, no horses," Rawley said. "Oscar didn't want men running out on him."

Across the feeble fire they kindled using a cigarette lighter and a pile of branches, the men determined they should make for the pilgrim highway. It was the closest vestige of civilization that any of them knew of, and they could part ways when they got there if they wanted.

Unspoken was that none of them had anywhere to go. Mateo spoke of a family in eastern New Mexico, of a "back home," but his voice was moonshine-frayed, mournful, and it was plain he and Alma and Rosy would never recross the immense distance that separated them from where they'd been before. Rawley said he'd been with Oscar since Caput Lupinum was founded. "I was the first to get branded," he said. "You know that wolf's skull posted by the gate? Was me that killed and skinned and polished it." Dulcinea, cupping the faded second brand on her neck, would only say that she could remember nowhere before Caput Lupinum.

"We can't go back where we came from either," said Xavier. Magdala saw him look at her. Wind surged across the desert then, knocking the fire out. In the light cast by the young moon, even her father's face became ghoulish and unfamiliar.

"We can be pilgrims now," said Magdala, wanting him not to be sad, wanting him to hope as she hoped.

Xavier said nothing. Rawley laughed. "Sorriest excuses for pilgrims I've ever seen," he said.

In the morning, they set off in the rough direction of the pilgrim highway, moving through the slatted shadows of saguaro arms and ocotillo spikes. Magdala's father did not carry her. When she looked at him, asking without asking, he stiffened. "You want to be on the road so much, *be* on the road," he said. But after a moment, he found a long mesquite stick and handed it wordlessly to her, and he never let her fall far behind him.

Before noon, they made it to a road, a battered two-lane finger of asphalt that Mateo recognized as the northbound state route. He said it would intersect with the pilgrim highway. They had not gone far down it when a thing emerged from the canyons, a thing which had once been a javelina and a man and a coyote and a prickly pear, but was no longer any one of those things. Mateo saw it first, stopped short, and held perfectly still as the rest of them caught up to him. Magdala absorbed the sight of the thing in pieces: dark snout and bristled head trailing into a naked human abdomen with a motley assemblage of legs, at least six of them, some that dragged or floundered brokenly along and others that strode forcefully through the dirt. Xavier unholstered his gun and cocked it, but Mateo's hand on his shoulder stopped him from shooting.

"What is it?" Magdala whispered to Dulcinea.

"It's a stuffed man, same as we get desert fruits from," she said. "Just not . . . rooted."

They stood still as the creature maneuvered closer, its black eyes focused straight ahead, its wide nostrils heaving. It was not heading for them, but seemingly for nothing, the line of its stride meaningless and unbroken. As it crossed the road in front of them, the sound of more hooves, more feet, followed. The group stood motionless as an entire stream of creatures emerged from the canyons and then passed through, one after another. All were formed from the same undead materials, limbs and trunks and heads conveying nauseatingly lush tangles of cactuses across the desert. Some were human in part, but most were not.

The silence that lay underneath the creatures' steady murmur of footsteps was broken all at once by Rosy's piercing cry. Alma rocked the baby frantically, even laid her hand across Rosy's mouth, but they soon found that it didn't matter: The creatures acted as if they heard nothing. None altered their paths. None even looked at her.

"They can't hear?" Magdala whispered.

"No," said Rawley aloud. "They just don't care anymore. They got the desert inside them now, and they know where they're going to, as sure as a lizard knows to go underground in a storm."

"Don't look," Alma said. "I've heard before of men getting desert sick without their lips ever touching desert fruit, just from looking."

"How long do you have to look before you get sick?" asked Magdala. The longing to see them was like an itch, almost a pain. She recognized in them the sickness that had stricken her when last they were in the desert, and felt a kind of likeness to them.

"Don't look at all and it won't matter," said Xavier.

The stream of creatures came and went, but in the flat, unending landscape, they did not disappear for a long while after. Again and again, Magdala's eyes strayed toward them. Alma had the notion that they should each tell stories to distract each other. "We'll make a game of it," she said, her voice too bright, her hopefulness forced. "I'll tell one today, Mateo tomorrow, and Xavier next, then Dulcinea—"

"Not me," said Dulcinea.

"All right. Rawley, then. Four days will take us to the highway anyway," Alma said.

"Let's say the best story gets a bottle of whiskey," said Rawley. "Make it interesting. We'll let little Magdala be the judge."

"How do I judge it?" said Magdala, pleased by his acknowledgment.

"You choose whichever one you like," said Rawley. "For any reason you like."

"I'll tell one," said Xavier. "I'll do it now. You got any of that liquor left, Mateo?"

"Sorry, brother."

"It's no trouble. Just all of you listen close now. And I don't mean only to me. I want you to hear the wind crying down in the canyons. The stuffed men walking." His eyes followed, for only a second, the creatures on the horizon. "I'm gonna tell you the story that my mother used to tell me, of how the Hopi know the world began and ended."

MASAUWU THE SKELETON GOD sat at a fire while the world was born, waiting for Man to come crawling up from the bottom of the canyon so he could teach him how to be alive. Man came to him, wearing no shoes, wearing no faces, knowing no names, not the god's and not his own. Masauwu looked Man full in his no-face; he dropped melon and squash seeds into the soil, then he dropped corn. Say it with me, Magdala, you know this story by heart: He said, you wanna live here, you must abide by certain laws. I'll make a way for you, feed all your appetites, but you can't get too hungry.

The corn grew up high before their faces. Through the corn, Man looked on him. Masauwu was sometimes half-handsome, sometimes only bones and stars and cold wind, but he wasn't a liar. Man shook his hand. Now the corn was four women. Man named them Blue and Red and Black and Yellow, and every year those women came to the fields with new crops of children.

Masauwu, he owned those corn maidens. They could come out with the rain, but when the rains dried and the sun hid, they had to go away. Go and come back, like a dance. They used to come around Man's fire, playing games with him. Man fell in love, decided he wanted the blue maiden for his wife, and stole her away so she couldn't go when the rains stopped.

After that, the rains went on and on. And on and on. But they got hot and poisonous. They would scorch your throat, eat through flesh. Under those rains, only monstrous things could grow. There was nothing to drink, nothing safe to eat. Masauwu saw what had happened and knew just what it meant. And with his bone-eyes, he saw

Man had built himself a house in the middle of the desert, where rain hardly ever fell, and there he and Blue were playing house, sipping from straws of cactus, not a solitary care for the rest of the world.

Masauwu beat down the door. Said to Man, I gave you the world and you swallowed it whole, then asked for one more helping. In the green country, the rain has gone rancid. In the green country, your fellow man is dying. You want a world, or you want a wife? Man said, I want a wife. And so Masauwu stomped his feet and broke the Remainder loose from the green country. Left Man and his corn-maiden lover to starve and thirst and live, just barely. And we are all their descendants.

"It's blasphemous," said Alma. "All that talk of Masauwu and corn maidens."

"You don't like it," said Xavier, "tell your own version."

"I dreamed once," said Magdala, "that I saw the green country."

"No one ever can see it," said Dulcinea. "You would die there in a second."

Late in the afternoon, they passed a man perched on the head of a saguaro cactus. Beneath his thinning thatch of hair, his pale head was deeply sunburnt. His robe was white, with blood stains tracking down the hem.

Mateo crossed himself at the sight. They gave the man a wide berth, though he did not acknowledge them as they passed. Magdala could not tear her eyes away. The look on the hermit's face was something between bliss and stubbornness, his eyes gently shut and his mouth hard-set. There was no question that he was alive, but he did not seem to feel the needles that must have been digging into his flesh.

Before long they came to another person seated on a cactus, and another; down the wide sweep of a ravine, they found an entire forest of saguaros mounted by people in white sackcloth.

Rawley let out a low whistle.

"They got tents down there," said Mateo, pointing at the circle of white dots in the center of the cactus forest. "Could ask to stay the night."

"How do you know they're safe?" Alma asked.

"Don't know for certain," he replied. "But they don't seem dangerous."

"Don't seem dangerous? They're the sorriest-looking crop of wretches I ever seen," Rawley said. "The ones that aren't cancer-riddled are old or crippled or both. We've already got the heads of wolves. No sense in pleading for a little when we can take it all. Bet they've got good eating. Canteens of cool water. Maybe even a little whiskey, though I confess I'm not holding my breath."

"How can you talk about robbing them?" Alma said. "They've done nothing to us."

"Not much interested in the compunctions of a woman who's been living fenced like a pet pony," Rawley said, and spat on the dirt for emphasis, like Oscar used to do. "Come on, Mateo," he said. "You're a sensible man. Don't you agree with me?"

Mateo hesitated, his eyes fixed on the rolling landscape and its scores of hermits. "Let's just walk on," he said at last. "It's not worth the trouble."

"Magdala needs rest," Xavier said firmly. "She and I gotta stop, if no one else will."

Magdala flinched at the weight of all their stares on her. "I can go on," she assured them.

"There's no need," Alma said, and in front of the men, Magdala was almost embarrassed by the kindness that in the dark of the bank vault had been a comfort. "Rosy needs to nurse anyhow," she said.

Rawley shook his head. "I'll be out here if you need me," he said. "Make camp right there." He jerked his chin toward an outcropping of rock, sun-exposed and yucca-studded.

"Don't be foolish," Xavier said to him.

Rawley stood a moment with his jaw clenched. Then he nodded and followed the rest of them down the hillside.

None of the cactus-sitters stopped them or spoke to them as they trailed through the saguaro forest; none even opened their eyes. It would have been easy, Magdala thought, as Rawley had said, to rob them. But she felt their vulnerability like a mirror reflecting her own, and a greater part of her wanted to shout a warning. *You could be shot! Hit! Everything could be taken from you!* The cactus-sitters somehow didn't know. She wondered if anyone had told them that they could have found healing, for deformities and sicknesses both, in Las Vegas.

They had almost reached the tents in the center of the cactus forest when a small man with a hunched back emerged from one of them, leaning heavily on a stick of juniper.

"Welcome," he said, tilting his head up to meet their eyes. "I am Renato. And who are all of you?"

"We're just passing through," Xavier said. "But we'd be real obliged if we could stay the night in your camp. Maybe get a little water."

"We would love to offer you food and shelter, on a few conditions," the man said. "The first is that you come without your guns. Bury them in the desert or entrust them to us, it makes no difference. We are all unarmed here, and we ask as a gesture of good will."

"No one here is armed?" said Mateo.

"No one. I promise you."

The men exchanged glances. Xavier slid his gun from the holster, unloaded it and presented it on the flats of his palms to the old man. A moment later, Mateo did the same. They looked expectantly at Rawley, who stood motionless with his hand on his rifle.

"No chance," he said. "This doesn't leave my side."

"Don't think they're planning on a stick-up," said Mateo.

"What do they want the guns for then?" Rawley shook his head. "No chance."

"He wants to fend for himself, let him," Alma said to her husband.

"You can find shelter in the ravines to the west of here," Renato said, not unkindly. "Burros often dig for water there."

Rawley's eyes were wide as his gaze fell across them. Magdala thought she'd never seen him so afraid before, not even when Oscar had a gun trained on her. His mouth opened, then shut. At last, he stalked away. "Find me in the morning," he said over his shoulder. "Or don't. I'm not risking it."

In the shade of late-blooming acacia, Renato and two of his fellow hermits served them a meal of stewed mesquite peas and roasted crickets. As the dishes were set before them, Magdala remembered Rawley saying she would never have to eat beetles as long as she stayed in Caput Lupinum, and she felt a small pang of loss, strange and unwanted, for the town they had left. But the crickets were not repulsive as she had thought they would be—they had a pleasing, almost-meaty taste that crackled in her mouth—and Magdala ate all that the cactus-sitters served her. When she had finished, she sat watching as Renato lifted spoonfuls of stewed mesquite to the mouth of one of his fellow cactus-sitters, a woman named Catalina, whose wicker chair had been wheeled out to the table on a set of casters. Renato sat patiently while the woman worked to swallow and chew, gathering up more food onto the spoon only when she nodded her readiness. Magdala knew she was not supposed to stare at people, but she could not stop watching. She thought she had never seen one grown-up caring for another like that, patiently but without fuss, as if it were the most ordinary and comfortable thing in the world.

"You folks been out here long?" Mateo said to them, after a while.

"Fifteen years now," Catalina answered. "The first faithful of our order left Las Vegas twenty years ago, searching for something one of their number had dreamed: a chapel carved out from the cliffs, empty for a hundred years, whitewashed by wind, a sanctuary where they could find peace. They hired the trail guide Barabbas Knight to lead them. He said he knew the place. But instead he robbed them of all their worldly possessions, abandoned them in the desert. For months they wandered, searching. Then one day, a revelation." She smiled. "Perhaps there was a chapel in the cliffs, somewhere, but there is peace to be found *here*."

"You saying it's peaceful to straddle a cactus?" said Xavier.

Renato and Catalina exchanged a look of amusement. "It is," Renato said, "for some. In the right frame of mind. In the right place, the right time. But we do not demand that everyone in our order practice cactus-sitting. Only those who feel so called. There are many ways of being in the world now," he concluded. "We all find one we can endure."

Magdala was bewildered. If the cactus-sitters had come from Las Vegas, they had seen the shrines of Alma's stories firsthand. She felt certain that one saint or another could have healed Renato's curved back, Catalina's paralyzed limbs, all the ailments and deformities that burdened the rest of them. She felt, then, for the first time, a pinprick of doubt pierce through her surety in Saint Elkhanah. But she pushed it away. There had to be some reason why the hermits would not or could not be healed by the Vegas saints. Alma always said the worthies did not choose to intercede for everyone. Perhaps the cactus-sitters had done something wrong, something they did not want to admit.

When every plate was empty, Renato showed the group to the empty tent reserved for strangers, then left them alone. As the sky darkened and the tent grew dim, the faint sound of the hermits singing their vespers came on the wind.

"Listen to that; we're practically in Vegas already," said Mateo.

"They're heretics," Alma said, harshly.

"How do you figure?"

"Didn't you hear him say they left Vegas? To wander? I'm certain they were excommunicated. And if they couldn't find another place to take them in, they must have some kind of barbaric, inhuman practices."

"Is that why they haven't gotten healed?" Magdala said, eager for a chance to settle the question. "Would it make Saint Elkhanah angry? That we're staying with them?"

"Magdala," Xavier said. "It doesn't matter. We're not on pilgrimage."

Something collapsed inside her at his words; she realized she had believed if they left Caput Lupinum, they would have to go to the holy city, that they would be drawn inexorably to the shrine holding her salvation, no matter how many miles had to be crossed. She had never fathomed that her father would refuse her, not once he knew she could be rid of her clubfoot.

"I thought you wanted me to be healed," she said.

"Sure, if there was any chance of it. But there's not. It's a bedtime story. A road ballad. A romance." He turned to Alma. "If you could stop filling her head—"

"If you won't take me, I'll go by myself," Magdala cried, wanting to make him as frantic as she was, as desperate. "Or," she went on, "or, Rawley will take me."

"No one will take you," said Xavier. "You're not going, and that's the end of it." He took up one of the bedrolls curled in the corner. "I'll be here," he said, laying it out in front of the tent's opening.

Magdala watched him with her hands curled into fists, understanding the brand on her neck not as a mark of protection but a mark of ownership, hating the easy curve of his spine as he lay on his side between her and the desert, the simple fact of him enough to keep her in. Her salvation all depended on him, she thought, and he didn't even care.

As night deepened and the vespers faded to the softer nocturnal chorus of mourning doves and cicadas, Magdala fell asleep despite herself; as her eyelids got heavy, her fury retreated. When she woke it was still dark, and from outside low voices came: her father's and someone else's.

"Not a survivor," she heard Xavier say. "So far, she is," the other voice answered. Magdala rose to her feet and peeked out the flap of the tent, her ears prying stray words apart from the low hum of their murmurs. One of the cactus-sitters had kindled a small fire just beyond the tent; they sat propped on a flat stone, stirring the coals with a stick. Her father sat across from them, his back to Magdala. "She still thinks there's some way out of this," he was saying.

She thought for a second of sneaking away from him, imagined herself stealing through the saguaros, past the cactus-sitters with their perpetually closed eyes. Then the hermit sitting across the fire said, "And you don't want to take her on pilgrimage?"

"I never even heard the name of Elkhanah 'til someone was warning me away from him. And it's all a scam, isn't it? Set any pile of bones on a pedestal, and people will come to see them. Thinking they're touching something that's not here anymore, that maybe never was. And they'll pay alms, maybe even play the slots on the way out."

"Would you take her if you thought it would work?"

"*Does* it work?"

The cactus-sitter made a soft sound of amusement. "I confess," they said, "I'm not liable to believe in the sanctity of a saint best known for his sharpshooting. Nor in any of the cowboy saints of Vegas. But who knows why miracles happen, or where?"

"So you think she could be cured."

"I believe," they corrected, "she will be healed."

"What's the difference?"

The cactus-sitter's head lifted and they caught Magdala's eye. "Little one," they said. "Did we wake you?"

Shyly, Magdala emerged from the tent and stumbled to her father's side. After a full day of walking, her clubfoot was so stiff and swollen that she could not disguise the pain of standing on it. The cactus-sitter did not pretend they did not see; their gaze was steady, unabashed. "Child," they asked, "have you ever ridden horseback?"

Magdala shook her head.

"Stay here a moment," they said, getting to their feet.

Left alone with her father, Magdala twisted her hands awkwardly in her lap and did not look at him, shame and anger and fear of losing his love all knotted inside of her. She half-startled when he reached for her hand and held it. The feel of his fingers and the heartbeat that thudded in his wrist disarmed her, and at once she wrapped her arms around him and said, "I'm sorry, I'm sorry," though not what for, letting him think she meant only her anger in the tent and not the two flights across the desert, their homelessness, the wolf's head on him. He held still within her embrace.

When the cactus-sitter returned, they were leading a small swayback mule ono a rope halter. "For you," they said to Magdala, holding the animal's lead rope out to her.

"We can't take this from you," said Xavier.

"You can," they said, and their eyes stayed on Magdala as they answered him. "Someday you will be back here to return it."

They left the cactus-sitters in the morning, Magdala perched on the mule's back and her father holding the animal's halter, the others trailing after them. Rawley was waiting for them on the ridge that curved around the saguaro forest, cooking lizards on a makeshift spit.

"I see you're still alive," he said as they approached.

"Barely," murmured Mateo. He had risen nauseous and weak-legged, complaining of his head. Desert sickness, Magdala had thought, fearing he'd looked too long yesterday on the roaming creatures. "Want of liquor," Alma had corrected her.

"They were good people," said Xavier.

Rawley withdrew the lizards from the fire, puffing at the smoke that rose from the most deeply charred. "You left 'em a whole mule richer," he said. "So they must be generous, or you're a wealthier man than you let on."

"It was a gift," Xavier said, patting the mule's neck. "A gift with an obligation." He looked at Magdala. "Given to understand that I'm charged with bringing this pilgrim to the holy city."

"Papa, really?" Magdala was afraid to believe him. "Do you mean it?"

"You got some feet to kiss," he said, a half-smile crossing his face.

"Guess we'll be parting ways at the highway then." Rawley got to his feet and ate the lizards as he walked, spitting bones at intervals onto the asphalt. "Mateo, you too?" he said around a mouthful.

"Looks that way," Mateo said wearily, his eyes on Alma and the baby. "I made a promise, and as I keep being reminded, I haven't made good on it yet."

"And how about you, Dulcinea?" Rawley smiled like he had smiled when they were serving him dinner in Caput Lupinum, narrow and ungenerous. "You sticking with me,

or are you going to shock some martyred virgin with your
sins and transgressions?"

Dulcinea flinched as if she'd been struck. "Not with
you," she said.

"Leave her alone," said Alma.

"Me and Dulcinea are old friends," Rawley said. "She
understands."

"Why are you kind to me but mean to her?" Magdala
demanded.

Rawley's look was poisonous when he faced her. "Don't
gotta be kind to either of you," he snarled, and she understood suddenly they were not friends anymore; that maybe
they never had been, despite all her hours in his passenger
seat and his smoky whispers in her left ear.

"You stay away from them both," Alma said. "Or you
can go your own way to the pilgrim highway. You should
count yourself lucky you're here in the first place."

"Mateo, you gonna let your woman speak to me that
way?" Rawley said.

"No one speak to each other," Mateo mumbled.

"There some kind of bad blood here we all should know
about?" interjected Xavier.

"No bad blood," Rawley said. "Just sore feelings." He bit
the head off the last of the lizards and swallowed without
chewing. "I'm gonna tell my story now," he said. "Listen
good, 'cause I won't repeat it."

THERE WAS A MAN born full of spite and loathing. From
the first day of his life, he dragged it along with him. But he
always kept a tight rein on it, like a hunger he never sated.
Then one day, he unchained it for just a minute and spit

on the face of a prisoner going to the hangman's noose. Thought, that man will be dead in half a moment anyway. Only the prisoner didn't die, not for real. After they hung him, he came back to life, traversed the earth, forgave everyone who'd wronged him except one person. Came to our man and said to him, "I've seen inside you. Seen who you are. And those thirty-three years of keeping it down, they don't matter. You'll be keeping it down the rest of your very long life, 'til you find someone to trade places with you." And he kissed the man on his forehead before he went, leaving a mark there like something burnt.

At first our man didn't know what he meant. But with time he understood. He didn't age. Wasn't a day older than when he'd first been cursed. And he could never settle anywhere after that. Everyplace he went, he was unwanted. People saw the mark and crossed themselves, said spells or curses, threw salt over their shoulders. And so he wandered, looking for some unlucky fool to take his place. An eternity of homelessness. Hard to find a man who would rather take that life than the short, sweet one he was given. Our man went everywhere, looking, searching and seeking in all the dark places. In jailhouses, madhouses, in every godforsaken hole in the earth he could reach. And as he went, the spite and loathing didn't go away; they got stronger. He hated every man who wouldn't take his place. Hated their smug no's and their readiness to meet death. Hated their uncursed souls and clean foreheads.

It was nine hundred years before he found one. A lonely desperado sentenced to hang. Would have done anything to cling on longer to life, even wander forever. He was an outlaw anyway. Would hardly have made a difference. But it all ends where it began because our man was so full of spite and loathing that he looked at the face of the poor, wretched desperado standing there in shackles, waiting for his turn at the gallows, and felt such contempt for the kind of man who'd take such a bargain that he spit on him. .And after that, the desperado wouldn't broker a deal with him. Said, "I'll keep my death, thank you very much." Spat right back at him.

Some folks say he's still wandering, looking for someone to take his mark and his everlasting hateful life.

Through Rawley's story and the silence that followed, they crossed long miles of flatland. Magdala slept through the hottest hours of the day on the mule's back, her face buried in the dark ridge of his mane and her dreams full of a lone man trawling for souls.

At night they camped high in the hills, the narrow mouth of a cave at their backs and the desert spread wide before them. In the distance, they could make out the glittering pale line of what Alma said was the pilgrim highway; she guessed three more miles and they'd intersect.

"I've been thinking," Rawley said, "maybe I ought to stay on with you folks a while longer. Could be good opportunities for a man like me in Vegas."

"You won't find someone to trade places, not even there," Dulcinea said.

"Sharp teeth on you," said Rawley, igniting a cigarette. "Why do you suppose I'm the man with the mark?"

She gave him a dark look. "I'm the one you spit on."

"You leave that girl alone," said Alma. "I told you once already. Not a chance you're coming with us. The deal was that we go together to the pilgrim highway. Then you're on your own. You want to go to Vegas, find your own route."

"You don't own the highway, on my last recollection," Rawley said.

"Leave off it," Mateo said wearily to both of them and to no one. "Could I trouble you for a drag, brother? I got aches that still aren't fading."

Rawley passed his cigarette behind Alma's head, trailing a soft brown line of smoke. "It's good jimson," he said, "but it's not liquor. Don't be expecting a miracle."

Alma's lips tightened into a thin line. "Put that cigarette out before something gets a look at the light," she said.

Rawley puckered his lips and exhaled an *O*. "You think I'm scared of stuffed men?"

"I don't care if *you're* afraid. I have a baby here who I'm planning on keeping alive."

"You can't tell me I got to stomach a whole day of you without jimson at the end of it."

"Mateo, are you gonna let him talk to me like that?" Alma demanded, but Mateo shook his head.

"You don't gotta be so tiresome, Alma," he said. "He only wants a smoke."

Rawley blew smoke. "Have a puff with us," he said. "Nothing in the pilgrim rulebook that says you have to be miserable all the time, is there?"

"All right," said Alma slowly. "Give it to me then."

"Open wide," Rawley said, and he pinched the cigarette between two fingers and maneuvered it slowly, with drunken languor, toward Alma's mouth. She seized it from him before he reached her lips and ground the cigarette into the dirt until the spark died and threw it over the cliff.

Rawley cursed and got to his feet and fumbled for his gun, fingers sliding clumsily across his holster until he found purchase.

"You put that thing away," Alma said, her voice rising, her eyes on the baby who lay wrapped in a blanket on the ground beside her.

"You gonna let your woman make the rules here?" Rawley said to Mateo.

"You're the fool who put the cigarette in her hands," Mateo said imploringly, his hand on his forehead.

"No. It's the principle." Rawley squinted down the barrel of the gun to aim, swaying on his feet. "You gonna apologize to me, or am I gonna have to look past that brand on your neck?"

Magdala and Xavier were at a distance from the rest of them, Xavier's body curled like a wall around Magdala, his eyes on the horizon. "Papa," Magdala whispered. "Help them."

"Not my place, Magdala. He has to choose whose side he's on."

"I'll take a bullet before I apologize to you," Alma said.

Rawley let out a hard raspy growl, then twisted the gun in his hand and swung the barrel at Alma's head. She flinched back, hands uplifted, and the gun caught her wrist with a crack that splintered bone. Alma howled and lunged at him, knocking him backward. His feet skidded on the rock; he stumbled on the precipice of the cliff and fought wide-eyed to stay up.

"Mateo, get a grasp on your woman," he growled.

"Alma, sit down. Shut your mouth. Let the baby feed," Mateo said. "He's only gotten so high on the jimson because his stomach's empty. He'll be better come morning."

Alma looked at him and her face tightened, her brows met in an arch, her mouth rose into a purple knot. She did not cry. She sat down and held Rosy close to her chest.

"I'm gonna tell you all how the world *really* ended," she said after a moment. "This is a real proper hagiography, not any of your old folk stories. So listen well."

A THOUSAND YEARS AGO, everyone forgot who God was. People could speak to each other across miles, across oceans. Heal any hurt or sickness. Build towers in a matter of weeks. Grow fields of food in a single lightless room. Amid all these miracles, churches stood empty, or they became bars, dance halls, casinos. Even the holy city of Las Vegas was once a place of vice and wickedness. But on the inside, people were shriveled up and halfway dead as soon as they were born. Their souls flickered like candles. They cheated and betrayed and slaughtered each other out in the open. They saw suffering and said nothing and pretended they felt nothing until it was true.

Only one man stood apart. Saint Sheldon of Las Vegas, the very first to be canonized by the Holy Church. At the dusk of the world, Saint Sheldon stood in a shimmering tower at the heart of Las Vegas and pleaded for mercy for humankind. God came down from heaven to look his favored one in the face. He said, "Tell me one reason why I should not blast humankind from the earth in a flood, as before."

"Your lovingness," said Saint Sheldon.

God said, "My lovingness is exhausted."

"Your patience," said Saint Sheldon.

God said, "My patience is exhausted."

"Your compassion," said Saint Sheldon.

God said, "My compassion is exhausted."

"Then, your glory," said Saint Sheldon.

And God said, "They have not exhausted that." He made a deal with Saint Sheldon that day. He would not destroy humankind completely, but he would leave a small Remainder in the hungriest and loneliest portion of the world. And as a show of his lovingness, his patience, his compassion, among them he would disperse workers of miracles. Saint Sheldon himself, they say, walked the earth as the poison rain fell and was untouched by it. God said, "If in a thousand years of suffering they do not take heed of my glory and repent fully, I will expunge the Remainder from the earth and begin again."

Already I know He'll be starting over. We will all be expunged, to the last of us. And good riddance.

They woke to monsoon downpour, a heavy, flat sheet of rain falling across the horizon. Dawn was hours off; the jagged edges of the clouds lit purple-black when lightning struck. Xavier fumbled to get their canteens open and leaned them against the shelf of rock so they would collect rain, his movements clumsy-frantic. Magdala was the first to see Alma was gone, and Rosy was alone on the rain-soaked dirt, shrieking and red-faced. She clutched the baby to her chest, feeling from Rosy's saint-touched fist no comfort, only panic. As she huddled into the narrow space beneath the rock, the rest of them followed until only Mateo stood in the rain looking over the cliff, searching for some trace of Alma.

"She never had desert sickness," Dulcinea said. "Never wandered."

"Someone took her, or she went for some purpose then," Xavier said.

Their eyes fell to Rawley.

"I didn't lay a hand on her," he said. "Just 'cause she never was struck desert sick before now doesn't mean she wasn't wandering."

Dulcinea looked darkly at him. "You hated her," she said.

"Didn't hate her," Rawley objected. "Just wished she hadn't hated me so loudly."

"We'll find her," Xavier said. "Only so many ways to go, no trees to hide her."

"Hold up," Rawley said. "You're tellin' me you wanna get drowned looking for a runaway woman?"

"Don't need to," Mateo said, his voice hollow. "Water's clear. You can see."

Rawley and Xavier walked to the edge of the cliff and looked down into the basin of floodwater, then drew back. When Magdala made to follow her father, he warded her off, but she persisted, pushing past him to see the twisted doll-like form lying face down in the arroyo. Her breath stuck in her throat; she covered Rosy's eyes as if the baby would be wounded by seeing. Rosy wracked in her grasp to get free, choking out angry, snarling sobs. Crushing the baby to her chest, she stood in the downpour, her legs locked stiff, contemplating the body that had been Alma, until she felt Dulcinea's arm around her shoulder. The older girl was crying without making a sound, tears trickling down her chin. "He killed her," she whispered to Magdala. "I *know* he killed her."

"Why would he do it?" wondered Magdala.

"To get to you," Dulcinea said. "And maybe me. She wouldn't have let him do it and so he murdered her." Her voice had a low, swollen sound to it.

Magdala did not ask the question she wanted to ask, the question that Dulcinea seemed not to want to answer, which was what it meant for Rawley to get to them. "I won't let him hurt you," she said, and Dulcinea's breath hitched; she almost laughed.

"We'll make a cross," Xavier was saying to Mateo. "Enough wood here for that. We'll carve her name."

Mateo's eyes were red-rimmed and glistening, but he did not shed tears. "We bury a suicide like that, we'll be answering for it," he said.

"You think that's what it was?" Xavier glanced over his shoulder at Rawley. "You don't think . . . it could've been—"

"She tried it once before," he said. "After one of her stillbirths. And she told me she'd do it for real if we didn't get out of Caput Lupinum, though she had the good sense not to." His eyes drifted from the floodwater at his feet to the cloud-smeared horizon. "I just thought, she finally was on her way to her stupid goddamned saints. Isn't that what she wanted?"

Xavier was silent a moment. "We'll take Rosy to Vegas for a baptism," he said, his voice as low and as patient as when he used to soothe Magdala in the time before Caput Lupinum. "Finish Alma's work."

"She had no work," Mateo said wretchedly, "but to harangue me for how unkindly I was and leave me with a milk-hungry burden three hundred miles from civilization."

As the rain slowed, the last clap of thunder sighing huskily at a distance, Magdala watched the men begin the work of burial. She could not lift her eyes from the sight of the body that had been filled with Alma before but was empty now, heavy and formless across Rawley's shoulder, looking indistinguishable from the carcasses of the animals he hunted. It was wrong that he was the one to lay her down in the earth and not her own husband, Magdala thought, but Mateo wouldn't even look at her body.

"She was the only kind, good creature in that whole damned wolves' den," Dulcinea said.

"Can't we tell them?" said Magdala. "She would never have jumped on purpose. She dreamed of Las Vegas."

"They both know that," Dulcinea said. "Somewhere deep down, they do. But if they admit it, they have to punish him, and they couldn't bear it."

They reached the pilgrim road before noon, the men sinking down beneath a strip of plywood with the words *VEGAS 320* spray-painted across it, to be nourished by its meager shade and by the promise it made to them. They saw no one else until they came upon a roadside campsite, a tarp held up by a cluster of tent poles, and a foam cooler resting in a battered red wagon. The men gathered beneath the tarp watched them warily, guns cocked, so they walked on and said nothing.

"They remind me of Oscar," Magdala said to Dulcinea.

"Wolf-men everywhere," she agreed.

The following day, they passed a cluster of roadside cairns, makeshift graves of stone and wood caving into the monsoon-softened earth. The graves became more densely packed as they went on, until they came to cairns whose accoutrements had not yet been stolen: water-logged saints' pictures, stubs of candles. Past noon, they caught up to a crowd of Texans coming from some tenement or shanty-town, their first-generation religion glinting rustily around their necks. "We been learning the rosary, been praying to Mary and every other idol you can think of," one man told

Xavier, fingering a crucifix on his chest. "What else can you do?"

They all had some patron saint driving them along, revealed to them through the ballads and pamphlets that circulated tirelessly back and forth down the pilgrim highway until they became tuneless, desperate melodies or torn scraps of paper barely legible. The man with the crucifix carried a crumpled leaflet that spoke of Saint Antonio, whose shrine held an ewer of his blood, consecrated as holy water; a drop on your forehead cured lustful thoughts and a drop in your eyes cured blindness. On the ground, Magdala found a frayed prayer card bearing the image of Saint Araceli, a beatific woman with dark skin and long, flowing black hair and a wolf sitting placidly at her feet. Some way down the road, a fight broke out between a devotee of Saint Marisol of the Salton Sea and a man who was certain she was no true healer of the lungless and the drowned, only a heretical Californian legend. Everyone needed something, or loved someone who did. Magdala had never seen so many people with clubbed feet like her own, nor so many with limbs wrapped in makeshift casts, stiff with disease, replaced by prosthetics of pipe and wood. She wondered how many of them were going to the shrine of Saint Elkhanah. She wondered how many would be healed.

The most prosperous of the Texas pilgrims had RVs to shelter them, but most were traveling on foot. At night, they settled down like herd animals in close-packed bunches with their heads inward, the children in the middle. Small fires burnt yards apart. Magdala looked longingly at the food reserves that many of the families carried with them: bulging sacks of corn flour and dried beans; pocket-sized glass bottles of agave nectar; luminous green sarsaparilla bottles filled with liquor or prickly pear juice. At one point an old woman came and knelt before Rosy like a worshipper, cradling the baby's cheek in her palm, then produced a glass jar of some fruit long fermented and handed it to Mateo.

Mateo looked stricken. As soon as the woman returned to her campfire, he grabbed the lid and twisted violently. Juice sloshed over the sides and into his lap; a scent rich and choking-thick wafted up from inside. "Mangoes," he said desolately. "Wasted on a baby."

"Was a gift for her," Xavier said. "Might as well use it."

Mateo hesitated, his fingers trembling on the damp sides of the jar. Then he steeled himself, determined, and fished a sliver of fruit out and mashed it inside his palm until juice tracked golden down his wrist, flowing to his elbow. He pushed the mashed fruit to Rosy's lips, and his baby sucked noisily, desperately, choking almost on those pieces which had not been reduced to mash within his fingers.

With the jar half-emptied, Rosy retreated into sleep, and Mateo set the jar down lidless on the sand and cried softly, harshly, while he watched the baby's sleeping face.

"Why did she give us fruit?" Magdala asked afterwards, her eyes on the remaining spears of canned mango, her entire body inclined toward the jar. She knew they had to keep the food for Rosy now that Alma was not there to nurse the baby, but she thought she had never been so hungry for anything.

"Bet she's not seen a baby in a long while," Xavier said.

"We oughta sell tickets," said Rawley, prodding at their fire until the flames threatened to leap from the pit. "Something makes me think these people would pay."

Xavier shook his head. "They've had it as bad we have."

"They've been on the pilgrim highway since Amarillo, that's what one told me. But they haven't seen shit. Half of them think the monsoon is a good omen."

"Could be," Xavier said, straight-faced. Then he admitted a laugh, rueful, tired, and so did Rawley.

They stayed among the Texans another day and came at twilight to a piece of plywood that read *VEGAS 300; ALABASTER, 2*. Someone ahead of them cheered. Down the long, rolling slope of a hill, the tee-shaped silhouettes of a shantytown protruded into the dusk. Closer, the scents of charred meat and horse manure overcame the wind to reach them. A sign directed them to holster their weapons.

"Never thought I'd want to cry for the sight of a pilgrim stopover," Rawley said.

The road bottomed out into a patch of cracked tarmac, and they walked beneath the hood of a one-time gas station that was now just a couple of blank-faced pumps slouching blearily away from the sun, with a row of horses hitched to a rust-worn railing. Their ears had been tagged, their hindquarters branded. A boy of thirteen or so straddled the railing between two skeletal brown ponies, holding an assault rifle.

"You wanna buy?" he yelled belligerently. "You could trade that mule you got."

Magdala, sitting astride the mule, shook her head vehemently; she could not bear the thought of exchanging the gift that the cactus-sitters had given her. Her father moved on. Ahead, a corpulent little man was selling pieces of bone on knotted cords; relics, he called to the crowd, the bones of saints and martyrs, Saint Elena's knuckles and Saint

Sebastian's clavicle, direct from Vegas, with healing powers equal to the leading competitor. "No need to go any farther!" he crowed. "Sacred relics right here."

The crowd thickened near the doors of a white stucco church reborn as a bar, the windows shattered and the doors removed; a partition of sheet tin had been set across the empty doorway. Past this building, pilgrims crept along shoulder to shoulder, like uncoordinated parts of some massive and sluggish animal. Shrill laughter echoed from the walls of the shanties. The mule tried to shy but had no space to do anything besides stumble to his left, nearly treading on Rawley's toe. As they pushed through the crowd, Xavier held tight to the animal's halter, heading with determination for a sign written in wide swaths of white paint, fluorescent in the brassy lantern light, which read out *ACOMODATINS.*

"Not much of a leg up on the bare ground," Rawley observed.

"Magdala and the baby at least ought to sleep somewhere safe," Xavier said. "Mateo, you willing to put something up?"

"Rosy can go without," Mateo said, but still he handed Rosy into Dulcinea's arms and followed Xavier to the door, which was two pallets bungee-corded to each other and nailed with lopsided enthusiasm to thin, slatted walls. A woman peeked through the slats in the door at them, staring motionless. Only when she saw Magdala on the mule did she shove the door open far enough for her body to fill the gap.

"What you got?" she called.

"What'll you take?" said Xavier.

She swept her eyes across the men, shook her head. "You got nothing."

"How about my crucifix?" said Mateo, digging the bit of gold out from underneath his clothes for her to see.

She laughed. "You think you're the first pilgrim to make me that offer?"

"Do you want his gun?" Magdala said.

"Hush." Her father shook his head. To the woman he said, "Can't part with that, I'm afraid. Look, is there something else we can do?"

The woman shrugged impassively. "Come back when you got something worth having. I can't be giving away something so precious as a roof and walls for free."

"I bet you I can turn my crucifix into a whole pile of Vegas chips," Mateo said to Xavier as they withdrew back into the crowd. "Just give me an hour."

"What do you aim to do?"

"Just an hour," he said again, and then he vanished into the bar.

Xavier and Rawley exchanged glances. "No good can come from that," Rawley said, half-amused.

"You wanna go in after him?"

"Papa," said Magdala. "Can we go and get water?" To their left, a water pump rose like a font from the dirt, attracting a cluster of dusty-faced pilgrims with bottles and jars and buckets.

Xavier eyed the swirling mass of travelers, "Dulcinea, you go with her," he said. "Nail your eyes to my daughter."

After days of groundwater unearthed from dirt-choked watering holes, the taste of the water from the pump was a small miracle. They bent their heads until their mouths were below the spout and drank insatiably, then splashed water on their faces and on Rosy's heat-flushed cheeks and the mule's dust-sheened chest. The disturbance around them as a crate was dragged across the pavement only registered afterwards, as a frenzied stream of speech began to carry above the din of the crowd. Magdala's water-bleary eyes searched for its source and found a man standing barefoot and wearing a thin, dust-colored garment. He was small, but the crate raised him above the heads of the people and animals surrounding him. "When the end of the earth is here, it will be you! You! You!" he cried, jabbing his finger at passersby. "You will pay the cost! And sooner than you think."

"Who is he?" she said, looking across the mule's lowered head at Dulcinea.

"Some kind of priest, I guess. I've never seen his kind," said Dulcinea. Her eyes swept the crowd. "We should get back to your papa."

But the man drew her eyes; Magdala looked away, but still the man's speech carried to her ears, its coherence fading as he became more excited. He slipped loosely between languages, his sentences half-complete, his words blurring together. As they approached him, Magdala made out the word tattooed across his forehead: *H E R E T I C*. Her eyes met his and he stuck his finger out. "You!" he cried.

Magdala froze beneath his gaze, her arms stiff around Rosy. He said again, "You!" and she stepped closer as if the words were an order. "I know you," he said, his mouth twisting into something like a grin. "One-legged woman."

Magdala shook her head, glancing anxiously down at her clubfoot as if he could make the words true by speaking them. "Not me," she said.

"Magdala, come on," Dulcinea whispered, tugging on her arm.

"I've heard your story." The man crouched low so they were almost the same height. "Sung it in a ballad of twenty verses. But *she's* not there."

He meant Rosy, Magdala thought, unless he meant Dulcinea. Her heart pounding beneath her ribs, she held the baby close to her chest. "What happens to me?" she whispered.

"Magdala!" Her father's voice came across the square, overpowering for a moment the street preacher's hold on her.

She whirled to face him. "He's telling me something," she protested.

"You don't know who this man is. Why he's trying so hard to get tetanus at a road stop, telling us all we're hell-bound when he's surely going to the same place. Come on."

The man climbed down from his crate. He was small enough that her father could look down at the top of his head. He looked full into Xavier's face, owl-eyed and un-flinching. "You're going to die in the desert," he said. "You're going to die, and your body is going to jerk in the wind like a dead branch."

Xavier tore them both away then, and Magdala could not see on his face how the words had affected him. "If we're gonna do this," he said to her, "if we're gonna go all the way to Vegas, you can't be talking to any stranger who approaches you. There's dangerous people out here. Dangerous people everywhere."

Magdala said nothing, neither contrite nor sure enough of herself to argue. She handed Rosy back to Dulcinea and let her father lift her onto the mule's back. "It's a heap of unneedful things on offer here," he groused as they pushed back toward the bar, Dulcinea on one side of the mule and her father on the other. "Cans of oil for cars not running. Sunday clothes like anyone still has more than one shirt to their name now." They moved past a corral built hastily from sticks, a partition assembled from two car doors cutting through the middle. A couple of malnourished, balding goats sniffed futilely at the dirt on one side, and a much stranger thing slouched on the other. It wore a thick exoskeleton of cactus spines, its skin withered to parchment beneath, its body buckled by the weight of what had overcome it.

Quickly, Xavier tugged the mule away. He slapped Magdala's face to the side when he caught her looking.

"They have no business caging that where people are gonna be," he muttered.

Magdala lifted her hand to her cheek, hurt not so much by the force of the blow as the thoughtlessness and ease of it, the fact that he'd hit her in front of Dulcinea and didn't seem to care if Dulcinea saw him. "Why'd you do that?" she demanded.

Dulcinea was watching them with a look on her face Magdala could not read, holding Rosy crushingly close.

"You know better than to look," said Xavier.

Before Magdala could protest, they were interrupted. "You want to buy, sir?" said a man standing inside the corral, feet from the creature. He leaned against the flimsy fenceposts, smiled widely. "The behemoth is full alive, though you wouldn't know it. There's enough jimson to kill a bull in that animal's system right now."

"What would I want it for?" Xavier said. Magdala saw that he was looking in spite of what he'd told her, darting short indirect glances at the mass of animal flesh.

"This one's unrooted," the man replied. "You know what that makes it? Power. Some men, they chop the arms clean off and make it walk; it'll drive their carts like a horse. A behemoth never tires 'til it sets down roots again. Isn't it a miracle?"

"An abomination," Xavier said, and pulled them away before the man could say anything more. In the shade of the bar, Rawley was waiting for them.

"You find trouble?" he asked, his eyes moving from Xavier to Magdala to Dulcinea.

Xavier shook his head. "Let's find Mateo and get out of here. Forget stopping for the night. I don't like the look of this place anymore. Like they're waiting for a show to start, these people. They're on pilgrimage because they don't got anywhere better to be."

"Same as us then," Rawley said.

At the doors to the bar, they waited for some snatch of Mateo's voice. Hearing none, Xavier exhaled a sigh. "Don't trust you out here," he said to Magdala, "so you'd better come with me. Dulcinea, you mind the animal."

He pulled her down from the mule's back, and she followed the men as they cocked their guns and shoved the tin doors aside with a dull clang that announced their entrance. The bar was moonlit and the air almost opaque with jimson smoke, a soft-colored cloud through which the faces of the gamblers were hideous and obscure. They sat on stools harvested from pews, awkward bulky structures, and rested their elbows on a slab of plywood. Mateo sat in the middle of it all, slumped across a canning jar still half-filled with liquor. He mumbled an incoherent reply to Rawley's greeting, slumped further to one side, and examined them through heavy-lidded eyes.

"Where's your gun?" Xavier said, looking at the place on his hip where his holster hung empty.

"Lost it," Mateo murmured and looked dreamily into their faces. "I had this whole room eating out of my hand, then it gone south and now I can't get back."

Rawley kicked at the legs of his frail wooden stool until it wobbled enough to send Mateo to the floor in a heap. When Mateo stayed down, Rawley growled in exasperation and heaved him up. "You got water?" he addressed the bartender. "Cold or scalding, either one."

"We're not scalding him," Xavier said, and tossed one of Mateo's limp arms across his shoulder. "We'll put him on the mule, and Magdala will walk a while."

They had fumbled in a line almost to the door before one of the gamblers stood, still holding his hand of cards between pinched fingers, and drew his gun on them. "You can't think you'll be leaving without paying what you owe," he said. "We didn't cross the whole Sonoran to get cheated."

"How much he owe you?" Xavier asked.

"He told me there was a girl who'll make good on his debt."

Magdala's father laid his hand on her shoulder. "You're not laying a finger on my child," he said to the gambler. "And that's the only time I'm telling you."

"It's not your girl he wants," Rawley murmured beside him. "He put up Dulcinea, I guarantee it."

"It's a grown girl he offered," the man insisted, sliding back against the bar until he no longer faced them all the way, his aim wavering a little. "I swear he did."

Magdala was relieved when her father shook his head. "You're not taking a girl, grown or otherwise," Xavier said. "Not from us."

"He's got debts to pay," the man said. "You gonna settle them elsewise?"

"Mateo can settle his own debts," Rawley said. "You wanna take something, take it from him. We're just the fools who agreed to share a road with him."

The man holstered his gun, then drew a short, dirty-looking jackknife from the smaller pouch at his side. He advanced slowly with drunken unsteadiness, watching them suspiciously. Mateo remained insensate, slumped toward Xavier, as the man grabbed Matias's wrist and held the jackknife close against his thumb.

"Don't take that one," Xavier said.

"He's not getting a choice in it," the man answered.

"Any other one but the thumb." Xavier drew closer to the man, arms crossed. "You really gonna cripple him for a debt stacked up in an hour?"

"I take his thumb or yours," the man said, voice swelling. The other gamblers halted their game and looked through the field of smoke to see what would happen.

"I won't tell you one time more," Xavier said, drawing his gun.

"I won't tell *you*!"

"I don't have patience for this," Rawley said. He shrugged free of Mateo's limp weight and placed himself between them and the gambler, unholstered his gun, cocked it and held it to the hollow of the man's throat. "Take the win of staying alive, brother," he said, nodding at Xavier to proceed to the door.

"You goddamn *cheats*," the man shouted, his voice lifting hysterically. He made a grab for Rawley's gun and Rawley, fumbling to hold onto the revolver, fired a shot that landed in the man's throat. The man choked on his pain, wobbled and convulsed, and crumpled to the ground.

"Magdala," her father said. "Get out of here and don't look back."

He didn't need to say it twice: She was already crawling for the door as the other gamblers rose from their seats and began shooting blindly into the smoke. Their bullets sank into the doors, into the bar. Magdala glanced over her shoulder in time to see one sink into Xavier's thigh. Xavier fell back into a table, splitting the plywood with a thunderous crack, and it toppled down, spraying moonshine and broken glass. Rawley cursed and hauled him up to his feet and made for the door, firing a final shot at nothing on his way across the threshold.

"Mateo," Xavier reminded him, spitting the word out from clenched teeth.

"I'll go back for him. Just hold on a minute."

Outside, the night was in its fullest bloom; passersby had drawn their guns, made uneasy by the sound of a fight inside. The mule was nervous, his ears pinned back flat, his eyes big and white and rolling. Dulcinea struggled to hold the animal still. When she saw Rawley come out with Xavier, Dulcinea did not ask if Mateo was there, if Mateo was dead, she only waited for Rawley to set Xavier on the mule's back and then pulled the animal forward. Magdala ran hard to keep up, heedless of the pain in her foot, more than once stumbling and falling and forcing herself back up. They ran until they were far past the clump of shanties, and only then pulled the mule up short. Magdala keeled over and gasped, clutching at her clubfoot, and looked over at her father to see the wound soaking brightly through his pant leg.

"Looks as if they're still both living," Dulcinea said, turning to regard Mateo slumped across the rack of Rawley's shoulders. Rawley let the man sink lower until he was nearly dragging, then, with a grunt of effort, hauled him up onto the mule behind Xavier.

"You gonna live, brother?" Rawley said to Xavier.

"You don't think the same men who just shot at us might stitch me up, do you?"

"Wouldn't count on it."

"We have to get to another town."

At their backs came the hollow clang of gunfire. Rawley cursed. They got moving, Magdala leaning on Dulcinea so she could bear the sensation of her foot hitting the sand.

Behind Xavier, on the mule's back, Mateo awakened slowly. He fumbled at his waist, found his gun missing, and looked bewildered at the rest of them as if someone else had been responsible for its loss. "Where is it?" he asked.

"You know what you almost did back there?" Xavier shouted. "They robbed you blind and would've robbed you lame too if we hadn't stood in their way."

"You leave me alone. Wasn't any fault of mine that they're cheats," Mateo whined. "I figured pilgrims would be virtuous."

"You can't gamble and get drunk in a room of strangers; they're pilgrims, not saints," Rawley growled. "Can't believe you got out of there poorer than you came to it."

"It'll have to be you who buys the bottle of whiskey for the storytelling," said Mateo, slumping down weakly against Xavier's back. "On account of Alma's death. You know." He looked wide-eyed at them. "I haven't told my story yet. You got your ears open, little Magdala, our judge?" He didn't wait for her nod before he said, "Then you listen, because I'm gonna tell you how the old world ended and the new one began. And it's no work of God. No work of Masauwu the skeleton either. Just the work of men."

IN THE FIRST DAYS of the poison rain, all the rich folk stayed in their houses. And for a long time, they could almost pretend nothing was happening. They could get other people to fetch them food and aluminum suits and everything else to keep them comfortable. Let other people get burnt, they said, let them die, there's so many millions of them we won't ever run out. Only, those people—the people who would risk death for a couple days of subsistence—ran out sooner than they thought. Soon the rich folk were eyeing big eaten-away holes in their roofs, sweating in their aluminum suits, eating the last cans in their pantries, getting worried that they would have to face what had happened outside the walls of their big old beautiful houses. It was getting to look hopeless. And for some people, it was hopeless. But for others it wasn't.

See, it didn't take long for someone to notice that there are a few places in the world that don't get much rain, nor much poison. Alma's beatific Saint Sheldon wasn't just a holy man. He was a businessman, and he knew good money when he saw it. The world's fortunes are on the downswing, Saint Sheldon said to himself, but that doesn't mean mine got to be. And Saint Sheldon invited all his richest friends to come and live in the city of Las Vegas. Some of them even made it there. But once they did, they realized pretty quick that in the Remainder rich people aren't rich people anymore, really, just a bunch of dressed-up mouths that want feeding. Saint Sheldon looked out the windows of his casino, down into the city of Las Vegas. He said, somehow those people down there are still eating. They could take care of us like they did before. But they got no reason to do it. Unless they think there's something we got that they need. Something they can't scavenge or grow or wring out of the desert themselves.

Well, before long, Saint Sheldon heard tell of an old woman living in the trash heaps of Vegas. That little old lady should've been easy pickings—she was stiff as a board with arthritis—but somehow, some way, she could lay a hand on a baby or a child and put a blessing on them, keep them from all peril and hurt until the day they came of age. And for that, people venerated her as if she was a living saint. Brought her gifts of food and flowers. The roughest desperados in the Mojave wouldn't think of touching her. Now, Saint Sheldon didn't know how she was doing it, or why, but he knew an opportunity when he saw one. He had that woman killed, in secret, and then he robbed her grave, polished up her finger, and put it in a glass case in his casino. Charged admission. And, all of a sudden Saint Sheldon had himself a packed casino and a mountain of alms and a nice big fence under construction to keep the poor out of Las Vegas.

There's not much people won't do, you see, for their children. Saint Sheldon knew it. He founded a church on it.

"We gotta quit for the night," Xavier said after a while. "They're not chasing us, and the mule'll drop dead with our weight on him much longer."

"You don't have a thing to say, brother, about this story I told you?" said Mateo.

Xavier pulled on the mule's rein, and the animal came to an abrupt stop, eager for rest. Mateo, who had been hanging on only loosely, fell to one side and crumpled to the ground. "Not a word," Xavier said, looking down at him. "Don't matter whether or not it's true. Changes nothing now."

"Ease up on him," Rawley said, hauling Mateo to his feet. "Haven't you ever been too shit-faced to stand?"

"Not Xavier," Mateo said. "Xavier's made no misstep since he spilled out from his mama's womb."

"You shut your mouth," Xavier said. "Rawley, help me down. I got no strength."

They laid down with no fire, a knot of limbs. Desert winds blared savagely across their backs. In the predawn hours, a gunshot woke them. Magdala rose a second before the others, sticking her head up from the cradle of her elbows to see Rosy lying bloodied and dead-stiff in the sand. Her scream seemed to come from somewhere other than inside her. She did not feel the seconds that went by as Mateo stood across from them, squinting at his dead child down the barrel of the gun he'd taken from Xavier's holster.

Rawley cocked his own weapon and aimed at Mateo's head. "You better think again if you're planning on a massacre," he warned.

"I think I can fire off a shot before you," Mateo said. "But I'll have to choose carefully." He swung around, graceless, stumbling, and aimed at Magdala. "We'd make better time without a cripple girl-child holding us up."

"You hurt a hair on her head," Xavier began.

Mateo aimed his gun at Xavier then, looking ponderously down the barrel. "Maybe little Magdala's not the trouble," he said. "Maybe it's you. What do you think, brother? Should I fire a shot? Spare you the trouble of living in this godforsaken wasteland?"

"I'll shoot," Rawley said.

Mateo crouched low, aimed his gun at Dulcinea. "Go ahead," he said. "Shoot me. But first I'll land a bullet in your harlot's skull."

"Not his," Dulcinea protested in a voice very near to a whimper. "Shoot me if you want, but don't say that."

"If you're not his, whose name is still there on the left side of your neck? Brands don't go away. You get a man's name burnt into your skin, you're his for life, don't matter if you get another man's brand later, don't matter what anyone tells you. Don't matter what cliff or flood offers you sanctuary."

"You leave her alone," Rawley said.

"You gonna be chivalrous now?" Mateo said, and his laughter was sharp and broken in his throat. "You gonna protect the lady's reputation *now*, after what all you done? Does Xavier know what you did, when Dulcinea was just the same age as his daughter?"

Rawley fired at him, and the shot echoed long across the walls of the distant canyons before the wind carried it off. "Goddamn," he whispered as Mateo crumpled. "Goddamn. You ever seen anyone so stupid?"

"Wasn't stupidity," Xavier said. "There was one round left in that chamber, and that was before he went and shot Rosy."

Magdala hugged her knees to her chest; she was crying; she was thinking that Rosy was supposed to grow up and ride a white donkey through the mountains and comfort the sick in a hundred villages before being martyred.

"You dig the graves," she heard her father say.

"Not digging another grave," Rawley said. "I'm tired of that now. We'll find a canyon and throw him down. He'll make a fine breakfast for some coyote."

"This the man you called brother? Lived with him for years, hunted with him. And you wanna feed him to the coyotes?" Xavier shook his head. "Fine."

"He won't be the first pile of clean-picked bones on the pilgrim road."

"What about Rosy?" asked Dulcinea.

"Throw her down too," said Rawley.

"I can bury her," Magdala whispered. "I can make a little grave."

"Wasted work," Rawley said and dragged Mateo's body away.

They followed the road north into noon, passing nothing but for a few plywood signs with letters heat-faded and vague. *PHOENIX, 20*. Spray-painted pictographs promised a high flood area. The mule shied at a plastic bag in the wind, and Xavier answered with a grunt of pain. His bullet wound glistened and wept through the hole in his pants.

"You all right there, brother?" said Rawley.

"Just fine," replied Xavier. "Hungry, more than anything."

Phoenix's carcass spilled languidly across the desert, stucco and brick razed to a flat one-story line, the colors dusk-pale, suburban outskirts extending in a thick ungenerous sludge out from the city's body. Last chance highway stops lined the road, *PINK TURTLE INN* and *NO-TEL MOTEL* in unlit neon, iron bars across the windows with paint peeling in broad strips and empty swimming pools encircled by chain link, their floors painted sickening teal or else left gray, uniformly surrounded by rows of plastic loungers lying on their sides. The studded heads of saguaros rose greedily to the level of the rooftops, their flesh wind-burnt and nicked.

"Huh," said Rawley. "I thought this was a city."

"City enough for me," said Xavier.

The wind cracked loudly through a sagging plaster roof and Rawley drew his gun; Xavier, too, though the chamber was empty. The sound abated when the wind stopped, and the men holstered their weapons. Under the rising sun, they came to an empty city hall building with the ashes of some long-ago fire dried on the steps and a limestone statue of Cortés on a rearing horse out front, lifelike in the motion-less, unliving town.

Without speaking, Xavier prodded the mule up the building's steps and reached for the marble door handle. The door yowled on its worn hinges and slowly creaked open. He choked on the whorl of dust that rose up, then tapped the mule's sides again and disappeared inside.

"Reckless idiot," Rawley said. "Best case he finds noth-ing, worst case, he's trading shots with some holed-up lunatic, and him with no bullets in his gun."

"Go and get him," Magdala urged.

"No chance, little lady. He dug his own grave. We'll give him an hour and then I say we cut our losses."

"Magdala, come on," Dulcinea said, her eyes on Rawley. "We'll go and find him. Don't worry."

Magdala followed obediently, dragging her foot along. Dulcinea stopped every ten paces to wait for her, then took Magdala's arm under her own and nearly dragged her up the steps. "If your papa dies, we're both done for," Dulcinea said.

"Papa's not dying," Magdala said. Then she snuck a fur-tive look at Dulcinea's face. "Why?" she asked.

Dulcinea wrinkled her nose, exhaled with great disgust at something inside herself. "Magdala, I never told my story," she said. "I gotta tell you my story now."

The door opened to them. Their eyes swept across the twin staircases, the oil paintings now ghoulish and obscure beneath a sheen of dust, a medallion in blue and gold spanning the floor. Magdala's clubfoot whispered across the marble.

"Tell me," she said. "But I don't want it to be scared by it."

"I don't want to scare you," Dulcinea said, and she held out her arm for Magdala to lean on as they began to climb the stairs. "But I might have to, a little, for this story to get told."

THE GIRL WAS BORN FIFTH to her mama. After there were already four hungry mouths to feed. When she was born, she screamed and screamed and wouldn't be soothed. She bit her mama's breast when her mama tried to nurse her. This is no child of ours, but a child of the desert, a coyote-child, her mama and papa decided. So they left her on a low, flat rock beside the pilgrim road and hoped the desert would take her back. They thought of her like a ground squirrel burrowing down into the sand, or like a woodpecker making a nest inside a cactus. They imagined her running through the arroyos on four fast paws, a tail tucked between her legs. They told the four hungry mouths back at the house that she was going home.

She didn't go home. A man came along and took her. He had a business selling people in Las Vegas. She lived in his business for seven years. But he didn't sell her to anyone. She was almost like his daughter because he knew her from a baby.

When she was seven years old, a man came riding through town. He rode a black horse and had a string of coyote teeth around his neck. He stopped in and the people-seller said, "What do you want?" and the man said, "None of these, they're all too old. I want the child."

And the people-seller was maybe a little sad to say good-bye to his girl, but not sad enough that he didn't like the trade the man made. So the people-seller put ropes on the girl's wrists and new clothes on her back, and he said, "This isn't a good man who has you in his grip. And when you become a woman, he'll be finished with you. I know his kind."

When the man took the girl, he knew as soon as he saw her that she was a coyote-child. The first thing he did was he pulled her teeth out and strung them on his necklace. The second thing he did was cut off her fingertips. The last thing he did was spread her open wide and rip the coyote out from inside her until she couldn't howl. And then he carried her off on his big black horse, and no one ever saw or heard from her again.

Tell me you understand, Magdala. You aren't a coyote but a little cactus wren. Your bones are so thin. If he got ahold of you, he'd find no howl to rip out. And I don't know what would happen to you.

With the story finished, silence overcame the staircase. A blanket of dust sat oppressively on the wood steps. Dulcinea toed a conspicuous mark left by the mule's hoof.

"I don't hear anyone," Magdala whispered.

"That doesn't mean anything yet," Dulcinea said. She held Magdala's arm gently and lifted her up the last step.

They had an entire row of doors open to them, a long narrow corridor that ended in a painting of a corpulent man in velvet-looking clothes.

"He's dead now," Magdala breathed. "Everyone in the paintings is dead now."

"Lucky for us," Dulcinea said. "Let's open the doors and see where your papa got to."

Magdala reached for the nearest door and pushed until it reluctantly slid back. The inner room was empty except for a desk and a stiff, ragged sofa, stained thoroughly with some thick black sludge that had never faded. The second door was held shut with a link of barbed wire, which Dulcinea could not or did not try to outmaneuver. Behind the third, some long-dried skeleton had hung himself with a noose made from a pair of neckties. Dulcinea shut the door on that room so hard that it rattled on the hinges. Magdala touched the jamb of the fourth door, and her finger came away wet and gleaming.

"He's been here," she whispered.

"He has or something has," Dulcinea said nervously.

Magdala squared her shoulders and pushed tremulously away from the wall to the last remaining door, which was loosely shut, too obvious, too visible along the dust-smothered line of the wall. Then she looked and didn't stop looking until Dulcinea came down and wrapped her arm around Magdala's head like a blindfold. Xavier sat with the mule on the floor. The mule was breathing the shallow and raspy gasps of a creature in great pain. With one hand her father held the animal's head by the nostrils and with the other he was feeding himself.

"He's mad," Dulcinea whispered. "He's mad or that's the devil, that's all there is."

"No," said Magdala, thinking of the deer with the snake in its mouth, the putrid wound on its flank. "He's sick." She stumbled across the floor toward him. One look from her father slowed her pace; some distance remained between them when she stopped, her gaze fixed helplessly on the animal that had carried her through the desert.

Xavier went on feeding from the mule, but as he chewed, he turned and looked at her imploringly. With his mouth full, he asked, "Don't you think we better leave town?"

Magdala said his name. Her voice came out reed thin. She glanced back at Dulcinea, her entire body poised delicately on her good foot. "Papa, do you want to go?" she said.

"This meat's not tender," Xavier said. "Knew back when the cactus-sitter gifted him to us, but I was greedy, I was hungry." His voice dropped to a whisper then, became pleading: "Always, always I have been ravening."

Magdala mouthed the word *ravening* and looked helplessly at her father, the blood smeared around his mouth, the look of utter surrender in his features.

"Go and fetch Rawley, we'll have a meal. All of us, but I've gotta have the wolf's share; it's I who made the killing."

Magdala touched the brand on her neck. Her fingers traced across the letters, forming her father's name in silhouette; tears threatened. She said, "Papa, please."

"Magdala, come here; partake."

Magdala came toward him, slipping loose from Dulcinea's grasp. Her father was still eating, both hands digging greedily into the mule's flesh. As she approached, he turned again and looked intently at her, eyes narrowed. Magdala reached the mule's flank. She swallowed hard. "Come on, Papa," she said. "Let's leave him."

"Sooner or later, you eat or get eaten, that's what they say," he said. "Well, Magdala, I can feel it trying to eat me from the inside out, hollowing a space in me that it can fill. But it's *mine* to fill, isn't it?"

"Yes, Papa, but—"

"You can't afford for me not to eat this mule, that's the fact of the matter. Tell me, what would you do without your father? Big man, shadow long enough for you to hide in, strength enough for you to forget how strong you're not. Only thing standing between you and your annihilation. When you think about it."

"I'm getting Rawley," Dulcinea said.

Magdala stood still for a long moment, her eyes moving between her father and the mule. At last, she lowered herself to her knees, then sank lower into a posture of prostration. She descended until her forehead brushed the carpet.

"What do you think you're doing?" Xavier said.

"If you're so hungry, eat me and not him," pleaded Magdala. "It's my fault that you're sick, that you're here. Eat me and not him."

For a long second, her father said nothing. His fingertips pressed lightly like five darts into her back, and she did not shy away, she did not even breathe. Then the pressure let up, and she felt as he stood falteringly.

Magdala lifted her face from the floor. Her father was wiping his bloodied hands on his knees. He was trying to cry, but he was too dried out for tears. She rose tremulously to her feet and slipped her hand into her father's sticky, hot one, then pulled him toward the door. She did not let herself look back at the mule, whose soft and shuddering moans followed them out the door. They traced the mule's hoofprints back down the staircase. Staggering from the wound on his thigh, Xavier nearly fell and pulled himself back up and did not look at Magdala, would not let his eyes touch her.

Rawley and Dulcinea stood on the other side of the limestone statue, conferring anxiously, Dulcinea's arms crossed before her chest. When they saw Magdala and Xavier come out, Rawley drew his gun and aimed at Xavier's head.

"Real pity it's going down this way," he said to Xavier.

"No," Magdala cried, looking between the two of them, then at Dulcinea, whose eyes would not meet hers. "If we can get to Vegas, he can get better. Some saint could heal him."

"You there, Xavier?" Rawley said, approaching with slow, light steps, only the toes of his boots on the sand. "You somewhere inside that bundle of bones, or is it only the desert now?"

Xavier did not respond. His leg was bleeding again, his own blood mingling with the blood of the mule in a dark tapestry down his pant leg. Rawley waited a beat, then cocked his gun.

Magdala pulled Xavier's gun out of his holster and held the revolver awkwardly in both hands as she aimed at Rawley. Desperately, twice, she pulled the trigger. The gun clicked impotently at Rawley, who stopped advancing and watched them for a moment, his eyes moving between Magdala and her father.

"He's gone, girl," he said. "There isn't nothing left inside him for you."

"He's just sick," Magdala said. "Can't we stop a while? In one of these houses? Can't we rest until morning? He's bleeding so bad."

"Won't be any different come morning," Rawley said. "You get on my back, we'll make good time across the desert tonight. We'll find ourselves a town. Not Vegas. Somewhere they don't have so many rules. And you and me and Dulcinea, we'll have ourselves a real nice time."

"Let her stop the night," Dulcinea interjected. "Just one night."

"Who do you figure is calling the shots here?" Rawley said.

Magdala looked helplessly to Dulcinea. The girl's face hardened. She seemed to decide something. "You drag us along now," she said, "and I swear to you I'll make every step an awful labor. Fight you everywhere we go. Scream the truth of you to every town we come across. But you let her stay with her father for one night, and I'll go willingly—do whatever you want."

Xavier stumbled brokenly along the road through Phoenix, unable even to keep pace with Magdala. At length, the city subsided into a graveyard of houses, piles of timber and shattered glass half-eaten by those termites too thrifty to be killed by lack of water. When Xavier could go no farther, they camped in the ruins of a house with two standing walls and listened to the wind break hollowly between the slabs of stucco. Xavier lay on his back, boneless, insensate, still beaming at the moon. Dulcinea laid her blanket across his limbs, but the stiff knobs of his knees and elbows protruded sharply from beneath the wool. When she looked at Magdala, her eyes were wet. Before she left Xavier's side, she crossed herself.

Rawley whistled a long, lilting string of notes and sat with his ankles crossed, his back to the wall. He looked at his feet and he looked at Xavier and he looked especially at Magdala, who had been kneeling before her father, but now had her body flattened and her forehead on the ground. She was praying. Occasionally, she opened her eyes and looked at Xavier's face. She did not look at Rawley. The moon was high when she ceased and sat upright. She pulled her club-foot out from underneath her and said, "I never told my story."

Rawley uncrossed his ankles and raised one eyebrow, nodded for her to go on.

Dulcinea said, "You don't have to, Magdala."

"I want to," she said. "It was unfair, me being the only one who didn't get one just on account of me judging the others. But there's not gonna be any whiskey, is there? There's not gonna be a prize to judge for. So I can tell my story."

"Make this long night pass, then, girl," Rawley said. "Tell us something worth hearing."

THE LITTLE GIRL and her papa lived in a big, tall house with a hundred rooms. They had friends in the house; everyone knew them. In the rainy season, they all put out buckets by the door and gathered up all the rain until the buckets overflowed. They shared bread, they shared meat. In the daytime, the girl's papa went out into the desert with his gun and his boots and a rag on his face to keep the burn off, and he said she could go anywhere she wanted inside the big house.

After a long time, things got different. There wasn't good meat to kill in the desert anymore, and everyone kept getting sick and they didn't know why. Sometimes they thought it was each other, sometimes they thought it was the desert, and sometimes they thought it was God. They started making bonfires outside at night and throwing things in, whatever they had. Somebody was supposed to be having a baby, but the baby came out too soon, came out dead. They wanted to put the baby in the bonfire and send it up to heaven the way they sent up their books and their good jewelry, like gifts, like ways of saying sorry, so God wouldn't make anybody sick anymore. But the girl's papa said that was wrong, he wouldn't let them, and after that things weren't the same anymore.

Now the girl's papa left a lock on the door to their room when he went out to the desert, and only he had the key. The girl was peeing in a bucket and watching the sun go across the sky and drawing pictures in the dust on the floor. She started to have desert dreams when she slept, dreams where she was something else, where she crawled through the world like she was as much a part of it as a tree or a rattlesnake or the sky, and she felt sick when she woke up on the floor with bruises on her forehead from walking into the walls to find that she was still only her, separate and alone. She pleaded with her papa to take her out to the desert with him, but he said no, only if it ever got too dangerous in the big house. She thought on that and asked, "Dangerous like what?"

And he said, "Like if our friends wanted to hurt us."

She thought of the baby her papa wouldn't let go into the bonfire, and all the times he'd refused to share the food he brought home for her, and all the things people yelled at him, the names they had for him, because he was different

from the rest of them. And when she could, she started telling stories about her papa, stories that made people think
maybe he was working for the god of death, maybe he was
the reason people got sick. She made up that he brewed
potions in their room and marked crosses upside down on
the floor, and she drew pictures of his secret forms, showing
how at night he became a skeleton and a bat and a wolf.
And they believed her. They stopped taking meat from him,
they started staying out of his way. Then one night after
their bonfire, they came up and burnt down the door while
the girl and her papa slept, and the girl's papa woke her up,
saying, "Magdala, Magdala, we gotta go, no time," and she
was so happy to be in the desert, no more locks on the door,
being what she dreamed.

And that's how the girl killed her papa.

Magdala slept deeply and long. When she woke, the sun
had already risen, and the air was fiercely hot. Her father
was only bones beneath his clothes, clean and sun-polished,
as if he had died months ago. Rawley was gone, and
Dulcinea too, and she sat beneath the white sun on the hot
brick and wailed and wailed until her voice gave out.

EXILES

I WAS A YOUNG MAN of twenty-five, freshly reborn from my baptism in a shallow dish of twice-recycled holy water. "Don't open your mouth, whatever you do," someone had warned me. "It'll poison you." The church had faux velvet carpeting and faux walnut pews and faux stained glass in the windows. Someone told me that in the old days, they used to officiate marriages there: ill-suited couples wearing party clothes, reeking of tequila, staggering to the pulpit where some underpaid Rent-A-Minister stood with his collar wrinkled, a Bible open in his hands but not to be read, only there for visual effect, shorthand for covenant.

I was the third person they baptized that day. They were baptizing everyone they could get their hands on back then. Afterwards, there was a party in a casino. Someone had found a few helium balloons. We sipped moonshine from champagne flutes and sang hymns with our hands lifted, our eyes shut, all very pious, everything in order. Someone fell on the floor in spasms and spoke in tongues and I listened obligingly, although in secret I despised him as a show-off. I would have died before I told the other converts what I was capable of; I wanted desperately to tell them what I was capable of. I was a farm boy from Sonora; I knew I didn't belong.

Late at night, when we were all so drunk that I thought no one would remember, I told them I had healed a boy possessed with demons. I told them I had healed an entire field of blighted melons. I told them I had healed my mother when she was sick enough to die. My fellow converts laughed uproariously and toasted my name. *Arturo! The living saint!* In the morning, the priest admonished me not to make jokes about that sort of thing. "The Church, you understand, does not recognize the existence of the saint-touched," he said, glancing over his shoulder as he spoke like the word itself was contraband.

Not long after that, I went to seminary. You had to eat somehow. In Vegas, it was the priesthood or life as a blackjack dealer in a casino, a ticket-taker at a peep show, a waiter pouring jimson coffee in some greasy spoon. And the Church had grand ambitions back then. A franchise every fifty miles throughout the Remainder; licensed trail guides to shepherd pilgrims down the '93; official branded merchandise produced in the old tire factory outside town. Opportunities for advancement for any man who proved himself worthy, or so they liked to say.

That was forty years ago now.

When the girl found me, I had been living for a long time as a scavenger in the desert. I subsisted on the beloved possessions of the dead and the discarded trash of the living. I had a shack of ocotillo sticks, a vinyl sleeping bag, a tin lunch box full of Zippo lighters. I spent my mornings tracing the paths of wild burros to watering holes and my afternoons following the carrion birds that flew in low, dense packs through the desert, settling down in a heap when they found an animal carcass. They never ate what the desert had already taken hold of, so they were safe to glean from. I'd stand a few paces back from them and wait until they had finished, then approach.

In all my years in exile, I never killed any creature, and I never ate the fruits of the desert. I crept through the landscape like a thief in the night, wanting not to be seen or felt. I cooked scraps of thigh meat and coils of intestine in the coals of low fires. I boiled bones until the marrow streamed out and sipped the broth the marrow made. I went days without eating. I caught a glance of myself in a cracked mirror and would not have recognized the skeleton staring back at me if he hadn't borne my own brand on his forehead.

In every way that mattered, I considered myself dead. I was only maintaining the sack of bone and flesh allotted to me out of some vestigial Catholic terror of the sin that can never be uncommitted. Alive by a technicality. Whenever I found anything that surpassed my barest needs, I went to the house of Mrs. Whitemorning with a sack on my shoulders. She did not make any grotesque attempts at genuflecting or expressing gratitude; she stood stone-faced in the doorway as one of her charges, a girl of sixteen or so, older than the rest of her children, loaded the things I brought onto her shoulders and struggled into the secret depths of the house with them.

The girl never spoke to me before the day she held me at gunpoint. At twilight, stoking my fire, I looked down and recognized her by her clubfoot. When I felt cold gunmetal on my neck, I lifted my hands. My fire stuttered and died beneath me.

"I'm going to the shrine of Saint Elkhanah Fleetfoot in Las Vegas," the girl said from behind me. Her voice was low and flat and strange, as if she were unaccustomed to using it. "I saw the letters on your forehead and I know *H E R E T I C* is just a priest who got found out. So you can bring me through the desert, or you can get a bullet in your brain. Which will it be?"

I could not contain my laughter. I had been expecting a demand for food or valuables. A wholesome and reasonable stickup. She wanted me for a *pilgrimage*? For *that* pilgrimage? I entertained the notion that the girl was a demon, sent to tempt me as the devil had tempted Christ during his forty days in the desert. *Leap and see if God doesn't kill you.* But I had already succumbed to temptation. I had been weighed and found wanting. I had leapt and fallen, and God was even now killing me slowly. There was nothing left to see.

"You're wasting your time," I told her.

She didn't dignify that with an answer. She walked around me, keeping the gun to my head all the while. Standing before me, she was taller than I remembered, her face still soft with half-shed childhood, dark flyaways crowning her head. I could have fought her off and possibly won. I could have told her to just shoot me and possibly she would have done it. And in either case, I would not have faced the prospect of returning to Las Vegas, nor the absurd and profoundly tedious trial of a pilgrimage meant to end in a miraculous healing. But some part of me, patient and perverse, had been waiting through ten years of exile for even the thinnest wafer of an excuse to go crawling back and find out if the archbishop had meant it when he said *on pain of death*. I did not protest when the girl slipped a lasso around my neck. She tightened it until I gagged, loosened the rope a little, then tightened it back up with a nervous jerk as if regretting this show of conscience. She had a tattoo on her neck, brash lowercase letters rendered in whitish-pink: *Xavier.*

"I'll kill you if you make a move," she assured me. I did not make a move. The moon rose and I followed her lead. She was heading north, not toward the pilgrim highway but toward the old state road, which passed through two hundred miles of uninhabitable country. I hadn't met with that part of the desert since I had come stumbling away from Las Vegas with a fresh brand on my forehead, drunk with grief and too tenderfooted to know better.

"Other roads to the city," I said to her.

"Been on the other ones," she said. "Didn't like them. This way, we won't meet with anybody."

"Nobody human."

The girl scowled at me, twisting the dark, thin line of her mouth. "That's what I want," she said. "Be quiet."

By dawn, we'd made at least ten miles; I wondered at the girl's endurance, though I could see the strain in her legs, how she trembled when she lowered her clubfoot to the dirt. Still, I was tiring faster than she was. I could feel the desert on my lips, in my throat. Sand has a taste, distinguishable, depending on where you wander. I was breathing strange dust now. She wouldn't hear me when I spoke of thirst. She seemed to be immune. People in the Remainder had been telling stories, longer than I'd been living, of people born in the desert whose bodies craved unworldly things: they grazed on the stubble of cactus, sipped from ewers of wind. I began to wonder if she was one of them. She never asked for directions. She squinted at the sun or at the crown-shaped shadows of the yuccas to determine her course. Twice I thought I saw her inhale the wind like a predator catching a scent.

Eventually she heard my breathing grow raspy and halted, and she surprised me by looking sorry. We ascended an abrupt red slope and she inhaled again, wrinkling her nose, then led me a little higher. In the crack between one ledge of rock and another, a little stream of water opened to us, murky stuff, infested with life. She nodded at it. "You want to drink," she stated.

I nodded. By then my voice had left me.

"Then don't move while I dig," she said, and so desperate was I from thirst that I could only conceive of obedience. I sat down on an outcropping of rock and observed the girl, digging with her hands formed into clubs, half-fists, little paddles that pushed through the dirt and the rock. Old scores of scratches already crisscrossed her knuckles. No telling what her life had been before Mrs. Whitemorning.

"Come here," she said to me.

I had never left my suspicion of groundwater behind, and I knew that the clearest water was oftentimes the most dangerous. If we drank from the vein she'd unearthed, years from now we might sprout tumors. If the girl had children, if she still *could* have children, they would be born weak and sick. The animals one saw in these stretches were like living warnings. Two-headed or three-eared, stumbling on legs that ended at the knee. Were I stronger, I would have refused the water and died of thirst amid the sagebrush. But my tongue was heavy in my mouth, and my throat bristled with invisible needles, and I clung to life like a parasite, hungry and needful. I lowered myself onto my hands and lapped like an animal, swallowing as much soil as I did water.

"Thank you," I said, and she flinched; she would say nothing. She did not drink herself.

My thirst forced the girl to dig for water twice more before she deemed it time to stop and rest. For this purpose, she found a cave inside the hills, a low-ceilinged crevice barely large enough to slide a body inside. She threw her boot inside, and a rattlesnake glided irritably out into the sun, casting black eyes on us, the low shuddering click of its tail lingering after its body had already vanished. When I hesitated to enter, she shoved me inside, then braced her outstretched feet on a boulder and went to sleep with her back filling the mouth of the cave, barring my exit.

Confined in that dark hole, panic unfurled inside me like a night-blooming flower, and I thought of murder as I have never thought of murder. Terrible thoughts entered my head, hot and sharp and quick: *You could, you could, you could.* The possibilities fell before me like beads on a string. I did not know myself in that moment. I put my head between my knees and shut my eyes as if I could keep myself out. When I heard the girl ask if I was awake, I was frantic with relief. "Yes," I said, "Yes, please," and she yanked with an abrupt twist on the rope until I came out headfirst, resurrected into the cool twilight, heaving gasps as I inhaled something besides my own rank scent for the first time in hours.

"Something's coming," she said to me.

The dust storm fell heavily on us. You cannot imagine a storm like that until you've been inside one. Dust in everything: every crack in your skin, every orifice. The wind lashing at you so viciously that you can do nothing besides wait for the end. I could have sought shelter, but I would not return to the cave for anything; she even tried to shove me inside, but I resisted, my throat burning, my eyes screwed shut. At last she gave up on me and crawled inside, taking the shelter I refused. I made a wall of myself at the cave mouth, and now our places were reversed. When the storm passed, I collapsed flat on the ground and let her out. She looked at me with bald contempt. "Come on," she said, "come on," and dragged her clubfoot across the earth, digging a shallow ditch as she went. She filled out the shadow of me as we moved across the dirt.

I WAS A CHILD of five, of seven, of twelve, my childhood swallowed whole by the farm on the Remainder's rancid crust where eight generations before me had lived and died, at first in spite of the unforgiving heat and then in spite of the poisonous rain and at last in spite of the collapse of everything. Crooked monuments of juniper wood marked their graves in a field where inedible melons still came up during monsoon season. In the mornings, I rose with my mother and settled down among the rows of squash as she ripped out the weeds that had erupted from the soil overnight. "You will salvage this for us," she would murmur, and I never knew whether she was issuing a prayer or a command. She would kiss my forehead before she left me to my labors.

It was family lore that I had once healed a cricket with broken legs. If it was true, I had been too young to remember, and I did not know how to repeat the miracle. But still I sat in the fields all day long, my cheeks darkening from one shade of brown to another, beads of sweat forming and then drying on the hollow of my back. My brother Tomás was charged to bring me water, provisions, anything that I might need. My brother hated me passionately. While he hammered down fence posts and swept floors and hunted rodents, I sat among pumpkins that rotted from the inside out and Apache giants that grew teeth where they should have grown seeds and green cushaws that were consumed by tumors. All my sitting did nothing to deter their degenerations, and our harvests were as miserably small as those of our neighbors, and we began to understand that all my sitting could do nothing to deter our degeneration either.

"Arturo the holy one," my brother sneered when the last squashes died on the vine, splitting open a putrefied delicata with the toe of his boot. "Arturo the saint-touched. Tell me, Saint Arturo, is this your handiwork? Are you the one we have to thank for all this?"

By then our mother was days away from her burial among the inedible melons and her ancestors. By then we were only months from packing our very few things and salting the earth so nothing worse would spring up than what had already come and leaving nine generations of graves behind us. I did not know: was I the one we had to thank for all this?

The desert grew stranger as we traveled northward. The vegetation became uncanny-lush, leaves and trunks dyed to a deep, rich shade for which I had no name. Vines hung in fat, choking ropes from the paloverde trees and roots knotted thickly into the dirt, cracking the earth, upsetting the lazy flow of the soil. The girl stumbled across this jungle, catching herself on her hands, screwing up her face as if she wanted to cry. Slack hung in the lasso.

I soon realized something was alive on the hillside in front of us. I thought at first that only I could see it, but then the girl stopped short, blinking, assessing the figure in the distance. She licked her lips, drew breath, and unholstered her gun.

"Do I gotta blindfold you?" she asked. She must know stories, as I did, of people driven to insanity by the mere sight of the stuffed men that roamed the desert. But this creature was merely human.

"*You* think so," she said scornfully when I told her so.

The man came haltingly down the embankment toward us, bleeding profusely through a blanket wrapped around his torso. His blood was dark on the blue fibers. He was a big, broad-shouldered white man, somewhat younger than me but at least twenty years older than her. He wore a dingy sleeveless shirt; he had not been shaving his beard, although hardly anyone still did. We all breathed through armor out here, our words guarded. For all we knew, his gunshot wound could have come from an innocent. He could be a killer; he could be a rapist. Or he might be the innocent himself. Anyone might have shot him. He could be innocent and killer both. He dwarfed the both of us, but he was unarmed.

"He's desert sick," the girl said.

"Hey, please, help me," he called, speaking a harshly accented northern pidgin I hadn't heard in years. He advanced nearer with the drunken stagger of a man dying for lack of water. He wasn't desert sick like she'd thought, only hurt.

"I'll kill you," the girl screamed at him when he got too close.

The man hesitated, clutching his abdomen. He looked wildly from her to me but found no quarter. He was nothing to me; I could not be responsible for him.

"Get on your knees," the girl demanded.

He must not have understood, for he only lumbered closer still. The girl's entire body trembled, the gun rattling in her shaking fingers. Her face was twisted in an expression of terror. But still she did not shoot. He was so near, but she did not shoot. I wondered if she was only afraid to kill or if she was really harboring moral compunctions.

I thought: I owe her nothing, instrument of my death that she is, and less than nothing to this stranger. But something wrenched inside of me when I thought of seeing him perish there on the ground. Ten years of scavenging and I was still not inured to death.

"Please, get on your knees," I said to the man in pidgin. I had not spoken that language since I had left Las Vegas; it had been for me a pastoral language, one that I learned and spoke for people who had come to the holy city from the Remainder's northernmost fringe. I felt somehow dishonest, speaking it again.

As soon as I spoke to him, the man obeyed, collapsing gracelessly to the ground. The girl looked at me with her eyes narrowed, and I did not know whether she was surprised because she had not guessed I spoke pidgin or because she hadn't expected me to intervene on the man's behalf or both. "Ask who he is," she said haltingly, as if testing out a new power she had not known she possessed.

I did not want to be her collaborator. I did not want to help her take her second hostage. I had not spent ten years shrinking from the smallest slight against God or man only to become the right hand of the least prepared desperado in the Sonoran. "I'm not your translator," I said.

"Ask him!" She turned the gun on me.

Again and again she tested my indifference to my earthly existence, and again and again I clung miserably to life, making whatever compromises were demanded of me. I translated her question.

"Name's Boswell," the man said, his eyes moving between us. Trying, no doubt, to interpret the lasso around my neck, the gun in her hand. My halting compliance. I could imagine what he was thinking. What able-bodied man, even one elderly and half-malnourished, would permit a clubfooted child to take him hostage? "Who are you?" he asked.

No one had asked me that question in years. Mrs. Whitemorning did not care to know; the crows did not care. The girl seemed to think that she already knew. Inadequately, I said, "My name is Arturo."

I did not tack on the honorific *Father*, which no longer belonged to me, but as he scrutinized my robes, the brand on my forehead, I could tell by his expression that they signified something to him. "They'll be looking for you," he whispered.

There was not a soul living who wanted to know where I was. Still, I could not be unperturbed by the fear in his voice. The sensation that somehow he knew me. How many hundreds had passed through my confessional, visible to me only as blurs behind a lattice, a set of sins listed off in order of their seriousness? I might be intimately acquainted with him. I might have preached heresies before him; I might have baptized him in an unplugged Jacuzzi.

"What's he saying?" the girl interrupted.

I had no intention of repeating what the man had really said. "He wants to know your name," I said instead.

Her face was stricken. It was for her somehow a loaded question, I did not doubt it. "It doesn't matter," she said. Then, like an afterthought: "Magdala."

I wished then that I had not asked her name. Simpler to consider her only as my captor, the pitiless creature who had ripped me out of my solitude and immersed me in a bucket of unasked-for horrors and obligations. As soon as she had a name, she became historied. Someone had spoken those syllables over her when she was small and vulnerable. Or no one had, and the name she'd given was false. Easier, I decided, to call her *the girl*. But I gave Boswell her name.

"Where did you come from?" she said and turned the gun back on me when I didn't translate fast enough for her liking.

"Came from Reno, originally," he replied. "But I haven't been back there in twenty years, and I don't got a home now. I *was* traveling with a posse of shitbags down the '93."

I translated. The girl looked disapproving. "What shitbags?" she said.

Boswell hesitated, as if uncertain how much to give away. "Kind of people who shoot you in the gut and leave you for dead soon as you cross 'em," he said at last.

"What'd you do to cross them?" the girl questioned, suspicious now, uneasy. She had been pointing the gun at whichever one of us was speaking, but she kept it trained on Boswell from then on.

"Stole," he said. "A horse. *My* horse, really. Or the one I was riding. I was gonna ride out of there and not come back. They didn't take kindly to that notion."

"They stopped you from running away?" Her fingers were on her tattoo. No one would have branded themselves there, where the tight, knotted cords of the throat rippled close against the flesh. No one asked for pain like that. She could only have been marked by someone else, and she sounded like she was speaking around a ball of flame when she asked him that question.

"No," he said. "Probably wouldn't even have cared if I hadn't tried to take the horse."

The word *no* was clear enough without my translation. The girl considered him. "Why'd you wanna leave?"

"They were gonna get me killed, sooner or later."

"Why?"

"Gonna get themselves killed, too. It's one thing, what you do way out here. Another to break the law where the likes of the Deputy might see you."

Having exhausted her line of questioning, the girl reluctantly lowered her revolver. "You gonna work some miracle on him?" she said to me.

For a paralyzing second, I thought that somehow she had found me out, that even here in the most godforsaken corner of the desert, my reputation preceded me. I was afraid of what she might demand of me, what she might expect. I answered with panic. "I don't do that," I said. "I don't do that anymore."

Her brow furrowed with confusion. She had no idea what I meant, I realized. She had merely thought I would do something virtuous like treat the man's wounds because I was a priest. She really didn't know the Holy Church of Las Vegas, I thought with amusement.

"I don't know how," I said, and it was true.

The girl scowled. For a moment she deliberated, rocking back and forth on her good foot. Then, to my utter bewilderment, she holstered her gun and went to the man's side and crouched so she could look at him. She seemed unfazed by the mess the bullet had made of his abdomen. She told the man to lie down, then made a poultice from ground-water and a stalk of aloe that she cut from a plant nearby. This she ground into his gunshot wound with punishing force. He sobbed soundlessly, his whole body shaking, as she worked.

Twice the girl caught me watching her, and each time she glared as if embarrassed to be seen doing a kindness. No self-respecting pilgrim I'd ever met would have passed up the chance to accrue an extra shred of virtue on the road. Best to supplicate from a strong position. To be a good contender for mercy and grace. But she did not seem to think so. While she worked, she kept the lasso looped around her ankle so she'd have both hands free. I could have yanked and she would have fallen and I would have been loose. *Could* have. She must have seen the thought occur to me. She tied the lasso back around her wrist, her brow furrowed. Now she kept glancing back at me like she thought I might not be there if she looked away too long.

"Tell him he'll heal with the bullet inside him," she said to me as she finished cleaning the wound.

I repeated her words. Boswell could only nod back. He was looking at the girl with something between horror and wonder, his mouth opening and shutting as the shock of the pain reverberated through him. She was binding his stomach with strips of his blanket, tying tightly until he could barely breathe. When she'd finished, she used the remains of the blanket to tie his wrists and his ankles.

"Are you taking him hostage?" I asked.

"No," she said. "I don't trust him. What if it's all an act, and he gets up and takes the gun and attacks us? You want to fight him off?"

Nothing seemed less likely to me than the crumpled figure on the ground picking a fight with anyone, but I did not argue. It did him no real harm to be bound when he could not have walked if he'd wanted to. And he was not my prisoner. I wanted no part in her wrongdoing. I laid down in the dirt facing the fire the girl had made and let my exhaustion catch up to me. Across the flames, the girl's eyes were heavy-lidded, but she sat upright, her gun in her lap.

"Won't you sleep?" I asked. As far as I could tell, she hadn't even laid down since she had taken me two days ago.

She rubbed her eyes with the back of her hand. "Yes," she said. "In Las Vegas."

"After Saint Elkhanah heals you." I could not keep the derision out of my voice.

"Don't say it like that," she said, sounding wounded, sounding as if she'd expected more kindness from the heretic she'd kidnapped at gunpoint. I wondered what she would say if she knew what kind of man I really was.

$$\underleftarrow{}$$

I WAS A BOY of fifteen, standing in the parched Nevada earth before a dying man's crumpled form. My brother stood at my shoulder; ten of our fellow laborers watched from among waist-high rows of corn. Rodrigo the water-carrier was a relic of a man, old enough to recall the canonization of the first Vegas saint. His reward for fifty years of thankless work growing the crops that fed the holy city was a retirement of circling the fields with an ornery burro and a two-wheeled water cart. Every hour he came to us, like a small miracle. The promise of his return, the relief he bore with him, divided the hours of the working day into endurable fragments. What happened to him happened too fast to be seen: The burro spooked, the cart jerked sideways, the wheel broke, and Rodrigo was crushed beneath the cart and water barrel both. By the time we reached him, he was half-gone already. The crowd of us managed to pull away the splintered skeleton of the cart. His entire body was stiff with shock, his mouth open as if he too was in disbelief. A look of staggering pain crossed his face when someone tried clumsily to lift him. My brother tried to stave the bleeding with his shirt; one of the other workers ran to the village for help. All of us—Rodrigo too—knew that she would not be back soon enough. Still, he kept saying, "Please. Please."

I had healed my family's crops into shriveled weeds; I had healed my mother into her grave. I had no business healing anything. But the situation felt so hopeless that I thought my failure could not matter, and that freed me. I pushed past my brother to crouch at Rodrigo's side and rested my hand on his hastily wrapped wound. Said, "Can I help you?" He nodded, his eyes flinching shut. I closed my eyes too. I stayed with him. For an incalculable length of time, I stayed with him.

There was no moment when I felt the thing happening, only a bone-deep, slow-spreading weariness and a sense of compassion so stubborn and unbegrudging that I would have sat for a hundred years with him. All the while, he grasped my wrist with surprising force, his grip never slackening, as if he was clinging onto life. When the sun was low on the horizon, he struggled to his feet. Everyone but my brother was incredulous. As the crowd had dispersed, a field's worth of workers shepherding Rodrigo back to the barracks for the night, my brother shoved me to the earth. I landed on my hands and felt beneath me a soft furrow in the ground, almost a dampness, where the water barrel had spilled its contents. "Saint Arturo," my brother said, his voice choked with contempt and grief. "You *can* heal, huh? Just not Mama. Not our land."

"I can't," I said. "I didn't." But it seemed that I could, that I had. I could not face my brother after that. That night, when everyone else was asleep, I gathered my very few belongings and snuck out of the barracks and left for Las Vegas. I never learned whether Rodrigo recovered. I wonder even now if he was compelled to lead the same burro and a new cart around the cornfields for the rest of his life, if on every lap he sidestepped the soft furrow in the earth where his life was nearly extinguished. What the miracle had meant for him, if it had meant anything.

I fell asleep, collapsing into strange dreams, and woke with the desert sour in my mouth. The girl was watching me, looking impatient. Boswell stood near her, shaky on his legs. Sometime overnight, she had untied him. She shoved a half-filled plastic bottle of sand-colored water at me.

"I dug it last night," she said. "He's already had some."

While I drank, she stomped on the remains of the dwindling fire, then slid her gun out from her makeshift holster. "He's dying," she said to me, jerking her chin toward Boswell. She seemed neither pleased nor grieved by this.

"He looks better," I said. He had been unable to stand only a day before.

"He's not. His wound is infected. He's feverish."

Scrutinizing the man more closely, I could see she was right. He was flush-faced, unsteady on his feet. "Does he know?" I asked.

She shrugged. "I want you to tell him he can go with us until his life runs out or he can die here alone, it's no matter to me." When I protested, she rolled her eyes. "I can't do it or I would. It's not such an ordeal. Hurry up."

"What if he doesn't die?"

"Then he doesn't."

I had never before pronounced a man dead to his face. I had many times been asked to comfort the dying or eulogize the deceased, but I had not been the one to issue the sentence. I did not know how to do it with grace or compassion. In the end, I could do no more than repeat the girl's words to him, though it hardly mattered; by the look on his face, I could tell he had already known.

"Let me go with you," he said. "I want to die near home."

He had said before he had no home. I wondered if he was dreaming now of a childhood in Reno. A dog at his heels, a scant but lovingly tended garden, a meal that no one else knew how to prepare like that. His eyes were glassy and too wide. We let him walk with us.

We moved at a crawl, accommodating Boswell's wound and the girl's clubfoot. *Northwest*, she kept muttering to herself, like a prayer, like a promise. Boswell dropped after a few hours, sinking heavily down and looking at us imploringly. The girl holstered her revolver, then shuffled closer to him and bent and lifted him from beneath the armpits, straining against his weight. He dwarfed her. She held him up until he stood, tremulously, hands outstretched for balance. I was startled by the care she showed to him. I would have found it easier to have gone on thinking she was incapable of kindness.

"Ask him if he wants to stop," she said, watching him waver.

"Can you go on?" I said to him.

"Yes," he said. "I only need a minute."

"He wants to rest," I translated.

"He's dying," she said flatly, but she helped to ease him down onto a boulder and only stepped back when he was steady. She was not strong. Most of the effort was Boswell's. But Boswell thanked her.

"It doesn't matter," she said, seeming to understand him. I declined to translate.

We could not make a fire with the evening so wind-torn and the brush so sparse, so we stood close to each other to brace against the cold and waited for Boswell's life to expire. His breathing hitched but would not slow. He was refusing to die, his body struggling obstinately into night. The sun set and still he lived.

"Father," he said to me, as the moon rose high.

I flinched away from those syllables, as if refusing to answer to the title could protect me from the stain it had already left on me, body and soul. But he insisted. "Father!" he repeated, his voice raspy. I was terrified of what he would ask me, if he somehow knew that I used to heal people in conditions far less dire than his. But he only said, at last, "Please, I want you to give me my last rites."

I should, I thought, have exchanged my robes for a dead layman's clothes. I should have worn a bandana or a hat low on my forehead to conceal the Church's mark on me. As long as I squirmed inside that old exoskeleton, I could never hope to become anything besides a termite. I could feel the girl's eyes on me. Boswell began to cry openly. "Please, Father," he said. "Please, do not let me go to my creator without an act of contrition."

"What does he want?" the girl asked me.

"Last rites."

"And you won't do them?"

She would not understand, blithe and savage pilgrim-desperado that she was: I could not perform the sacraments without feeling my own unworthiness ooze into them like a slow poison. I feared that any act of contrition performed at my behest would only damn the supplicant. And, if I was honest, I was afraid for the Almighty to see my face. It had been years since I had last said a prayer. I knew better than to think it could be welcomed or answered. But even now I could not be unmoved by Boswell's desperation, his infant-like hunger for the simple comfort of telling his God he was sorry before he evacuated his corpse. And, after all, did I not know how to administer a sacrament with the hollow competence of a seasoned parish priest who never prayed unless he was in front of an audience? I would not, could not, heal him. But I could do this.

I knelt before Boswell so we were level with each other. I crossed myself, then him. I had no anointing oil, so I spit on my fingers and pushed a cross of saliva into his waxy forehead. He was weeping openly now, his entire body shaking.

"Have you been baptized in the Holy Church of Las Vegas?" I asked.

He nodded limply.

"And you want to say contrition?"

"Yes," he whispered. "Yes." His eyes were glassy, his forehead hot.

I stood on the edge of the meaningless and self-made precipice a moment longer, and then I leapt from it and said to him the half-remembered words in pidgin:

My God, I am deeply sorry for
Having offended you

He tailed my words, and, behind me, so did the girl. I heard her.

And I detest
All my sins, because of your
Just punishments

Boswell sputtered the final word and could say nothing more; he was too close to death now, trembling on the
threshold. I held his body upright, grasping his shoulders,
and went on, hearing the girl's voice tremble as she spoke
words she didn't even understand, barely audible beneath
the wind.

Most of all because they offend
You, God, who are all good and
All deserving

Boswell was dead. I held in my arms a cadaver. Yet the
girl kept repeating my words, and so I persisted, driven on
by the inertia of the ritual, the needful pull of the verse, the
terror and ecstasy of speaking to one who could destroy me.

Of my love

Her gun clanked; I thought, for a moment, she was
going to shoot me, and I glanced over my shoulder, but she
was kneeling. The clanking sound had only been her revolver as she hit the ground. Her hands covered her eyes so
I could see her face only through the lattice of her fingers.
As if she were embarrassed to feel whatever she was feeling.
I turned back around and faced Boswell, his face slack, eyes
too open, and I gripped him as if he were a cliff's edge, and
said:

I firmly resolve, with the
Help of your
Grace

Bile rose in my throat. The feeling of weightlessness
was lost. I became again, irrecoverably, myself. I dropped
Boswell's corpse and the prayer went unfinished. The girl
didn't seem to realize.

I WAS A PRIEST of thirty-two, fresh-faced and well-fed in my black robe, but achingly hungry for the admiration of my superiors, or at least my parishioners. I had neither. On Sundays, I preached homilies that bored my audience to sleep. On weekdays, I entered the confessional. I had a wax potted fern, a leather-bound Bible. Through the afternoons, my parishioners trickled in and out, bearing guilt disproportionate or inadequate to their wrongdoings, bearing thinly veiled exhilaration at forcing a sheltered man of God to hear their transgresses. Bearing desperation so palpable that their confessions were like pleas. *Father, I cursed God's name when I learned my husband was dying from the cancer in his stomach. Father, I have been skimming off the top when I empty the register at night; it's just—I must afford the medicine somehow. Father, I have thought of burying myself alive, my head sprung up from the sand like a cactus.*

From my seat, I threw down prayers of contrition to repeat-after-me-now with the rote and ruthless motions of a blackjack dealer, trying never to listen too closely for fear that I would hear something that moved me to work a miracle. Early in my career, only once, I had tried to lay hands on a sick child and heal them. But I felt nothing when I did it, and the child died days afterward. I supposed then that I was impotent. I supposed I was free of the burden it would have been to work miracles. And the longer I sat in the confessional, the less I feared, for had I not heard everything and responded to none of it? Their sufferings were nothing to me. Nor their transgressions.

I passed the hours by watching a slit of sunlight move across the floor, impatiently waiting for the slit to vanish into the corner as the sun sank lower in the horizon.

When my shift was over, I drank in silence with my fellow men of God on the rooftop of the Glitter Gulch, the twenty-foot-high neon silhouette of a nude cowgirl intermittently blinking in and out of life at our backs, our parishioners suffering and sinning and hurtling toward death on the streets below.

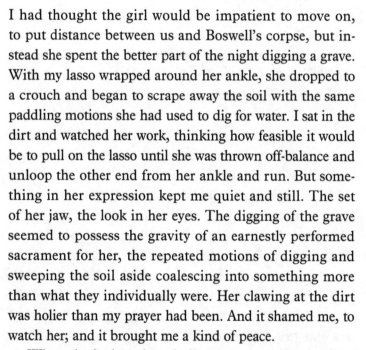

I had thought the girl would be impatient to move on, to put distance between us and Boswell's corpse, but instead she spent the better part of the night digging a grave. With my lasso wrapped around her ankle, she dropped to a crouch and began to scrape away the soil with the same paddling motions she had used to dig for water. I sat in the dirt and watched her work, thinking how feasible it would be to pull on the lasso until she was thrown off-balance and unloop the other end from her ankle and run. But something in her expression kept me quiet and still. The set of her jaw, the look in her eyes. The digging of the grave seemed to possess the gravity of an earnestly performed sacrament for her, the repeated motions of digging and sweeping the soil aside coalescing into something more than what they individually were. Her clawing at the dirt was holier than my prayer had been. And it shamed me, to watch her; and it brought me a kind of peace.

When she had made a shallow trench wide enough to hold a man, she slipped my lasso back around her wrist and dragged Boswell to his grave by the arms. After all the care she had shown the grave, I was taken aback by the careless way she handled its contents. "You could close his eyes," I said, but the suggestion only drew from her a look of contempt that was so peevishly adolescent that I would have been amused if she didn't have a rope around my neck. She left the man bundled awkwardly, one arm behind his back, and heaped dirt on top of him until he vanished.

"Something'll dig him up, like as not," she said under her breath, surveying her work. I was not deceived by this show of cynicism. I had watched her work through the night's coolest and most hospitable hours. But she did not glance back at the grave once as she pressed onward, and I had the sense that it was the work of burial itself, not the extinguished life it was done for, that had meant something to her.

We had walked the state road for only a few hours when riders materialized on the horizon, a clump of thrashing limbs that, from a distance, appeared as one enormous and many-headed behemoth. I would have believed such a creature walked the Mojave. I felt both relief and dismay when I realized we were only encountering other human beings, and ones probably better equipped than ourselves for the desert. The girl tensed up on my lasso and froze like prey when she saw them. "I should've known," she muttered. "He *told* us." Her eyes swept across the barren landscape. The Sonoran, for all its many sins, had the decency to offer cover to the slinking creature. In the Sonoran, we could have crouched in the buffel grass, amid the sage. But the Mojave was all bare earth and lonely Joshua tree silhouettes. There was no chance the men hadn't already seen us.

"What do we do?" the girl whimpered. As if I were the one leading the pilgrimage. It rankled me, her insistence on acting as if I were really her guide only because she had told me I had to be. I did not want her to forget what she had done to me. I did not want her to think she was for-given merely because we had together watched a man die and buried him.

"You do what you want," I said. "I'm already a captive."

The girl sucked air between her teeth. She had, at least, the decency not to look wounded. The sounds of hooves on the dirt, low and shuddering like thunder, reached us. In a hollow gesture of resistance, the girl lifted her revolver and aimed shakily at the oncoming crowd.

The horses the men rode were like no horses I had ever seen: mangled-looking beasts, their bone structure primitive, their stride high-backed and unsteady. Desert animals, half-feral and angry, straining at the iron bits jammed into their mouths, lifting their feet to kick at imag-ined nuisances. Their heads shaped like clubs, their eyes small or swollen or in one case missing entirely, their bris-tled coats patchy and bruise-colored. But the men on their backs were a more familiar species. They all wore the same sun-bleached denim uniform, bandanas cloaking their mouths from the dust, weather-beaten Stetsons pushed down low on their foreheads.

The leader drew up on his horse's rein and looked at the two of us, the girl with the revolver in her trembling grasp and me. "Father," he said, solicitously, tipping his hat. At his nod, the other men drew their guns. He spoke the same pidgin Boswell had spoken, though with a sharp accent that suggested he'd been born on the Remainder's barely habit-able northern fringe. I suspected these were the men who had left Boswell for dead. I only wondered if they were still looking for him.

The leader drew his revolver last, and slowly; while the others had aimed at the girl, he pointed his weapon at my chest and watched me, a smile quirking the corners of his mouth. "You're an awful far way from home," he said. "Sent on some holy mission, I'm sure. Official Church business?"

He had the slinky patience of a predator playing with its food. I thought I had known a thousand men exactly like him. Some of them were bookies. Some of them were bishops. I was still deliberating over what to say, whether to attempt a lie in spite of the brand on my forehead, when the girl cried, "We have no valuables."

At the man's look of confusion, I translated for her, deciding that the sentiment was far from the worst thing to express to a group of men wearing the costumes of bank robbers. But when I repeated her words in pidgin, the man only grinned. "Don't know about that," he said. "I think you're plenty valuable."

I could not fathom what he meant. If he hoped to ransom us, he was in for a disappointment. Possibly there were no two people in the entire Remainder more unwanted. But I did not have time to ask what value we had to him, or to disabuse him of the notion that he had anything to gain from taking us. He swung down from his horse's back and crossed the short distance to us on foot. The girl held perfectly still as he approached, her gun hanging uselessly in her hand at her side. At the last second, she threw down the weapon and broke into an unsteady run. She made it no more than five paces before he caught her.

The men were clearly practiced in taking captives. They tied us at the wrists and secured the ends of our bonds to the horns of their saddles as if we were cattle, assuring us that we were well within kicking distances of their horses. Then they set off at a trot, fast enough that the girl had to stumble and put her full weight on her clubfoot to keep pace. She gritted her teeth against the pain of putting her twisted limb down flat, her bound hands reaching out ineffectually when her stride broke as if trying to catch herself. She did not speak to me, but every once in a while, I caught her glancing in my direction, as if she wanted to know I was there, that she was not alone. I refused to meet her gaze. I did not want to be her comforter.

After an hour or so, she wearied enough that she fell and did not catch herself. For a few gruesome seconds, the horse dragged her before he came to an uncertain halt, sensing the dead weight behind him. I waited for the rider to dismount and put her back on her feet, but he only glanced over his shoulder at the girl's crumpled figure and spurred the horse onward. The girl uttered a half-smothered cry and reached blindly out with open hands, clawing at the earth. She could find no purchase. I feared how she would look when she lifted her face. I cried out in protest and felt the agonizing passage of seconds before the leader turned his horse inward and brought the rest to an abrupt stop.

"Goddamn, Jeroboam," he said, shaking his head. "This is an *asset*, don't you understand? You get her off the ground and put her up there with you."

"It's always my horse you're burdening," whined Jeroboam. His mouth clamped shut the second the words were out, as if he were willing himself not to say what he'd already said, and he cast a furtive, fearful look at the leader before he slid down from the horse's back and lifted the girl from the dirt. She flinched away from him with as much force as she could manage. I could tell she was in pain. Gouges of blood and soil had made of her face a patchwork. Her lip was split, her eye already swelling.

"You want to ride?" Jeroboam said impatiently, as if he had been ordered to do the girl a very great favor. Uncomprehending, she didn't answer, and after a second, he lifted his hands in exasperation and stomped back to his horse.

"Do you want to ride with him?" I asked her.

"Not with him," she said, lifting her chin, regarding the man with loathing. Her meaning was clear, even if her words were not. In the end, no one made her ride. The men took a slower pace after that, and proudly, stiffly, she walked another hour.

At sunset, our captors made camp in a thatch of mesquite. They tied us at the wrists and ankles and left us a little ways from the rest of them. Silently, we watched as they went about their night's work. One produced a book of matches from his pocket and made a low fire with a pile of mesquite sticks. Another dug a chunk of meat from the pack at his side and sawed it into six pieces, equally portioned, then served one to each of us. The girl regarded the meat with suspicion, refusing to partake even after the other men ate their parts. My teeth were too brittle to saw through the dried flesh, but I was so hungry that I satisfied myself by sucking on it until it softened enough for me to swallow. I occupied myself this way until the leader stalked over to us.

"My sincere apologies for that rough introduction," he said, lowering his bandana to expose a pale mouth and a wind-roughened, bald upper lip. "We been on the road a while, and I'm afraid Jeroboam has simply forgot how to treat a lady."

The girl was silent.

"She speaks no pidgin," I explained to him.

He nodded, unsurprised; hardly anyone south of Vegas did. "Well, you tell her I'm Barabbas Knight. Jeroboam is the one that dragged her. Over there is One-Eye." One-Eye, correspondingly, had an empty socket where an eye should have been. "And the one wandering off like he's stuffed is Barebones. Now Barebones is a churchman like yourself." He nodded to me. "And he's been our liaison to the Holy Church of Las Vegas for 'most three years now."

The man pacing a ways from the others had a cross burnt into his forehead, a mark that I very much doubted had been portioned out by the Church and might possibly have been self-inflicted. Though I tried, I could not imagine him inside a confessional, standing at a pulpit, straining the stitches on a black robe with those heavily muscled shoulders.

"I know him," the girl said when I had translated, jerking her chin toward Barabbas.

Against my better judgment, I repeated, "She says she knows you."

Barabbas Knight struck a match across his leather chap and lit a cigarette, securing the loosely wrapped bundle of jimson between thumb and forefinger. "That so? 'Cause I could swear I never met a cripple crippled quite your way."

"He doesn't remember you," I told her.

"I don't know him. Only his name. Someone told me his name. I can't remember." She shook her head. "It doesn't matter. Ask how come they took us. Ask if they want us dead."

I was not certain I wanted the answer to that question, but of course it would come out sooner or later. "She wants to know why you took us," I repeated.

"Well, that's easy," said Barabbas Knight. "One word. Money. Know that in almost every language." He grinned with chew-stained teeth at the girl.

"Ransom, you mean?"

"Ransom? Not exactly. You don't know, huh?" He scrutinized me, looking narrow-eyed down the bridge of his nose. "I guess you've been out here a while. The Church is paying handsome bounties on heretics these days. Wants them rounded up so they quit shit-stirring in every godforsaken corner of the Remainder. Between the two of you, I reckon we'll make enough to take a nice vacation."

I was, for a long moment, too incredulous to translate what he'd said. That they were taking us to Las Vegas. That the Church wanted to reclaim its heretic-exiles enough to pay for them. *They're looking for you*, Boswell had said. I could not fathom why the archbishop should want to reclaim the detritus he'd swept from the streets of his holy city.

Then again, I knew not everyone with brands on their foreheads had crawled away in shame as I had. Some of them had gone out triumphant. Some of them had carried their heretical doctrines and unauthorized miracles out to places the Church could not easily follow. When I still lived in Vegas, rumors of their wayward ministries would surface in bars frequented by travelers. On occasion, some desert-bleary pilgrim would even show up on the Strip clutching a pamphlet or repeating a story that openly defied Church doctrine, looking for a shrine that did not exist. Exile was not enough to protect the people's imaginations when Vegas sat like a poisonous fruit amid the hideous briar-patch of the Remainder, surrounded on all sides.

Haltingly, I repeated what Barabbas had said to the girl, realizing only as I finished speaking that he somehow thought she too was a heretic with a bounty on her head. The girl caught on faster. "I'm not a heretic," she said urgently, imploringly, as if this accusation were graver and more offensive than any other that could have been uttered against her. "Tell him."

I repeated what she had said.

"What are you together for then?" said Barabbas, grimly satisfied, seeming to think he'd already caught me in a lie.

The absurdity of my situation rankled like an old wound I couldn't stop reopening. "Not by any choice of mine," I said. "She took me prisoner."

Barabbas paused, then erupted into laughter. "She *took* you?" he said. "Listen, boys, listen to this. The crippled child kidnapped our man of the cloth, he says."

One-Eye and Jeroboam laughed in tense, dutiful brays that died a second too soon for Barabbas's satisfaction. He turned his back on them with a punishing gesture and looked back and forth between the two of us. "She's got a tattoo," he said to me. "Just the same as yours. I heard of them being on the neck. On harlots."

He couldn't read, I realized, and he didn't know or care enough to discriminate one set of letters from another. "He's confused," I told the girl. "About your brand."

The girl ducked her head, covering the ridge of scar tissue on her neck protectively with her fingers. She seemed as dismayed that they'd noticed her brand as that they were planning to abduct her on account of it. "I'm not a heretic," she insisted. "Tell him it says *Xavier.*"

I repeated her words to Barabbas, but his patience was fraying. We were not so funny a joke that he would keep laughing. "Don't know what *Xavier* is," he said, facing the girl as if she could understand a word he said. "But if we

can't sell you to the Church, we surely can sell you to someone. It doesn't trouble me either way."

I was reluctant to translate what amounted to a veiled
threat to her, not only for fear of how she might react. In
a handful of hours, the girl had been diminished in my
estimation from an armored creature of the desert to a
frightened child, big-eyed and bloody-nosed, even more vulnerable than she knew. Or perhaps *just* as vulnerable as she
knew. *Been on other roads,* she'd said. *Didn't like them.* "You
don't have to worry about the Church," I said when he'd
gone, instead of translating. "They'll laugh him out of town
if he tries to collect a bounty on you. They know a heretic
when they see one."

The girl refused to be consoled. "And then what do you
figure he'll do to me?"

There was nothing I could say to comfort her that was
not a lie. He might, of course, do anything. We sat watching
in silence as the men assumed their nighttime positions.
They slept in the approximate shape of a cross, their
feet facing inward. The one called Barebones kept watch
without being asked, sitting with his knees tucked to his
enormous chest and staring at the campfire that blazed
impotently into the overwhelming darkness. Despite his
standing guard, or because of it, the girl would not sleep.
As I made myself comfortable in the dirt, she sat stiffly and
studied her hands.

"We have to get out of here," she said in a whisper.

It did not seem to me that we had any real chance of
escape. We were bound at the wrists and ankles. Even if we
had not been, we could never have outrun them on their
horses—certainly not with the girl walking the way she did.
We would have needed to steal away undetected, and it

seemed that the men slept in shifts. "If you find a way," I said, "you let me know."

If she was stung by my lack of confidence, her face didn't show it. But after a long while, she said, "I know I shouldn't have took you."

I had never expected anything so near an apology from her, and yet hearing it brought me no satisfaction whatsoever. I held my tongue and kept my eyes fixed on the dark line of the horizon. I had nothing to say that I would not later have to repent for.

"I just don't understand why you didn't fight, even," she said. "It was like you didn't care what happened to you."

"You might have noticed, only one of us had a firearm."

"It wasn't loaded," she said, sulkily.

I looked at her in disbelief. The absurdity of the entire situation swelled to grotesque proportions. If I had only called her bluff, I could easily have lived out the rest of my years an exile in the Sonoran, unseen by man or God, forgotten by the Church. It was my panicked scrambling for life, my hungry infantine clinging to existence, that had landed me here. As I'd knelt before my fire, staring at her clubfoot in the dirt, I had been not in the place of Christ overlooking Jerusalem with the devil at his shoulder, but Abraham laying his son on a sacrificial altar, unaware that a goat would emerge from the undergrowth. And I, faithless coward, I, flinching away from the prospect of surrender, had failed to tie the limbs or pile up the kindling. So instead, the flames had engulfed me.

"I wish you hadn't told me that," I said to her.

The girl shrugged. "You know, I figured *you* would have a gun," she said, defensively. "Everyone usually does."

"I don't kill."

She looked sidelong at me, full of adolescent contempt. "What are you, a cactus-sitter?"

I had never heard the word before.

"You know. Those hermits out near Nogales. Well, they're hermits but all together. They meditate morning to night, and they don't arm themselves."

"Never heard of them."

"I met them when I tried to go to Vegas before, when I was small. They were kind to me. They gave me a mule without me paying anything for him." She sounded not like herself when she spoke now. She sounded softer, she sounded young. "I doubt any of them have survived," she said, and there was something like self-punishment in the way she condemned them to an imagined death.

I was distracted by the revelation that she had attempted to make a pilgrimage before. "This isn't your first trip to Vegas?"

The girl seemed to remember herself then. She looked suspiciously at me. "You don't gotta ask so many questions," she said. "It's none of your business."

"Thought I was your guide."

She flinched as if she was embarrassed to be reminded. "You're not my guide anymore. Because we're not on pilgrimage now. We don't have anything to do with each other."

I found myself strangely affronted by this pronouncement. She could not tie a lasso around my neck and then simply cut herself loose. We were in some way bound to each other until this journey was over, however it ended. "You brought me here," I said. "The way I see it, you're responsible for walking me through."

She regarded me with something between scorn and amusement. "Am not," she said.

"You are."

The girl was silent for a long moment. "What would the Church do to you," she asked, without looking up at me, "if you were turned over to them?"

"I don't know," I said. "They used to like drawing and quartering."

"Would God not save you from them?"

God would not spit on me if I was on fire. "You noticed a lot of divine intervention on my behalf, thus far?" I countered.

She chewed on this. "How come they exiled you?" she said, perhaps wondering if the Church had been in the right when they branded my forehead.

I had no reason to care what the girl thought of me, least of all now, when my life was no longer in her hands. But I found I could not bear to confess aloud that I was every bit as much a fraud as her Saint Elkhanah, he a two-bit con man transmuted by the Church into a healer of the lame, and I a healer of the lame transmuted by the Church into a two-bit con man. I did not want her to know I had embodied all the greed and self-aggrandizement and corruption that wrung a working economy out of faith and desperation. And not only had I embodied those things, but I had embodied them so fully that the Church itself had recognized me as competition. I had not realized until this very moment how desperately I needed the cheaply won moral high ground the girl had granted me when she held a gun to my head and slipped a rope around my neck.

"Doctrinal disagreements," I said at last.

"Mrs. Whitemorning always said she thought either you was atoning for something so bad you could never make it up, or you were just a filthy child-fucker trying to win her over," she said, looking sidelong at me.

She spoke so casually that I almost didn't hear the edge in her voice. It had not occurred to me that she might think my transgressions were so venial in nature.

"My sin was pride," I said, to put her mind at rest. "I thought God wanted me for something. I was disabused of that notion."

I WAS A PREACHER–BUREAUCRAT of fifty-six. Bloated and malnourished from my diet of deep-fried entrails and filched communion wine, I hid my gut beneath a formless black robe while I stumbled mechanically through the liturgy. The collection plate came back empty most weeks. As I traversed the monotonous track set out for me, Las Vegas mutated and grinned dementedly at itself in the cracked mirror of the Mojave.

I was surprised when I received an invitation to the home of the bishop of north Vegas, a man who had been my immediate superior for ten years, but in whose presence I had been only a handful of times in my whole career. I had not thought he knew my name. I fantasized that I had been admitted somehow into the upper echelons of the Church, to sit among those men of real power who resembled the rest of us only in the light of day. I even had the audacity to wonder if I had done something in the half-hearted discharging of my ecclesial duties that had commanded the Church's attention. I dressed in the least ratty of my vestments and combed my thinning hair.

The bishop lived in the penthouse of The Silver Nugget, a second-tier pile of cement that compensated for its squat, unassuming exterior with the most ostentatious lobby I had seen outside the Sunlite: high-pile, wine-colored carpeting and damask wallpaper in opulent, sultry colors, rows of slot machines respectfully concealed by bedsheets. I climbed five flights of stairs and emerged into a room heady with the odors of jimson and what I would later recognize as pineapple. In the corner, a woman wearing a feather boa and a sequined gown was playing an out-of-tempo litany on an upright piano.

I had expected it would be a party, that there would be other guests besides myself, but I found I was alone. I realized my host was in the room only when I turned my head and found him sitting motionless at the head of a lacquered wood table, incongruously small in the room's vastness, his head half-obscured by an enormous vase of silk orchids. He was dressed not in his vestments, but in a pool-blue shirt printed with swollen, hallucinogenic-looking tortoises, and he looked on the whole twenty years older than he had looked when I had seen him only a handful of months before.

"Arturo," he said from among the flowers. "Come and sit down. Let's eat."

And we did: more than I had eaten, cumulatively, in the entire preceding week. A man with heavy-looking tumors on his forehead and his bare scalp brought out two platters of what appeared to be steak, and proved instead to be a javelina's gamey flank, slathered in a bloody-looking desert-fruit compote so it had the look of rare meat. From there, the dishes only became more artful and less edible, food disguised as other food that no one alive had eaten, but that everyone thought they knew from sun-bleached billboards and old cookbooks. The thin, warped bodies of cactus wrens, cooked as though they were chickens; pads of prickly pear, cut into thin strips and cooked in lard until they resembled fried potatoes; hand-pies assembled from powdery mesquite flour and stuffed with a dark, gelatinous stew of rodent organs.

Dinner went on for hours. The bishop barely spoke through it. I realized after the first few courses that he also barely ate through it, scraping his food around his plate without bringing his fork to his mouth. I had the strange feeling I shouldn't have been making such an effort to choke down the food; that it was really only for decoration, and I was the only one in the room who didn't know. The bald man carried away our dishes and brought out new ones at sporadic intervals, heedless of whether either the bishop or I had finished eating. All the while, the woman at the piano played incessantly the same shambling minor-key tune, striking sour notes and falling out of the rhythm more and more as the night wore on.

The staggering quantities of food, the piano music, the lustrous darkness, all sunk me into a state of confusion that was almost like dreaming. I was not the only one. As the moon rose and the man with the tumors took away cavernously large servings of some facsimile of pineapple upside-down cake, I saw the bishop's eyelids droop. I sat watching him seem to fall asleep, beginning to wonder if I should see myself out. Then, suddenly, he said in a voice so low that I could have missed it, "Come and lay hands on me, my child."

At first I was too taken aback to obey or refuse his demand. He mistook my dazed hesitation for a refusal. "If it's money you want," he said. "I'll pay right. I'll pay whatever you want. I'll give you this whole building, if you like it. Throw her in the bargain." He dazedly swung his arm in the direction of the woman playing the piano. "Well, not the building," he amended. "Give you whatever else you like. You want to be a bishop? You want a good place in the Church?"

"What is it that you want me to do?" I said, though I knew already. I simply could not fathom how *he* knew. It felt as though he were calling me by a name I'd become unused to hearing spoken aloud. It echoed foggily; it rang too true.

"I *know* you," he said, loud and accusatory now, rising shakily to his feet. He had either spilled something in his lap or peed himself. "*Saint-touched*. You can heal me. Come here. Lay hands on me now. The doctors say I only have weeks left."

I contemplated the possibility that I was in the middle of some kind of sting operation. If I laid hands on him, I thought, the lights would all come on, the woman at the piano would draw a gun from underneath her feather boa, I would realize the pineapple upside-down cake had been poisoned. But martyrdom and inquisition seemed to me, then, almost preferable to another twenty years of inglorious monotony.

I approached him. The bishop pulled aside his shirt to expose his turgid abdomen. The Day-Glo hues of the neon lights from the casino across the street made him appear alien, ghoulish. I had not worked a miracle in forty years. I rested my hand on his stomach and felt the illness sprouting tendrils inside him, crowding out his organs, driving his immortal soul toward its reward or punishment. And to my shock, I felt the same compassion that had arrested me in the cornfields fifty miles east of Vegas, not a feeling that came from within, but one that intruded upon me from without. I closed my eyes and kept my hand flat on the swell of the bishop's abdomen. For hours, I stayed with him. At dawn the next day, I left The Silver Nugget drained, delirious with exhaustion, bewildered by this miracle that—even then, I knew—neither giver nor recipient really deserved.

For months after that, I awaited the announcement that I was to be made a bishop. I awaited wealth and influence. None of it came to me. My disappointment curdled into fury. A year later, I preached loudly of the saint-touched. In the pews, amid the dust and the old hymnals, my parishioners woke from their stupors. And so did I.

The rusty scent of dried meat cooking woke us. Dawn was stretching pale and woolen across the Mojave, bleaching the Joshua trees and the junipers, the boulders and the sand, so that everything, including the earth, looked white.

"Thought you two would die of sleeping," said Barabbas Knight, talking around a half-chewed hunk of meat. "Come on now, get something to eat."

As she had the night before, the girl refused the meat he offered. I wondered if it was distrust of the men or distrust of the food itself that kept her from sating her hunger. I could not have refused the meat if it had been rancid. Barabbas glanced at the girl and, determining that any additional food rations would only be wasted on her, lifted another piece smoking from the spit to his own mouth. He said, chewing, "You won't eat, Barebones sure will. Come get yourself something, Barebones."

Barebones regarded Barabbas doubtfully, then the meat that had been intended for the girl, and slunk cautiously over to it like a feral animal. He let his eyes fall across the girl and then me, and then he returned to his horse, with whom he shared his extra portion. The animal lipped eagerly at the meat. At the girl's look of disgust, Barabbas laughed. "That's nothing next to the rest of what I've seen those animals do. You ever sit a desert horse, girl? Or for that matter, a regular one?"

I translated for her. "A mule," she said haltingly. "When I was a child."

"A mule will carry you, but a desert horse, my girl, they'll *take* you somewhere. They don't get tired. They spook at just about everything, but they'll run forever. I think they got a bit of behemoth in 'em. I've heard road stories. Can't imagine it's pretty, the amorous union of regular old mustang stock and that walking sludge, but it does make for fine horses. Come on now. We'll get you saddled up. Make better time if you're not falling on your face." He seemed to halfway exhaust himself with the stream of speech that flowed from his lips. He gave no indication of remembering the girl couldn't understand him.

"He's going to let us ride," I said, when she looked questioningly at me.

The girl seemed pleased by this development, but she balked when Barabbas motioned to the saddle occupied by One-Eye, who gazed vacantly upon the desert with his remaining eyeball.

"I want my own horse," she said.

Reluctantly, I translated, expecting what would come of such a demand.

"You see an extra horse here?" Barabbas said, motioning to the clump of horses beneath the mesquites. "Even if we had one, I wouldn't trust you."

The girl understood enough to grasp that she had been refused. "I don't want to share," she protested, her voice rising in pitch, getting tremulous. She seemed to find the prospect of riding with someone else not merely unpalatable but frightening.

"Look, now," Barabbas said. "I'm not in the mood for a fight. You wanna share with Jeroboam? I'm sure Jeroboam would be happy to make a little space for you in his saddle." He chucked his thumb at Jeroboam, who had acquired in the pale sunlight the look of a corpse halfway resurrected.

"Not him either," said the girl. "I don't want to share a horse."

I looked between her and Barabbas, wondering who was more tractable between the two of them, deciding that the answer was neither, feeling the absurdity of my position as negotiator between one captor and another. "What if she rides with me?" I said. "Tie the horses together, if you want."

Barabbas laughed. "You two really think you're running some kind of first-rate con, don't you? A couple of real Vegas scoundrels. I halfway respect it." He shoved the girl toward One-Eye's horse. "Now get up there. You wanna make good time, don't you?"

With slow, tortured motions, the girl crossed the distance to One-Eye, who held out an empty stirrup for her to mount with a sarcastic courtesy he abandoned as soon as she fixed him with a glare. It fell to me to ride with Jeroboam, who seemed no more pleased by the arrangement than I was. "The horse won't like it," he kept muttering, almost in a croon, as I was thrown gracelessly from side to side on the animal's withers.

We had ridden most of the day when Barabbas brought the men up to a sudden halt and turned his horse off to the side. In the distance, perhaps a mile from the road, a plume of dust was rising.

I thought at first that we were seeing a dust storm gathering force. It would have been a rare and precious blessing to have so much notice. But Barabbas seemed in no hurry to get away, and neither did the others, although I felt Jeroboam squirming in the saddle behind me, restless, nervy, anticipating what I didn't yet know was coming.

Barabbas twisted in the saddle to face me. "You ever seen a crowd of berserkers on the hunt?" he said. There was something sly in the way he asked the question that discomfited me. As if there was some insinuation in the words I was supposed to grasp, a joke he expected me to be in on. The look in his eyes was feverish, hungry. I had never even heard the word *berserkers* before. I shook my head, afraid to commit to an answer.

"Oh, boss, we don't got to go out and watch them," said One-Eye. "It's nothing we haven't seen before."

"But our guests haven't," said Barabbas. "Awful discourteous of you, One-Eye." Deciding the matter was settled, he prodded his horse off the road and into the nodding sea of saltbush.

Jeroboam issued a grunt of displeasure, but beneath me, I felt the horse respond to his bootheels. We moved forward. Barabbas's whims seemed to be unquestionable policy for his posse. A moment later, One-Eye followed, trotting until he and Jeroboam were riding abreast, Barebones behind them. I could see now how the girl sat stiffly perched in front of One-Eye, back arched so that no part of her touched any part of him. She did not look at me, even as we rode side-by-side; she seemed to be focusing very hard on looking at nothing.

"Thought they would turn on us and eat Boswell alive, last time," said One-Eye.

"Would've been no loss," Jeroboam said with a nasal snicker. "But"—he lowered his voice to a murmur—"I don't like getting up close to them unless we got some good reason. Don't see why he gets such a kick out of it."

Barebones rode past them then, his horse advancing in a long-legged lope, and his proximity silenced them for a moment. As we rode closer, I could make out a loosely gathered crowd of humans. Gaunt figures, protruding from the landscape between outcroppings of cholla or prickly pear, their mostly naked white bodies washed-out beneath the sun. They danced frantically, their arms above their heads and their legs thrashing out, kicking the air, sometimes striking the bodies of their neighbors.

Closer still, I could make out some of their faces in the fragments of time between one harried movement and the next. They had the wind-ravaged, sunken-in appearances of people who had been squeezing a living out of the desert for a lifetime. I was chilled by the look of them and chilled again when I realized how closely I resembled them. The lank and thinning hair, the wasted limbs, the dark puckered-up sores around the corners of the mouth.

Yet, unlike me, they did not seem to feel their frailty. They danced with their entire selves, and they showed no apprehension of us as we rode closer. Instead, they were fully involved in each other. They seemed to have no hierarchy, no order. But still, there was something feigned in their wildness, a self-conscious delight in the brutal way they dealt with each other. It was, I realized, a performance.

Only when we came close could I see that in the middle of the crowd, contained by the loose ring of people surrounding it, was one of those unnamable motley desert animals that you came across sometimes in these lonely stretches. When they looked more human than not, they were called stuffed men. Otherwise they were behemoths. The distinction was only in the eye of the beholder. Both were assembled from cadavers, fused with one another into colossal, undifferentiated piles of human or animal and vegetable flesh. That creature with its many legs might be three men or ten, might be a man and an antelope, might be anything. The crowd screamed at the creature like masters scolding their dog, or else goading it on. They wanted it to attack, I understood.

Reluctantly, Barabbas drew his horse to a halt twenty yards from the crowd. The others hung back, even the seemingly unshakable Barebones content to keep a wide margin between himself and the spectacle unfolding before us. "It's not *right*," murmured Jeroboam, and I wondered whether he meant the behemoth or the crowd around it. Beneath us, Jeroboam's horse was anxious, dancing sideways, tossing his head until his mane whipped me in the face. Jeroboam did not try to rein in the animal. He seemed to agree that there was something to be afraid of.

"Who are they?" I asked Jeroboam.

"Hell if I know. No one knows, really. Essentially, they're batshit people who either started out batshit or got batshit after they spent a few years drinking Mojave water."

I could tell he was going to say more, but he fell silent when a man tore loose from the crowd. The man collided with the behemoth, lunging onto its back and throwing a wire garotte around its immense neck. Watching him, the crowd issued sounds of approval. They did not cease dancing; their movements only became faster and more frantic. As they thrashed and twisted, the man looked skyward for a lingering second, long enough that the behemoth nearly bucked him off. Fiercely, he reclaimed his position, biting down on the creature's back and holding its flesh in his jaw to keep himself up as he tightened the garotte. I did not want to see what I was seeing, but I could not make myself look away. I felt in that moment we were part of the crowd, complicit in what they accomplished. Beside me, the girl instinctively crossed herself.

At last, after an interval that might have been one minute or thirty, the behemoth collapsed, dead, and the man shakily dismounted, his mouth a broad, blood-stained stripe on his narrow face. He screamed, tilting his head back, and then—spent—crumpled at the feet of the animal he'd slain. The crowd answered him with a phrase intoned as one voice, *he is the desert now*, followed by a chorus of screams as thick with ecstasy and need as his own.

Barabbas, still mounted on his horse, issued a friendly whoop and tipped his hat to the crowd before circling back, apparently satisfied with what he'd seen.

"What do you think, Father?" he said, riding up alongside me. "He is the desert, huh? Something wholesome about it. Some say the *real* church is the desert."

I could not have answered him in any way that would have preserved the fragile façade of civility that existed between us. I felt weak and vaguely nauseous. "What do they mean, 'he is the desert?'" I said instead.

"Oh, they think you can only die good if you die into the desert." He laughed. "And the way you do that is you kill something and slip inside its skin. The bigger, the better, mind you. You can't achieve any kind of respectable immortality wearing a javelina. So that's how they'll bury him. In the skin."

"He's dead?"

Barabbas glanced over his shoulder. My eyes followed his. Already the crowd was dissipating. The behemoth's body lay slumped where it had fallen, like a pile of refuse.

"If he's not bad-wounded from that scrap, they'll finish the job for him," he said blithely. "It's how they like it. Would like as not die young, anyway. Three generations of drinking out of puddles in highway overpasses catches up with you."

Somehow his condescension toward the berserkers repulsed me as much as the grotesque ritual itself. He did not believe in or even respect whatever brutal creed moved the rest of them to applaud the butchery. It was only entertainment to him, a sideshow that broke the monotony of a long and tedious stretch of highway.

I had, until that moment, felt the kind of natural and restrained anger toward Barabbas Knight that was only reasonable given that he'd taken me prisoner, but I hated him now with a loathing that was bone-deep and personal. It had been years since I had felt such particular hatred for anyone besides myself. I did not know how to carry a rage that could not be satisfied in small rituals of self-punishment. If it did not smother me, it would come pouring out, violent and hideous, and I would be all the more unforgivable when it was sated. As we moved forward, I kept my mouth shut and my eyes ahead. For the rest of the afternoon, we traveled in a stupefied silence. No one seemed to want to acknowledge the horror of the thing we had seen.

At night, as the campfire burned low, something that was not coyote or human kept us awake with howling. One-Eye muttered, "Like to shoot that thing in its damn mouth," and Barebones, in a rare show of verbosity, grunted in agreement. Barabbas prodded at the fire, chewed on a cigarette he'd long since exhausted. "Preacher man," he instructed, looking at me. "Give us a homily."

I thought at first he must be joking. But at the short, incredulous bark of laughter that issued from me, he grew impatient. "Go on, stand up. Give us a homily."

There was perhaps something perversely appropriate about a band of outlaws demanding a sermon from a convicted heretic. Perhaps he thought I'd preach on the virtues of kidnapping and collecting bounties. That we were in some deep way one and the same. Or perhaps I was just the same as the berserkers to him, and he only wanted to pass the time.

"I have no Bible," I said.

Barabbas Knight, improbably, dug a small, weather-beaten leather book from the pockets of his vest and tossed it across the flames into my lap.

"Untie his hands, Jeroboam, you cur," he said. "No way to treat a man of the church."

Jeroboam's rough fingers slid across my wrists. He worked at the knots, sparing the ropes so they could be rebound. The ache in my wrists, contorted for so many hours by my bondage, was a thin, hollow pain; flipping through the dog-eared pages of the Bible felt like the lash of a penitent's whip. My shoulders felt heavy. I knew already there was nothing safe between those two covers, no passage that would not now loose a monsoon gust of rage within me. I had sworn never to preach a homily again. Even administering the sacrament of contrition to Boswell, a stranger against whom I bore no grudge, had nearly undone me. I would not preach again for anyone, but least of all for Barabbas Knight.

The girl said to me, "What do they want?"

"A sermon."

She made a face I couldn't read. "Why?"

"Hurry on up," Barabbas Knight said.

My eyes traced across the pages of the red-lettered passages in the Gospels: Christ healing the man possessed with demons, Christ resurrecting Lazarus, Christ collapsing beneath the weight of his own cross.

"You expect us to believe you earned your bread and wine in Vegas that way? Come on, give us the goods." Barabbas's amusement was wearing thin now. The spectacle of the black-robed hermit holding the Bible was no longer adequate entertainment. I realized he had not thought I'd refuse him.

"I have nothing to preach on."

An expression that was almost fear passed across Barabbas Knight's face before his look hardened into a contemptuous scowl. "Well, look at the proud Vegas heretic." He spat across the fire. "Too good to preach for his fellow outlaws. Did you ever guess, men, that we were too far gone even for hellfire and brimstone from an old man's tongue? Did you ever reckon we could be as bad as that?"

"Always hoped so," One-Eye said, earnestly. "Always did."

"Can't hardly trust a man like you," Barabbas Knight said to me. "Preacher who says he can't preach. Just a liar who got caught in a tight spot, that's all you are. You know, in the old days, really old, I used to lead tenderfoot pilgrims up and down this road? Those were different times, when you could straight-shot from Sonora clear up to Salt Lake City, no nighttime howling, nothing to make trouble 'asides a few of the wanderers, and maybe some overgrown coyotes getting hungry.

"I was good at it. Was damn near *famous* at it. Only had to kill one man for it all to go sideways. My name was mud all through the Remainder after that. I denied it, too. Swore up and down it wasn't me. But no one ever believed me. And after that, I was hearing those roadside preachers talk about the end of days, the fall of man, the whole stack of sin we done, collectively, and I got to understand the *lying* about the killing was even worse than the killing because that was a sin I kept carryin' with me. Isn't that something?"

Fury swept through my body. How dare he unburden himself to me? How dare he fling himself at my unwashed pastoral feet? "I don't give confession anymore," I said, and it was the mildest rejoinder I could manage.

Barabbas's face twisted scornfully; I saw in his eyes a wounded anger. "Jeroboam, tie his hands again," he said. "And throw that book in the goddamn fire."

Later, when the men were finally asleep, I felt the girl's eyes on me. "Why wouldn't you preach for them?" she whispered.

I was in no mood to be questioned. "I don't preach anymore," I said, and rolled over, facing away from her.

She was undeterred. A distant howl half-covered her whisper: "Why not?"

"Why does it matter to you?"

"I wish you would have preached for them. I never heard a real Vegas priest give a sermon before. I might never hear one, now."

How disappointed she would be, I thought, if ever she came face-to-face with the thing in which she believed so fervently. She was a better pilgrim than the Church deserved. "You wouldn't have understood anyway," I said. "I would have given it in pidgin."

She said nothing. Clearly, that excuse held no water for her. I remembered the way her lips had traced the words of the prayer I had dictated for Boswell as he knelt dying in the sand. She had not understood the words I had spoken then either. It was possible, I thought, that her faith was purer for being entirely unencumbered by understanding. Around us, the clicks and rattles and screams of desert creatures formed a wall of impenetrable sound. Into the night sounds I spoke, not a sermon but only a fragment of scripture.

"Consumed like smoke. Withered like grass."

"What?" she said.

I spoke fast, as if sneaking the words through before I myself understood them. I had given a hundred homilies just that way, escaping unnourished and without condemnation from my own pulpit. "My bones are burnt as a hearth. My heart is smitten, withered like grass. My bones cleave to my skin. I am like a pelican in the wilderness. I am like an owl of the desert. I watch and am as a sparrow alone on the housetop. I have eaten ashes like bread and mingled my drink with weeping."

She was silent for a moment, but I could hear her breath coming fast and labored. "Say the pelican part again," she said.

"A pelican in the wilderness," I repeated. "An owl of the desert."

"I can't stop thinking," she whispered, "that I should never have kidnapped you."

I did not know what to say. "I have eaten ashes like bread."

"I'm afraid Saint Elkhanah won't heal me now."

"I have mingled my drink with weeping."

"Tell me I can still get healed. Please."

I could not outright lie. I would not go so far. I only wished I could tell her it was not her fault. The righteous and the wicked alike starved on a Las Vegas diet.

"From heaven did the Lord behold the earth," I said. "To hear the groaning of the prisoner. To loose those that are appointed to death."

"To death," she whispered after me. "Please, tell me."

"From heaven did the Lord behold the earth," I said. "To hear the groaning of the prisoner."

The desert grew stranger as we traveled northwest. The high Mojave belonged entirely to wilderness, and everything, not only vegetation, not only animals, not only the living, was vulnerable to transformation.

The threat of thirst, ever-present but always quiet, never erupting into catastrophe, was dangerously easy to forget in the face of the dangers the desert stuck boldly in front of us. On the second night, Barabbas coerced the men into entering a roadside motel, a blocky compound painted a ripe shade of orange that looked impossible against the bleak desert taupe. He said they might still have beers in the fridge, he said they might have an indoor swimming pool, and his men flinched at this blatant show of madness, but obeyed because he pulled his gun on them.

Inside the motel was some horror unnamable to them. They emerged hours later looking shell-shocked, staggering, with Barabbas's slack body across their shoulders. Later, over the weak flames of the night's cookfire, Jeroboam stole a jimson cigarette from the unconscious Barabbas's shirt pocket and took slow, pensive drags and told us the floor inside had opened to a dark pit at least thirty feet deep, in which rattlesnakes coiled around the prone bodies of infants, the clicking of their many tails so loud that he and One-Eye couldn't hear each other speak.

When Barabbas woke, he said, "There's no living out here," under his breath, without his usual loquaciousness. The smirk was gone from his lips, the light from his eyes, and we avoided buildings after that. The open desert was a more honest danger. There, we only had to contend with our thirst and the maddening sameness of the landscape, which rolled on before our eyes forever and ever, unaltered, unbeautiful.

Despite her insistence on the first night that she would escape, the girl did not once try to make a run for it. She hardly had the opportunity. On the road, she sat in front of Barabbas with her feet hanging loose at the horse's sides, her entire body tensed, her eyes roving the horizon for the threat or distraction that would be her opening. At night, as the men sat laughing by their fire, she squirmed backward in her bonds until one or the other of them noticed and yelled half-hearted threats whose substance she didn't understand, but which were nonetheless sufficient to keep her from going any further. At all times we were bound at the wrists and ankles, and we were never left alone with the horses. I could see her frustration turning, hour by hour, into despair. But as she kept her unending watch, she would whisper sometimes: *From heaven did the Lord behold the earth. To hear the groaning of the prisoner.*

"Would you still go to the city?" I asked her. "If you got free now?"

"I have to," she said, seeming bewildered by the question. "All my life it's what I've wanted."

"Even if it might throw you back into these men's hands?"

"It wouldn't matter, after that," she said. She wouldn't look at me. With a defensive note in her voice that told me she knew I'd disapprove, she added, "I decided: if I haven't gotten free by the time we get there, and he learns I'm not a heretic, that he can't give me to the Church, I'll tell him I'll do whatever he wants as long as he lets me go to the shrine first."

I was speechless. I understood then really there was no *after* in her imagination, only the unimaginable transcendence of the long-awaited moment. The healing had, for her, assumed a significance far beyond the removal of a physical impediment. It would be a kind of death to achieve something so desperately longed for, I thought. Or a kind of rebirth. Who knew what the girl would be after she was made whole in her own estimation? *If* such a thing could ever have happened, *if* kissing the bones of a sharpshooter-priest fifty years dead could ever have accomplished it, *if* the cost had not been the rest of her earthly existence.

"That would be worth it to you?"

She looked contemptuously at me. She did not want to be made to ponder the reality of her situation. She must realize that Barabbas Knight had no reason to care what she offered when he could take anything he wanted without her permission. She had no leverage; she had no power. "It's all that matters," she said.

I could not convince her of Saint Elkhanah's fraudulence, of the whole Church's basic and all-consuming corruption—of that much I was certain. But I could at least convince her, I thought, that she should not lay down her life at its very dawn for the chance to kiss a skeleton's feet if there were another way to accomplish it. "Look for an opening," I said. And, to my own surprise, my vague dismay, I said: "I'll help you."

On our sixth day in the hands of Barabbas Knight, the dry bed of the Colorado River appeared like a dull-colored snake down the long slope of the hill we had spent a morning climbing. Before we descended, Barabbas drew to a halt and looked back at the rest of us. "We're getting close," he said. "In just a day, we'll be saying goodbye, see ya later, to the both of you. Should be trouble-free from here on out."

I couldn't translate, for we were riding in single file, the horses walking a narrow gap between two crusts of rock, but Magdala could see as well as the rest of us the heat shimmering on the concrete spires of distant hotel-casinos, the city roads circulating like narrow black veins through the patchwork of buildings. She knew we were reaching the end.

Although the dregs of Vegas sprawled through miles of desert, its innumerable motels and gas stations and drive-thru restaurants and flat-roofed bungalow houses were in a perpetual cycle of settlement and contestation and abandonment. The Strip itself was walled by twenty-foot-high slabs of corrugated tin and fortified by heaps of refuse that had amassed patiently over the course of decades, scrap metal and plywood mingling loosely with broken appliances and the bumpers of old cars. One could bypass this labyrinth of garbage only by entering through a single gate, a grandiose construction of chain link and barbed wire and bungee cords flanked by a row of defunct neon signs whose muted lime greens and magentas only intimated the glories of the city beyond. This was the holiest place in all the Remainder.

Before the gate, a clump of men dripping with guns stood watching us approach, looking shiftless, impatient. When we were not far, perhaps ten feet away, one of them lifted his rifle, a narrow, sleek weapon that could have filled all of our bodies with bullets in a matter of seconds, and yelled for us to stop where we stood.

Barabbas obligingly lifted his hands. "Name's Caspian Blake," he said without conviction. "Got a bit of kindling here for Mother Ecclesia's fires."

"Knight, you're on the blacklist," the guard said, with something like amusement. He stood looking dutifully stern until Barabbas lowered one hand and dug through his saddle bag for a Tabasco bottle filled with moonshine, which he passed with a flick of his wrist and which the guard caught, held to the waning sunlight, then tossed back.

"Come on now," he said to Barabbas. "You know he's still looking for you."

Barabbas's expression changed then. "He's back in town?"

"Since a month ago."

From behind me, One-Eye cried: "Fuck!"

"I'd keep a wide berth. If I were you," said the guard.

"Hold on now," said Barabbas. He threw a glance back at his men, then dismounted and approached the guard so they could talk privately. It was the opening we needed. Magdala's eyes met mine, and I squirmed loose from the saddle, throwing myself to the ground. I had intended to cry out, to create a distraction, but dots swarmed before my eyes when I landed, my lungs flattened, and I came back to myself to see Magdala galloping past me on Barabbas Knight's horse.

Seeing the animal's long-legged stride, the way she clung low to his neck as if she and the horse were one creature, I thought for a moment she really would accomplish it. She'd put enough distance between herself and the men that finding her in the hills wouldn't be easy. She'd hide out a while, she'd grind her bonds against the sharp edge of a rock until they frayed and she was bloody-wristed but free. But the moment passed so quickly that I had barely gotten my breath back before it ended. Seated up on the animal's neck, her wrists tied, she could not find her balance. The horse lost a step when he passed over an upturned rock, I saw her bounce, and when she landed, she slumped to the side and fell heavily into the dirt.

The horse, startled by her fall, tossed his head and ran all the faster into the hills, carrying off the escape that had been beyond his rider.

"You gonna just stand there?" cried Barabbas. "That's what you're gonna do?"

Barebones looked impassive. One-Eye motioned helplessly in the direction of the vanished animal. "They're fast when they're loose, boss," he protested.

"I got my charge still," said Jeroboam, nudging the back of my head with his toe.

Barabbas made a sound choked with rage. It was, he must have known, his own fault that Magdala had managed even a very abortive attempt at escape and lost his horse in the process. But he could not take the loss gracefully with so many witnesses looking on. The humiliation was worse than the inconvenience. He stalked across the sand to Magdala and lifted her by the armpits, then pulled her roughly after him across the dirt. Still weak from her tumble, she moved clumsily, wincing whenever weight landed on her clubfoot. Halfway across the short distance between her and us, Barabbas pulled her off her feet and carried her the rest of the way to One-Eye, who sat comfortably mounted with half-suppressed smugness, unable to disguise the pleasure he took in Barabbas's humiliation.

"Give me the horse," Barabbas said to One-Eye, his voice like steel. "You can walk."

"Aw, boss," One-Eye said, but he dismounted, casting a sidelong look of derision at Magdala as he went.

We spent the better part of the night retracing our steps back up the hillside, searching for the horse that everyone, including Barabbas, seemed already to know would not be found. Still, Barabbas's anger swelled like a blister, erupting at last when he found a pile of what he took to be horse manure and Jeroboam recognized as the droppings of a steer.

"Boss," Jeroboam said, with the frantic momentum of someone who had been working himself up to saying it, "if the Deputy's really back, maybe we oughta, you know, cut our losses a little bit. Maybe we don't find the horse, maybe we don't get the bounties on these heretics, but we put some miles between us and Vegas—"

Barabbas turned on him. His face had fossilized, the clear imprint of rage frozen across his white mouth and colorless eyes. For a long moment, he held Jeroboam in his stare. Then, abruptly, he turned on Magdala, who had followed after the men on foot in a kind of daze, her eyes focused nowhere, her expression empty of emotion.

"You!" he said. Then, in a low snarl, the contempt palpable: "You think you're too expensive to escape consequences; let me tell you that's not true. Church don't specify *gently used* when they ask for their heretics back." He held her by the neck, his height advantage magnified by the lip of rock on which he stood. Her feet came off the ground.

Her face went pale. He would kill her, I thought, without even meaning to. And he would like as not kill me if I intervened. I prayed, then: not for divine intervention, but for fearlessness. I prayed not like a living saint, but like a man standing on the precipice of a bottomless abyss. Like Abraham at the altar when his son lay bound and prone. Not hoping for a goat to stumble out from the undergrowth, not expecting it. I advanced on them and tore Barabbas's hands from Magdala's neck. He fought me—won—threw me to the ground and stood over me with his hand on his holstered revolver. And then, all at once, the unclouded winter sky broke open and a flood of rain came down.

I WAS A LIVING SAINT of fifty-eight, rising at dawn and pushing aside the wooden shutters on the sole window of my white-walled austere chamber to admit the pale Nevada sun. The leather-bound scholar's Bible already open to the intended chapter. *For thus hath the Lord said: The whole land shall be a desolation, yet will I not make a full end.* I was wearing rough, white linen shirts that scratched my skin and left a faint pinkish rash on my collarbones. I was fasting mornings and eating only vegetables at night. After my devotions, I sat before my mirror and practiced the expression of rapture that would come over my face when I worked miracles.

On Sundays, I abandoned the liturgy and delivered sermons of my own making. I preached of the kingdom of heaven on earth. I preached of the triumph of life over death, good over evil, innocence over corruption. I preached of the resurrection of the body with the soul. Before crowds of flush-faced, trembling, ecstatic acolytes, I laid hands on the sick and the injured. I had learned that my ability to heal came and went in blatant disregard of what I felt or what I believed. I never knew whether I would succeed when I stepped up to the pulpit. But that I managed to heal perhaps one in ten of the faithful, that they often departed with the same aching, old bullet wounds and growing cancers and chest-deep coughs and deformed limbs that they came with, hardly mattered. They blamed themselves for my failures; and, anyway, they were cured *en masse* of their despair. "We are in the presence of a living saint," they whispered.

Naturally, the Church was not ignorant of my doings. Within a handful of months, I was summoned to the Sunlite for a formal warning. As I sat in a scuffed leather banquette, the archbishop paced the room and threw out admonishments. The word *ego* was uttered. The words *heretical doctrines*. I bit back laughter. I regarded him with a contempt that was almost sympathetic. He did not have what I possessed. Of course he was threatened. But it could not come to anything. Let him try to stand in my way. I thought of the words God had said to the prophet Ezekiel: *Like emery harder than flint I have made you.* I was a living saint. I was assured of success.

Jeroboam and One-Eye, even Barebones, believed I had made the rain. They didn't say so, not outright, but they tiptoed around me with a new suspicion that was almost awe after that moment. Barabbas had no such reverence. The winter rain had broken the trance of rage he'd fallen into, but he was sullen and irritable the rest of the night, tying me and Magdala to trees so we could not even move

enough to get comfortable, chain-smoking until his cigarettes were gone, berating One-Eye and Jeroboam for
imagined slights as if he could drain his anger like pus
from a wound. The next morning, he announced that
they would not enter the Strip. "Gonna have to go south to
Paradise and see if Warden'll take the two of them into the
city and broker the deal for us," he said.

"I hate Warden," sulked Jeroboam. "Laziest piece of shit
in this half of the Remainder."

"Man makes good deals and he's honest. I'd do business with him before I'd do it with you," Barabbas said.
"Besides, we got no choice."

"Seem to recall you saying before that the Deputy had
left Las Vegas for good," said Barebones.

Barabbas turned on him. His forehead glistened, although the day was not hot. "Don't know what gave you
that notion," he said.

"You saying it, probably."

One-Eye indulged himself in a wolfish, delighted intake
of breath. Barabbas shot him a look that shut his mouth.
Jeroboam, wisely, was pretending to be deeply involved in
saddling his horse.

"Well," Barabbas said, after a long silence. "Either he's
back now or the guards are full of shit. Not saying the
second one's not possible, but I'd rather not take chances
and I think you, Barebones, more than anyone, oughta
agree, given what he's got you on if ever he catches you. So
to Paradise we go."

Magdala looked anxiously at me, wanting to understand.

"Someone is looking for them," I told her.

"Do you know who?" she whispered. "Would he help
us?"

"I don't know him."

"Do you think he's better than these people?"

I could not guess whether the men feared the Deputy because they lived outside the law, or because the Deputy lived further outside of it still. I had never heard of the Deputy, but I had lived in Las Vegas long enough to know that names did not hold fast to meanings. He might be as much an outlaw as Barabbas Knight, despite the moniker. "They're afraid of him," I said, uncertain whether that meant we should be afraid too.

Across that day we retraced our steps southward, the men throwing glances over their shoulders and begrudging each other every slight delay. They balked when at dusk Barabbas led the string of horses to one of the numerous roadside shacks catering to travelers. The unpromising heap of brick he selected bore a sign mounted above the door reading *RANDY ROCK HIGHWAY DINER*, its assets enumerated in smaller letters beneath: *steaks, pie, coffee.* Someone had tacked a piece of plywood onto the tail of the *R* in *DINER* to boast of *CHEAP DIESEL.*

"It's not safe," Jeroboam complained.

"Safer in here than on the road," said Barabbas. "He hasn't set foot in a place like this all his life, I'd wager."

The men exchanged glances, but they did not protest. They had expected to arrive in the city yesterday, and their food supplies were drained. Unaccustomed to the kind of hunger that I had come to know as an intimate companion, their bellies had been complaining all day long.

Lacking a generator, the inside of the diner glowed smudgy orange beneath kerosene lanterns. Barabbas blinked to settle his eyes, then shoved Magdala onto a slab of cracked red vinyl and motioned for me to sit beside her. "Now, me personally, I think I want a steak," he said.

"Extra ketchup. What for you, Father? Caviar and champagne? Or is that not rich enough for your blood?"

That wrung an anxious chortle from One-Eye but no one else. I sensed that no reply of mine could possibly mollify him, so I kept silent. The diner would have burnt its menus for kindling decades ago; they would serve whatever they could find now, approximating coffee with ground mugwort and crushing lizard meat into patties that they'd grill until unrecognizable. The diners inside Las Vegas were no different, although they enjoyed the relative advantages provided by working generators that could fuel their freezers.

Barabbas produced a handful of plastic poker chips and passed them off to Jeroboam, then slid into the booth across from me and instructed One-Eye to sit down. Barebones, always at a distance, remained on his feet. He had hidden his pistol instead of surrendering it to the plastic bin inside the door; everyone else had dutifully turned theirs in, even Barabbas, who handed over both his own gun and the revolver he'd stolen from Magdala. The look in her eyes when she looked at her weapon, empty though it was, was one of longing.

When I was in Las Vegas last, no self-respecting establishment would have asked its patrons to surrender their guns. They wouldn't have needed to. The bars and restaurants along the pilgrim highway were the domains of people unarmed and unready for fighting: stooped old women fingering weather-beaten crucifixes, broods of children in hand-me-downs looking solemn and monk-like, lone penitents maimed or sickly or simply half-dead from their passages through the desert. Only their guides, cowboys in flashy clothes, were likely to be carrying. Now there were no penitents, no guides; the diner was crowded with men whose faces telegraphed murder.

"Would they help us?" Magdala whispered.

I considered the *they* she meant: the grizzled man in the booth across from us who was doubled over so he could absorb the unnamable brown clumps in his soup more quickly, the bleary-eyed woman holding a coffee mug and staring vacantly at a clock whose hands hovered eternally on the threshold of 2:15. "They might help *you*," I said, although I somewhat doubted it. "They wouldn't help me."

"Because you're a heretic?"

She made no pains to speak softly, unused to being understood by anyone but me. I hushed her. "If you want to go," I said, "you should."

She shook her head. "I can't just—"

"Hey, enough of that!" Barabbas said thunderously, slapping his palms down on the tabletop. "Y'know, the longer I've put up with you two, the more eager I am to get you off my hands. You're the kind of trouble I could've left in the Mojave."

I was spared answering him by the arrival of a waitress, who slid identical plates of some potato-like substance and a piece of meat across the table to us. When her eyes fell on Barabbas, she tried without success to hide her shock of recognition.

"You see her face?" said Jeroboam, leaning across the table. "She knows you. He's been asking for you here, I'm certain of it."

"She's just never clapped eyes on anyone so handsome," said Barabbas, but he became anxious after that, hurrying us through our plates, the toe of his boot keeping up a steady rhythm on the floor. I ate ravenously. My first bite awoke a hunger that had long lain dormant in the pit of my belly. I felt desperate, I felt weak. I gulped two cups of water, and they would not portion me a third, but I would have emptied that too. Not since my days of scavenging had I eaten so ravenously. Outside the diner, with the night black and full around me, I fell to my knees and choked up everything I'd eaten, my stomach unused to fullness.

"Waste of good meat," One-Eye sulked.

"It's his last meal," said Barabbas, laughing. "Out not with a bang but with a whimper."

The men quickened their pace after we left the diner, abandoning the road for a more obscure path through desert scrub. The city skyline disappeared and reemerged at intervals, assuming a metallic, crystalline appearance as night deepened. We seemed to get no farther away from it or closer to it as we moved. The horses were half-desperate with weariness by the time Barabbas cut through thick undergrowth and drew up before the husk of a barn.

"Good enough for the night," he pronounced it, looking into the open black mouth of the structure. The men filed obediently in after him. Darkness hung heavily inside, punctured only by slivers of moonlight that stole through the cracks in the walls. I could make out the faint bodies of old machines and little else.

"They might not see us if we run," Magdala whispered. "Once they fall asleep."

"Unless one of them stays up," I said, glancing sideways at Barebones. I had the growing suspicion that he, like Magdala, was not beholden to sleep so long as he was in the desert.

"You two," Barabbas whispered across the barn. "Shut your mouths." He peered again through a gap in the wall, then looked over his shoulder at us. "You must be wonderin'. I want you to know that if you're thinkin' of runnin', it's the wrong damn time. The Deputy's probably seen us all together, and your name'll be mud to him. So don't waste your time. Tell the girl."

An edge had crept into Barabbas Knight's voice that I had not heard before. At the door to the barn, I had seen sweat glistening on his neck, moonlight reflected on his clavicle. The night was dark and silent and strange. We could not light a fire; for fear of being seen, we did not even risk a cigarette lighter. I asked what the Deputy would do to us if he found us.

"You saw what the berserkers did to that behemoth?"

"Yes." As if I could, for the rest of my life, forget.

"Something like that."

"Why?"

"Preacher man, you ask the wrong questions. He don't have a *purpose*; he's got an *appetite* and he's gotta feed it. He likes to chop people up an' stick 'em with irons until they beg for mercy, an' then he kills 'em."

"How do you know?"

"How *don't* you know? You were a Las Vegas priest. If I was you, I'd be holding weekly meetings, you and all the other black-robes, trying to get a handle on him. But then again, I've heard men say he works for the Church, and they keep it all quiet. Doesn't do anything they wouldn't approve of."

"Why is he after you?"

A shuffling sound echoed across the barn. The men all froze for a moment before determining the sound had come from inside.

"Rats or somethin'," Jeroboam muttered sleepily from his position in the corner.

"He's police," Barabbas said. "In one manner of speakin'. But really he's just a big overgrown berserker taken out of the desert."

"He's a berserker?"

"He was desert-born, at least that's what people say in Vegas. Grew up way out there, moving around, biting the heads off behemoths to earn his stripes. And you can guess what happened when the small-town boy came to Vegas. If he wants you, you're dead. That's it. Dead. We been running from him since a couple years back. Didn't think he'd be back." This he said with an edge of disgust. "Should never have tried the gates. Damn fool move."

Across the room, Jeroboam shifted. The sound of a snake's rattle filled the quiet. He scrambled to get away from the animal, then let out a raspy half-muted scream when he couldn't.

"You bit?" One-Eye asked.

"Well, it wasn't kissin' me." Jeroboam's breath was labored, his voice pinched and high. "Goddamn, it hurts. You gotta do something. Carry me to Vegas, or—it don't matter. Goddamn, it hurts."

I cannot now explain how I knew I would heal him. Only, I felt then, the sensation that had arrested me as a boy of fifteen in a cornfield and a man of fifty-six in a dark penthouse. A longing that came from without. That filled and nourished and made demands of me that I could never have made of myself, that made me both more and less than what I was. Later, it would be strange to me how little I thought before I acted when I saw him suffering. I did not even hesitate long enough to wonder if the snake was still there, somewhere in the darkness. But in that moment, his need was like a rope thrown to a man at the bottom of a vast, self-made chasm. I took the rope. I crawled through the dark to him.

"Where is the bite?" I asked.

"You gonna suck it out?" Barabbas said, his laughter shrill and panic-stricken.

Jeroboam pitched his head into my lap. The skin on his throat had swollen, feeling fever-hot on my fingers. I found the twin pinpricks from the snake's fangs. Jeroboam gagged and sobbed as I pushed down on the wound. As I held him, the men fell silent. The palm of my hand stayed flat across the swelling. I kept my eyes shut. I felt compassion for him that did not come from my own brittle, misused heart. I felt such a rush of exultation that I could have sung through my cracked, desert-dry lips.

How can I describe those moments? The labor, the heaviness of the burden wracking me, the joy that surged from my head down through my feet. The wound was hot and damp on my skin. He sank limply onto my thighs, no longer holding up his own head, and I thought he must be dead. Then he gasped, and I felt the swelling decrease beneath my hand, and I knew he would live.

"Shit fire," Barabbas said, sitting back on his feet. "Didn't know we had a living saint among us."

Magdala was looking at me, her face stricken, her eyes wide. Her gaze moved from the prone man in my lap to my hands and then back to Jeroboam once more, making herself believe what she had witnessed, digesting again and again a truth which stuck in her throat. "You heal?" she said. "Always?"

I saw on her face the same horror and dismay that I had seen on my brother's face, fifty years ago now, as he called me Saint Arturo. I said, "No," and then I admitted, "Sometimes."

"Did you let me stay clubfooted because I took you?"

What could I say to such a question? The answer was no, the answer was yes. I had not laid hands on anyone since I fled to the desert with a brand on my forehead. A few days ago, I had been afraid even to say a prayer. But it was also true that I had not tried. I had not wanted to try. "I didn't know I still could," I said.

"You could have *tried*!" she cried. "You didn't even try!"

"What's she saying?" said Barabbas.

"She's angry at me for helping him," I said. It was not strictly untrue.

"Well, tell her to shut up," Barabbas said. "Bad enough we got Jeroboam screaming to the rafters. We may as well put out a welcome mat for the Deputy."

"I never choose when it happens," I told her. "Please understand."

"Just try it." She thrust her clubfoot toward me. Tears streaked her face. "Doesn't God want me to walk right?"

No more than God had wanted me to remain comfortable and well-nourished and unbranded in Las Vegas, I thought, and her pious, childish entitlement suddenly enraged me. "And what business of mine is it if he does?"

This silenced her for a moment. "I thought you were good," she whispered.

"I told you enough times I'm not." *A heretic is just a priest who's been found out,* she had said. Some part of her had understood we were all rotten. She should never have hoped for more than bald-faced hypocrisy and an occasional psalm from me.

"You didn't even *try*," she whispered.

I sat in the dark all through that night. Imploring God, *you ever-distant father-tyrant, punish me for all my transgressions, visit upon me every suffering known to the devil and yourself, only find some scrap of goodwill in yourself enough to let me work this miracle, however undeserving I may be of the privilege. I put you now on trial. I demand to know why I can draw venom from an outlaw but not heal a child. I know she is undeserving. She comes to you clawed and grasping. But should you punish the creature you set in a bone-land for living like a skeleton? Have you any mercy?*

In the deepest hollow of the night, I reached for the girl's clubfoot in the darkness. I felt nothing: I could tell it would not work. Her eyes held mine and I saw fury in them. I felt the letters *H E R E T I C* on my forehead with as fresh a hurt as if they'd just been etched onto my skin.

I WAS AN OLD MAN standing unsteadily at the front of a courtroom, my fingers pressed flat, like the wings of a butterfly, on the pages of my Bible. The court of law had once been for mock trials. Empty camera stands crouched spiderlike before the bench; coatracks bore rainbows of unflattering polyester robes. It still was for mock trials. In a pistols-at-dusk shootout with the Holy Church of Las Vegas, the lone heretic can only fire blanks. I had been dragged that afternoon without warning from my confessional, through the chapel where I had given homilies and performed baptisms and spoken of the redemption of all mankind, down to the basement studio where a tribunal had now gathered to assess whether I had sinned against the Church gravely enough to deserve excommunication. Like all accused heretics, I had no advocate; I had no supporters. Yet I did not fear the outcome. I believed in my own righteousness. I had in my head all the time the words of the Lord to the prophet Ezekiel: *Emery harder than flint I will make you.*

The archbishop, refined and grim as a death's head in his wine-colored robes, stood before me and, for a long moment, said nothing. He knew how to command an audience. This was a ritual as much as the Eucharist. "Father Arturo," he said at last, very grave, very solemn, "you stand accused of heresy. You have laid claim to powers supernatural, advertising yourself as saint-touched. You have plied the masses with unfulfilled promises of healing and wicked fantasies of a kingdom of heaven on earth. You have been a blight to the unity of the Church. What do you have to say for yourself?"

I could deny none of it, yet I believed myself innocent. "I have laid claim to nothing I do not possess," I said, although this was not entirely true; I *knew* it was not. How many of the faithful who had come to me were dead now, or sicker than before, or the same?

The intimation of a smile slid across the archbishop's lips. He had been waiting for me to say exactly this. "Let us see, then," he said. A child with twisted feet was carried into the room. Where she had come from and how they had gotten her, I could not imagine. The crowd drew an awestruck breath at her appearance. At the archbishop's instruction, she was laid out on a table like evidence, her bent feet displayed. There was fear in her eyes, I could see; she did not want to be here. She had not asked for a miracle cure.

"Heal her, Father Arturo," said the archbishop.

I laid my hands on the child's feet. I tried to re-become the boy of fifteen whose compassion was well-deep. But that boy was so far from me that he was unreachable now, and I had never chosen when I healed and when I didn't. The girl cried and twisted away from my touch. In mere minutes, the crowd began to clamor for my execution. Children of Las Vegas, reared on the flash-quick stories of stage burlesques and romances, they grew bored of the drama playing out before them. In the face of their heckling, I relinquished my grasp on the child's feet. I was pronounced guilty.

In the depths of my self-pity, I did not spare a thought for the child. I did not wonder if she made it safely back to her family, if she even still had a family, how it must have felt to be carried to the front of a courtroom and put on display as if she were a sign or a wonder and not a living person. But I wonder now, and cannot stop wondering.

Barabbas roused us before dawn. We stole through country too rough to be ridden. The men left their horses in the barn with no assurance of getting them back. Inside the arroyos, their boots hissing across loose rock, they stumbled like children. Certain that the Deputy was not far behind them, they were anxious to reach Paradise and be rid of us. While Jeroboam yanked Magdala along, Barabbas let no slack into my bonds, sometimes yanking suddenly so that I came crashing to my knees, other times jerking the leash in short, fast motions as if he could fool me into following him. He could; I did. All my life I had never gone anywhere without some rope binding my wrists, someone urging me along.

We descended from the arroyos onto a colorless plain and staggered along patches of broken asphalt halfway buried by sand, crushed like glass. A peeling face grinned snidely at us from a one-legged billboard: *JUST*

BECAUSE YOU DID IT / DOESN'T MEAN YOU'RE GUILTY. Barabbas glanced over his shoulder, bristled when the wind snarled in the brush. *WE'LL MAKE YOU UNTOUCHABLE.* "Come on, old man, come on, you wanna die and the sun's not even up." The dawn was like a red-gold crown of spikes on him.

A highway sign promised we were three miles from Paradise. Here, wilderness melted into outskirts melted into city, every street feeling like the dregs of the last, the ending of something. A pack of dogs crossed the road in front of us, their collective colors shimmering like an oil slick, their bodies streaming wetly together, tail to nose to tail. Besides them and the snake, we had not seen another living thing for miles. There were no creeks here, not even puddles. But there were mountains. Spires of plastic and Styrofoam, glass and aluminum and rubber. Junk cars, their hoods hanging open, their innards long since salvaged. Now their gaping mouths held the broken legs of office chairs, the hollow bodies of fire extinguishers, the cracked eyes of television sets. Corpses in a permanent state of un-decay, monuments to a desert-brand of intangibility that no priest or billboard lawyer ever advertised. It was not feral dogs we had seen but wild ones, the garbage their natural habitat.

"How you know you're home: when you smell the rising shit of the dregs of Vegas," murmured Barabbas.

We had waded deep into the wreckage before the sound of an engine startled the men. Barebones drew his gun and the others hid, flattening themselves lizard-like into the piles of waste. "Goddamn it," Barabbas muttered to me. "It's him. Just know it is." He crouched low, behind the sagging frame of an old Cadillac. "Barebones," he murmured, "you shoot 'til that chamber is empty, you hear me?"

The way they slipped so easily into their positions, I realized they had always expected their pursuer to catch up to them at some point. All the time we had crossed the Mojave, we had been running away from and toward this Deputy, whose name they whispered with such worshipful awe and terror that he had become something more than human even in my own estimation. Barebones slumped his massive shoulders with something like relief. The wind rose and tossed bundles of plastic like tumbleweed across the road. When the rustling sound died down, the desert was silent. Barabbas held his breath, then released a long slow sigh, then held his breath again. His gun was still holstered. Slowly, he rose to his feet until he was crouching with his knees only slightly bent and peered across the body of the car.

"We'll keep going," he said. "Stay low. Belly-crawl if you gotta. We'll wash the filth off us if we lose him."

"Boss, you know he can sniff us out," One-Eye whimpered. "Come on now."

Barabbas yanked my leash. We crept with backs stooped, Magdala dragging her clubfoot. Our shuffling through the mounds of refuse made sounds painfully conspicuous. Each moment felt pregnant. The sky grew hazy above us. I followed Barabbas closely and watched the slow swinging motion of the revolver he had stolen from Magdala. I wondered if he knew it was unloaded.

The sound of a gun firing made me flinch. I had never become familiar enough with the sound to disregard how it tore through the wind, how it thudded in my chest. Reflexively, I glanced down to see if I had been struck. Then Barebones fell, an uninterrupted arcing motion downward, like a stone hitting the water, like a baptism, shot in the neck. The gun fired twice again after that, striking

Jeroboam and then One-Eye, throwing them down so suddenly into death that they had no time to cry out. Magdala pulled herself loose from her captor, yanking the rope from Jeroboam's limp fingers, and crossed the distance to me as if I could shelter her. I could not shelter her. I stood in the mounds of decaying plastic and trembled and waited for a bullet to come down invisibly from nowhere and end my life. But I did not die. Barabbas stood aiming his gun at different points on the horizon, luckless, desperate, until a bullet struck his leg.

Barabbas crouched low, his face tight, then rose and staggered onward. The leash obliged me to follow, but I knew we could not escape. When we emerged from the piles of refuse, the Deputy was waiting for us.

The Deputy was a lean man of indeterminate age. He wore no shirt, but his torso was covered by a scuffed, careworn plate of aluminum. The same makeshift armor overlaid his upper arms and legs and even his neck, ending just below his chin. By comparison, his bare wrists and shoulders appeared starkly fragile, the soft tissue of a hard-shelled creature. He moved stiffly beneath the metal, as if it were attached to him, even seeming to freeze on the cusp of motion to register pain before he extended his arm and fired his gun.

The shot struck Barabbas Knight in his other leg, and he crumpled to the ground. I, too, sank down, not knowing if I were placating my captor or his killer, or no one at all, but accustomed—by this, my third kidnapping in less than two weeks—to living in a posture of supplication. From the dirt, I saw the man approach us, I saw the steel caps on the toes of his boots reflect the woolen color of the sky, I saw the narrow black mouth of his gun exhale a lean jet of smoke. He spoke pidgin with an awkward, stilted accent.

"You have a lot to account for, Mr. Knight," he said.

Barabbas tried without success to spit. His tongue stuck on his dried lips, he braced himself on his elbows and got onto his knees. The Deputy kicked him back down.

"Confess your sins. Go on."

Barabbas coughed blood onto the dirt and glanced fleetingly at me. I saw in his eyes entreaty, longing. I did not turn my face away from him. I did not make him suffer by himself. "Get on with it, kill me," he said to the man.

"Mr. Knight, I don't plan on laying a single finger on you until we have some privacy. But I get the feeling your traveling companions think I'm some sort of degenerate, so why don't you tell them why you're on the ground?"

"Goddamn," Barabbas said. "You know as well as me that desert murder ain't no murder. It's necessity. It's what you gotta do. You got a whole string of pilgrims with you and one desert sick, you kill the one who's causing the trouble."

"Now that's the prologue to your very long story. Tell us the rest. Confess to this man of God all your iniquities."

"He told me he don't hear confessions," Barabbas said. "He don't wanna know."

The Deputy waited.

"What do you want? Three men in a Pima gamblin' hall? A woman and her little child in a Vegas alleyway? You an' I both know I can go on and on, but this man of God, he told me he don't *care*, and well he shouldn't, 'cause he's surely in the hands of the devil now, surely he is."

The Deputy absorbed this torrent of language with a look of vague disgust on his face. "Stand up," he said to me. He cut the ropes binding me to Barabbas and tied my captor to a tree. Then, so nonchalantly that I could hardly believe it had happened, he shot Barabbas in the foot, piercing the toe of his boot. Barabbas let out a stifled scream and began to cry in wracking infant gulps, face contorted and pale nose reddening.

The Deputy turned away from him, holstering his revolver. "You two," he said, speaking now not in pidgin but in the common language. "You're not part of this idiot's posse, unless I'm mistaken."

I glanced at Magdala. For the first time since our travels had begun, she could speak for herself. We'd never needed to get a story straight before. She did not look back at me. Her eyes were on the Deputy.

"He's a heretic," she said.

It was no real betrayal; the secret was emblazoned on my forehead. But it stung like a real betrayal would have. She could have said anything to him.

"I can see that," said the Deputy. "And you?" He stepped closer to her, reducing the distance between them to a handful of inches. Magdala stiffened, squaring her shoulders, lifting her chin so she could look him in the eye. His gaze fell to the brand on her neck. I could see from the way she clamped her lips shut, curled her fingers into fists at her sides, that she was suppressing the urge to cover the mark. For a long while she held perfectly still. But when he lifted a finger to touch the brand, she slapped his hand away without a second of hesitation.

"I'm a pilgrim," she said, with force.

The Deputy bared his teeth in some approximation of a smile. His front teeth were sharpened pieces of tin; he had calluses on the inside of his lower lip where the points wore at his gums. I wondered if he had lost his teeth or chosen to remove them. "A pilgrim and a heretic, huh?" he said. "What brought you two together?"

"He kidnapped me," the girl said.

My laughter startled them both. Distantly, behind us, Barabbas Knight uttered a low, plaintive moan that went unanswered.

"You can't trust him," the girl went on, before I could dispute this story. "He's a liar."

The Deputy looked at me, a brow lifted. "How long ago you arrested?" he asked.

"Ten years," I said.

"But once a heretic, always a heretic, huh?"

"I had no intention of coming back here."

"'Course you didn't. But you're here now, aren't ya? And, do you know what, I'm feeling generous. You want to turn him in, girl? I'll let you have a cut of his bounty."

The girl's eyes fell across me, but she was not really looking at me. Her gaze stayed unfocused. I knew an attempt to blind oneself to suffering when I saw it. She seemed to steel herself then. She was thinking, no doubt, of Jeroboam's healing, of the fraudulence and hypocrisy of which she thought I was guilty. She nodded her *yes*. The Deputy tied my hands behind my back.

The Deputy's motorcycle was a chimera of mismatched steel and iron pieces, mottled and bruised, but it held all three of us for the distance between the trash heaps and the Deputy's personal backdoor entrance to the Strip, a door hidden amid the piles of refuse, concealed by a bent lower half of a garage door turned sideways. I saw my homecoming through the steel-nicked wall of the Deputy's back and shoulders, watched the ground darken from a blur of sand to one of cement beneath the wheels of the motorcycle. The city had never been so hideous to me as it was in that moment, and I longed with a despicable longing to go home to that past where my forehead had been unmarked and I had belonged here, and its putrefaction had been invisible to me.

The man guarding the front door of the Sunlite lifted his gun as we approached, then recognized the Deputy and lowered it, scrambling to open the double doors so the Deputy could ride through them. I wondered at the status our captor had evidently attained in less than ten years. Some men could labor behind a pulpit for twice that time and receive less than a second glance from the archbishop for their efforts.

The Sunlite was unchanged. The windows were shattered in the upper twenty floors of the casino, exposing the interiors to the assaults of wind and sun, but the building remained standing and so remained a landmark, the red and gold marquee still sparkling, the cracked upper windows refracting sunlight. The lobby was a graveyard of slot machines and craps tables interspersed with glass-encased reliquaries. The archbishop's predecessor lay in a velvet-lined coffin beneath firelight, decaying at a leisurely—some would say anointed—pace. The scent of tobacco smoke still clung persistently to the carpet. Plush red fibers sank pliably beneath my sandals, and I remembered how it felt to come here a berobed supplicant, remembered the vague surety that I was losing something as I treaded across this lobby.

The Deputy had plainly been here before; his glance fell cursorily across the torchlit casino floor. But the girl, unused to the crumbling splendor of Vegas, looked with fascination on the hall of relics. Her pace, already stilted, slowed further still. Her Saint Elkhanah was not here. He was down the street. I assumed she would manage, after I had been turned over, to find him. She could not come so far and not find him.

On the fourth floor, we entered the archbishop's chamber and found him at his desk. I was momentarily taken aback to realize he was not the archbishop of my day, but that man's successor: a small person, unimposing, a vessel for the Church to fill. At first, I did not recognize him as the bishop whose healing had been my gateway to heresy twelve years ago. And then I knew. I wondered if it was on his orders that the Church was endeavoring to repossess its exiled heretics. I wondered if he even remembered me.

"Deputy," he said, getting to his feet. I had the thought, uncharitable and absurd, that he could never have survived in the desert. He had a soft look, like a balloon partway inflated. He was so pale that I could see the veins in his neck. His eyes darted from the Deputy to the door and back again, and I realized he was afraid. "What's this?" he asked. Only then did he really look at me. The letters on my forehead. I could see the second when recognition dawned on him.

The Deputy pushed me down to my knees. The archbishop circled his desk and came to stand before me. "Father Arturo," he said in the common language. There was repulsion on his face: it occurred to me that I must smell as dire as I looked. "I think you've aged half a century."

I would not ask for mercy. My eyes remained on the marble floor. A distorted picture of myself shimmered back at me. How the torchlight threw the shadows. When I had been here last, I had believed I was untouchable. The words of the Lord to the prophet Ezekiel had echoed in my head all the while, and I had idiotically misapprehended them.

I had disregarded that they were spoken to a man who plunged himself into a life of misery, of martyrdom continual and unceasing, *because* he had been made emery, harder than flint, and his adversaries could only touch him in ways that wounded him, not ways that made him dead.

Yet now, as there had not been before, there was joy floundering inside me as I faced the archbishop: a feeling powerful, delirious, bright. Something like courage, something like drunkenness. At last the consummation of my life's journey was approaching. Ten years in the desert, prostrating before a bundle of coals, ten days of unwilling pilgrimage, all culminating in this moment.

"How long is exile from the Church and its gates, Father Arturo?" asked the archbishop.

"For life."

"Why, then, have you returned to Las Vegas?"

I did not bother to recite the sequence of events, absurd and hardly credible, that had led me here. "It seems I am not finished with this city yet," I said.

"And you remember the sentence given to you if you should ever return."

"I will be drawn and quartered."

"Have you proselytized much since you've returned to town?" asked the archbishop. "Spread your heretic word far and wide?"

"To none."

"Well, I am pleased to hear it." He spoke to the Deputy now. "Will you be claiming his bounty?"

"It's hers," the Deputy said, meaning the girl. I heard her shuffle on the floor behind me, the slow drag of her clubfoot on the floor and then the thud of her boot heel. I wanted to tell her she was forgiven. Despite what she had done, I did not want her carrying the burden of me all through whatever would come after her pilgrimage. It was not properly hers to carry. But when I looked over my shoulder at her, she would not meet my eyes.

"I don't want it," she said. "I only came to see Saint Elkhanah's feet."

The Church had enterprisingly repurposed a set of batting cages into a prison for heretics awaiting execution, outfitting each chain link-enclosed chamber with a sleeping bag, a paint bucket and a worse-for-wear New Testament. The cages could have contained ten of us, but none of the other cells were occupied when the archbishop's men swept me past the defunct vending machines, past the rows of dust-glossed lockers, and shut me inside the cage nearest to the door.

A night and a day I stayed there, hearing overhead the carrion birds that preyed on the human waste in the sewers of Vegas, my eyes focusing and losing focus on a frayed poster of a blond man wielding a baseball bat. His expression was intent, his confidence unassailable. Someone had scratched *the faithful city has become a whore* into the cement floor beneath me. I was not the first heretic to mistake himself for a prophet.

At midmorning, a priest came for me. At first I thought he was to lead me to my execution, but he said he had only come to give me my last rites. Unlucky, to have drawn the straw of that responsibility. I am sure no other parish priest envied him. He stayed across the chain link from me, unwilling to imperil himself. He asked me if I wanted to say contrition. I looked him full in the face. He was a young man, blemishes still trickling down his jaw, straw-colored hair sticking up at awkward angles, his vestments slightly large in the shoulders. He did not yet know what or who he was. In four decades he might sit where I sat now. He was faithless, an utter hypocrite, and yet—I understood so vividly, as if I had always known—the sacrament would still be pure if he delivered it.

"Yes," I said, and I let him lead me through the words.

A few hours later, the door opened again. I readied myself for death. I was prepared to look the Almighty in the face and acknowledge my frailties before him. But the man who entered held the door open for me as if to set me free.

"You've been let go," he said. "Someone's waiting outside for you."

The girl stood outside the batting cages with her arms crossed before her chest, a revolver holstered at her waist that had not been there before. I recognized it as the gun she had used to stick me up. I wondered if it was loaded now. I wondered who had been the one to get it back from Barabbas Knight.

"Why did you tell them to let me out?" I demanded. "Why did they do it?"

She seemed not to want to answer. She threw a nervous glance over her shoulder at the squat compound where I had been confined. From the outside, it looked like nothing. There was a miniature golf course on the small faux hillside behind it. I wondered if the Church used the course as overflow, in fatter days for the trade in heretics. Perhaps the lesser offenders were confined there, among melting plastic replicas of St. Peter's Basilica and the pyramids. "Come on," she said, petulant, a little impatient, as if she still had a lasso around my neck. "Do you want to be free or not?"

I followed her down the road. The sun was beginning to set. She walked with purpose, fast and determined. Then, abruptly, she stopped. "I only ever wanted one thing," she said. "I don't remember wanting anything else. Were you ever a pilgrim?"

"Never."

"But you've been in exile. And I'm starting to think they're almost the same. The whole world being nothing to you. Only wanting the one thing you can't reach. Always going and never getting there. Sometimes I feel like I've been wandering alone longer than I've been alive. I want you to come with me. Please."

She meant to the shrine of Saint Elkhanah, I realized. So she had not gone yet. "Tell me," I insisted, before I agreed. "How did you get them to let me go?"

"The Deputy called in a favor," she said, not looking at me. She began to walk again. "I told him I would work for him if he did."

I was, for a moment, breathless with guilt. If I could have turned around and walked back into the batting cages, I would have. "Why?" I said, unable to manage more.

"You helped me." She looked defiant, as if she had expected me to argue with her. With the revolver at her side, she walked taller; she had the wolfish look of the desperado who had ordered me to lead her through the desert. I could almost believe that she knew what she was doing. "I didn't want to be the reason you were dead," she went on. Then before I could answer: "Please, I just want you to come with me. Don't say anything. Just come."

What could I say to this child who had pinned all her hopes on the wrong saint? Should I perform for her a catechism, should I write a lengthy treatise, should I sermonize until she surrendered her hope? I would not make her be alone in such a moment. It was the closest to repayment I could possibly accomplish. I told her I would go.

The pilgrims were fewer in number than they would have been in years past, but Saint Elkhanah Fleetfoot would always be able to pull a crowd. When we reached the doors at dusk, a line still spilled out onto the street. The pilgrims were bedraggled, weary, something desperate in their faces. Many had probably come from much farther than we had. They had come from Sonora, or from Texas, or from Wyoming. They had seen horrors that would not visit our eyes. But we each hauled along our own tragedies. I wore a bandana low on my forehead so no one could see my brand. Few literate pilgrims, these days, but the girl insisted. She stayed close to me, as if she could have protected me. The Deputy had secured my release, but on the condition I leave Vegas and never return. I was not supposed to be here.

The shrine was the lowest floor of a one-time casino; the upper floors were now crumbling and inaccessible. The bones of the holy saint himself were displayed in an elevator whose doors remained eternally open, a strip of small marquee lights shining benevolently down upon the glass case, mirrors on all the elevator's walls doubling, tripling the bones. To stand inside that elevator and look around would be to see Saint Elkhanah everywhere: the precise pins of those skeletal toes pointing in every direction; the steady, fossilized ankles always protruding upward, reaching for the legs that had been buried somewhere else, if they had been buried at all.

Formally, we were no under obligation to give alms when we entered the building, but the expectation was clear. The pilgrims in front of us were stripping layers of clothes as if removing their own skins, laying the road-wearied garments in a pile. Their gifts were worthless—almost everything here was worthless—but there was salvation to be found in the act of giving, or at least that was the rejoinder in Las Vegas: Whatever you possess, give that, and you will be rewarded with your due portion of divine grace. Remove your skin to save your soul.

We had nothing to strip besides the single layer of clothes on our bodies, or so I thought. Magdala dug inside her shirt and produced a battered old compass, then a worn gold crucifix, pilgrim-standard, but so often an object of road barter that I was shocked she still possessed it.

"Do you think it's enough for both of us?" she wondered.

"Enough for you, certainly."

She regarded me with a look that was half-petulant, half-stricken. "You have to come with me," she said.

"If it matters so much to you," I said. "But I don't need healing."

"Pray for your forehead," she said. "Pray for the scar to heal."

I saw then, all at once, the beautiful simplicity of her belief. It was like a piece of glass suspended in midair inches above an unrelenting floor. How deeply she would crack, how acutely this would hurt when she hit the ground. And yet how sublime the moment before, when all was still held in place, when she could justifiably believe that she would kneel at that corpse's feet and everything would be different when she rose, *she* would be different, body and soul, and so would I. I almost envied her, but I think what I really felt was a longing to be the same as she was, a wish for some innocence long since torn out of me.

We came closer to the shrine. The supplicants ahead of us—a man and a woman, middle-aged, the man gingerly putting his weight on a prosthetic leg of pipe—turned to face us. "Can you believe it?" the man said. "We're really here. We really made it."

"Seven hundred miles we walked," said the woman with him, resting her hand on his shoulder. "All the way from Las Cruces."

"Does it pain you, your foot?" said the man to Magdala, who seemed startled to be addressed by a stranger.

"Sometimes," she said, cautiously.

"Mine hurts me every day, although it's gone. I prayed for years to have relief, before I first heard Saint Elkhanah's name. You can't count on a miracle, I know. You shouldn't. But you have to hope, don't you?"

"Yes," said Magdala, softening now, no longer suspicious. "You have to." The man and the woman advanced to the front of the line. For a second, they stood before the bones of the saint, still with awe. Then the man released a deep exhalation, gathering himself, and leaned on his companion so that he could lower his body to the floor. She knelt beside him and they both prayed a moment, heads lowered, before they together rose and kissed the bones. I thought: soon he will know he shouldn't have hoped, and I wondered how many hundreds each day must lose their faiths. But then the man rose to his feet. "It's gone," he whispered. "The pain is really gone from it." He had a look of bewilderment on his face. As he walked away, his steps were tentative but firm, his leg secure on the prosthetic as it had not been secure before.

I began only then to hope I had somehow been wrong, that there was something solid and true beneath the Church's rotten veneer. For a glancing moment, I imagined my own pain done away with: the brand smudged out of my forehead. When we came to the shrine, we knelt together. Magdala began to pray, an almost inaudible stream of words pouring forth from her lips. Her eyes were squeezed determinedly shut; her intertwined fingers were white-knuckled. For a long time, she held still. I saw the pilgrims behind us stirring, getting impatient, wanting to know when their turn would come. I held them back with a look. At last, she returned to herself. She seemed to have gone somewhere distant, transcendent, beyond where I could possibly have traveled with her.

She rose enough to kiss the skeletal feet, touched her lips lightly to them, and then stood. I saw—before she could see, although she must have known, she must have felt—that her clubfoot was still just as before. After she lifted her face from the feet of the saint, she stared down at it for a moment, waiting to see if anything had changed, wanting to see the world remade. She stuck out the foot to take an experimental step and came heavily down, sinking to the floor. I was not strong enough to lift her back to her feet, but still I tried, at least to bolster her as she shakily stood. I held her by the arm and let her half-collapse against me until she gathered strength enough to stand, to face her clubfoot and the rest of her life clubfooted.

She did not cry. She did not protest or lament. She did not turn back to try again, as I knew pilgrims sometimes did when the saints failed or declined to intercede on their behalf. She did not, for a long moment, say anything. She wore the expression of someone who has seen the ghost of a person either beloved or detestable to them.

"It is not your fault," I said to her.

"I know," she said, her voice rough and clotted with restrained tears. "I know," but it was vivid to me that she didn't. *I should never have kidnapped you,* she had said to me when we sat with our wrists bound in the Mojave. *I'm afraid he won't heal me now.* An exacting and unmerciful saint she had imagined for herself; more bearable, perhaps, to think she might be unworthy and not Saint Elkhanah Fleetfoot.

"You are good. You had belief. You saved my life," I insisted, and I did not only mean that she had secured my freedom on the eve of my execution. I could have knelt before my campfire for twenty years more before I succumbed to the privations of the desert and sank down into oblivion, but I would have been dead for every moment of it. I *had* been dead every moment of it until I had a gun aimed at my head and a lasso around my neck and a pilgrimage forced upon me.

I could not tell whether she believed me. "You can't stay here," she said, wiping her nose with the back of her hand. "Where will you go?"

I did not want to leave her then. I felt a kind of vicarious despair when I thought of the life she had sold herself into, what she would see and know and do, who she would become. But I did not want to make her sacrifice purposeless. The dregs of Vegas lay before me and beyond it, the whole of the Remainder.

"Show me the road to the cactus-sitters," I said to her.

At the edge of the city, she unholstered her revolver and handed it to me.

"I have no need for a gun," I said.

"You do," she insisted. "You don't gotta use it if you never need it."

I understood, from the fierce half-desperate look on her face, that she would not feel peace if she knew she'd sent me out to the desert unarmed, vulnerable to the attacks of wild animals and violent men and sixteen-year-old desperado-pilgrims. "What about you?" I said as I reluctantly accepted the revolver.

"I have a feeling I won't be left long without one," she said, glancing back over her shoulder as if the Deputy might suddenly appear there. "It's loaded now. Not like before." She smiled half-apologetically. "Don't let anyone take it away from you."

I WAS EMERY harder than flint, the brand on my forehead and the memory of my trial still fresh, scavenging from the body of a man I had found lying face-up in the bottom of a canyon. My hands shook and nausea rose in my throat, for I had never robbed a corpse. I felt I should have said a prayer for him; I should have lifted my face to heaven and inquired after the state of his soul. But I did not want to know what he had been before he became this: clothes coated in a thin resin of red canyon-dust, flesh slick and bloated and sprouting club-shaped buds of prickly pear. I avoided his eyes as I pawed through his clothes. I had found already a leather wallet, a useless and quaint artifact. What did it mean, that the man possessed something like that? Who had given it to him, and who would keep such a thing in their pocket? It made me want to guess his age; it made me want to know his name.

He had a pocketknife with the blade broken. I flicked this aside as if I were one of the carrion birds that, already, I had begun following. I had seen them throw pieces of bone

and sinew away carelessly, leaving a small mountain of unwanted pieces on the ground so they could more easily get
to what they desired. But this man had nothing of worth,
and somehow that made it worse, because I could not even
claim there was any utility in what I had done to him.

After I finished digging through his clothes, I sat back
on my haunches and looked at the crows circling over my
head, and I thought if I could only make myself weep for
the man, he and I would both be redeemed somehow. Yet
I could summon no tears. I could not transcend the filthy
banality of this thing I had done to keep living, this thing
I would do again and again in pursuit of tiny scraps of left-
over life, until I followed the crows unthinkingly, until I
recognized my guilt like an old friend standing politely and
soundlessly beside me, until I could divide a man into a
series of useful pieces without ever considering what he had
been when he was still whole.

In all those canyons I wandered, I found sometimes
scratches on the wall, recent or very old. I used to trace my
fingers along them, reading or perhaps pretending I was
the writer. I was so impossibly lonely that I thought I would
die, although I knew well that no one could die from loneliness: the desert is what murders the lone traveler, through
hunger or thirst or coyotes or heatstroke.

I was always repeating the words of the Lord to the
prophet Ezekiel then. Not as a mantra, but as a lament.
I had been made emery, harder than flint. And so I
went on. With the loneliness and guilt and the letters
H E R E T I C, I went on. As a scavenger, I went on. And
then I found Mrs. Whitemorning.

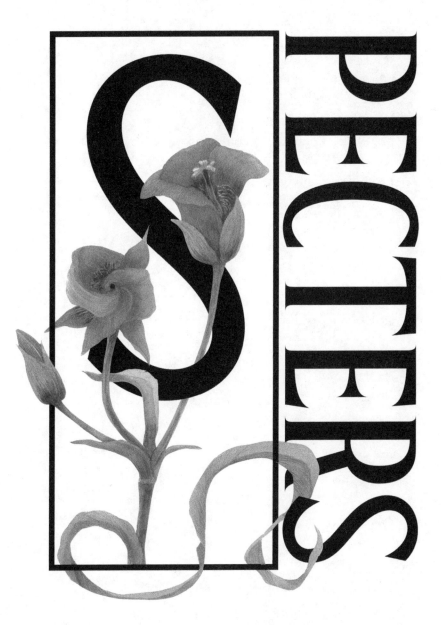

THE WOMAN CROSSED the dregs of Las Vegas on a big horse with rolling white eyes: a desert horse, monstrously ugly, but strong and inexhaustible. Excitement flared its nostrils. Dusk was hanging heavy on the horizon, glistening through the windows of the high-rises and cracking on the asphalt. The woman was coming home. Toward the heart of the city she descended, beneath a series of cement over-passes where coyotes tore at garbage and unlucky gamblers tried to sleep. The Strip gleamed lonesome from a distance. A sagging billboard imposed the words *IN A WRECK?* upon the landscape.

Wearing shapeless clothes, hair braided into a crown across her skull, she cut an indistinct figure. But the va-grants knew her by the wooden prosthetic that stuck out of her right pant leg. Murmurs followed her as she rode by. One man crossed himself as she passed. Another reached out with a shaky hand that only managed to brush the horse's hind legs.

She did not holster her gun until she reached the pink, claw-shaped motel with the empty fountain, where already the Deputy was in his room, waiting. She bent in the saddle to open the door and rode across the threshold. Inside, she stayed on the horse while the Deputy lit a cigarette. The room was less a room than a cave, with the windows all broken and curtains flapping limply in the gaping holes that remained. On sunlit days, heat thickened the air and bleached the carpet.

"The lead you had was right," she said. "Twelve bodies in the Lake Mead crater. All laid out in a row. Not even hidden."

"Jesus Christ," he said. "They got any valuables left on them?"

"Not really," she said, avoiding his eyes by looking instead at the twisted bedsheets, the filthy yellow walls. "Nothing good."

"You didn't look."

"No."

"And why not? Mother Ecclesia could use some more pocket tracts." He was almost laughing, his tin canines flashing violently in the front of his mouth. "Lead crucifixes. Maybe some of them little aluminum charms they pin to the saints so God doesn't get confused which part wants healing."

"Fuck off," she said softly.

He laughed until he coughed. Then his face hardened. "They were pilgrims though, weren't they?"

She shrugged. "Weren't *not* pilgrims. Only men, from what I could tell, but I don't think the group started that way."

"You think it was your wolf-men that did it?"

She *knew* it was. But she didn't want him thinking she cared overmuch. "Unless there's someone else out there slaughtering men and kidnapping women."

The Deputy pushed himself upright on the bed and ground his half-finished cigarette into the carpet. "Were they fresh, those corpses?"

"A day, maybe."

"Then they likely haven't skipped town yet."

"Guess not."

"So go and get 'em, then."

By *get 'em*, he meant kill them. There was no confining men like that, she knew as well as he did. But even after five years, even when the men in question were as bad as these ones, she was not used to the way he threw away other people's lives so casually. "Need bullets," she said, though she didn't, and if she had, she could have gotten them from someone else; she liked to have a stockpile. Just in case.

"Fresh out," he replied. When he lied, he always lied like that: without commitment, without conviction, throwing words over his shoulder.

"Fine," she said, childish, surly, and cued the horse backward until his hooves clattered on the threshold. The wind at her back felt damp. She thought, she hoped, it would rain one last time before monsoon season ended.

"Bury them good," he called after her. "Bring me a trophy."

"I always do."

"And keep it quiet. I hear there are witnesses again, we're gonna have to have a conversation."

He spoke as if she had wanted witnesses to any of the small and half-justified atrocities he ordered her to commit. As if she were putting on a performance, the way he did with his flashing metal teeth and loud engine and lovingly staged acts of sadism. She did not dignify the accusation with a denial.

She stuck her head into half a dozen of the worst snake holes in Paradise before a bartender stumbled over his words saying he'd seen no posse of men with tattoos of wolves on their necks. She didn't even have to pull her gun on him before he was admitting in a lowered voice that they'd rented out his basement the day before and were still camped out downstairs.

"Was just business," he whimpered. "You're the merciful one, they all say it. You won't tell him, will you? I'm not deserving of what he'd do. I promise you."

Magdala never mentioned anyone to the Deputy if she could help it, but she felt no compulsion to give the bartender peace of mind. She descended the staircase to the bar basement and cocked her revolver before she opened the door, her heart thundering in her chest.

When she heard a scratching at the door, she hesitated only for a second, then twisted the handle and swung the door open into a waist-high sea of coyotes. They had anticipated her better than she had anticipated them, and the coyotes lunged at her with the thoughtless, needful hunger of animals half-starved, their teeth lashing, their bodies hunched low.

With her back pressed to a sliver of open door, Magdala fired almost without thinking. She emptied the chamber and let the last surviving dog creep away into a corner on three working legs. There had only been five of them. If there had been more, the fight would have been fair, and she might not have won.

For a moment, she stood in the heap of animals and inhaled their musty pent-up odors, the sharp tang of their blood. She was thinking she had walked into a trap of cruel and idiotic construction until she saw in the corner the girl of eight or nine years old, pilgrim-thin, eyes so big in her face that she was like the ghost of a child.

"I couldn't stop them," the girl said to her.

Magdala couldn't tell whether it was an apology or only a stunned statement of the facts. She looked between the child and the dead coyotes, trying to work out why the animals had not attacked such easy prey when they'd had the chance.

"Were there men here?" she said. "With wolves on their necks?"

Slowly, the girl nodded.

"Where'd they go?"

The girl's eyes fell to the pile of coyotes. "There," she whispered.

For a long moment, Magdala looked at the animals, trying and failing to find traces of the men they supposedly had been. It seemed both impossible and certain that the girl was lying. The Deputy, she thought, would be irate she couldn't take any trophies. "How?" she asked.

The child had no answer. She shifted her weight and Magdala saw a bullet had embedded in her foot. Magdala felt her own culpability like a blow to the chest, only made worse by the girl's apparent failure to fear or loathe her for what she had accidentally done. In her five years with the Deputy, she had never hurt a child.

"You have parents?" she said at last, inadequately.

The girl's face crumpled, and it seemed as if she might cry. Then, with a visible effort, she took command of herself. "Dead," she said, almost proudly, throwing her black braid over her shoulder. "Dead and gone."

Magdala examined her from across the room. "I'll get someone to yank that bullet out of you," she said at last. "But you can't say your name to them, can't say where you come from, can't say what you seen. Do you understand?"

The child nodded.

Magdala opened the basement door and the wind cut through her. It was the cold watery wind of the after-monsoon, no longer sticky and thick but empty, clean, nascent. While the girl stood in the doorway, Magdala brought the coyotes into the street one by one, laying them on the wet pavement, steam rising in curling white tongues as heat consumed the monsoon moisture. For a moment, she stood before the pile of them. She had thought she would feel satisfied or victorious or at least safe when the Caput Lupinum men had been caught, but she felt none of those things now.

She knew she would not be stopped, and yet her motions were furtive as she tied the carcasses end-to-end with a length of rope and hitched the long, dead trail of them to the horse's saddle. When she was finished, she laid her palm on the horse's neck and tapped twice with the base of her hand. The animal stooped and she swung her good leg across its back. "Come on," she said to the child, who obeyed without hesitating.

They dragged the chain of bodies into the dregs of Vegas proper. After the rain, the road looked diseased, monsoon water stagnating darkly inside potholes, flies murmuring on the filmy surfaces. But before dawn, the water would dry up. The flies would retreat to their deep-buried wells of groundwater, their protected shelves, their putrid dens of everlasting life.

Magdala thought sometimes that Vegas would not see another monsoon season. She could feel the finality of this one that was now dissipating into the desert night. There were priests in some outlying parishes, quietly but with great urgency speaking of the end times. That was heresy, but one so unappealing it posed no threat to the Holy Church of Las Vegas. It was heresy Magdala could not really convince herself to believe.

"Did they tell you who they are?" Magdala said to the child, once she had finished burying the coyotes.

The girl said no.

"I knew them once," said Magdala. "Some of them, at least. I belonged to them."

The church where Magdala took the girl was an inglorious thing living in the bones of a fourth-rate casino. Its unlit sign, painted in brash green letters, was the only one on the street. The other structures were nameless and empty: shelters for vagrants, simple trash heaps, impenetrable piles of rubble now only related in a vague, ancestral way to buildings. Magdala dismounted outside, threaded the horse's reins through a chain link fence, and held out her forearm so the child could climb down. The girl gripped Magdala's outstretched limb two-handed with a fierce, hungry grasp and hung suspended for a second with all her weight on Magdala before she landed.

So late at night, the church was not a house of worship. It was only another hole into which soft-bellied creatures could crawl. They sprawled across the bus-seat pews and the unfinished floor, clutching old clothes or loosely woven fragments of yarn—charity blankets, made with scornful indifference by Vegas nuns who only half-knew how to sew. In the foyer, Magdala leaned on a cane of juniper wood and led the child to the night priest. He was of the lower orders of the Church's inscrutable food chain, but still he had guards on either side of him, swollen-looking men nearly suffocating in their own boredom. The priest looked at her and stiffened in his seat. He barely saw the child. Doubtless he thought she was there looking for a fugitive. When she showed him the girl's foot, he visibly relaxed. He instructed the guards to send for a nun, the work of wound-tending decidedly below his station.

Magdala began slowly to edge backward toward the door as if to go, then stopped and stood still for a moment. Her eyes moved to the altar with the cup of blackish wine, the hard heel of bread balanced on the golden plate. At last she looked to the life-size crucifix mounted on the wall: Christ bloodied, his face melting with heat and age, a lei of plastic flowers draped unceremoniously around his neck. She got slowly to her knees, the gesture painstaking, then lowered her forehead to the floor in prostration.

A nun emerged from the back of the church, looked with something between fear and astonishment at the woman lying across the floor, and motioned for the child to follow her. When she came back, she was alone. She stood in front of Magdala, afraid to interrupt, until Magdala stood, gripping the back of a pew to hoist herself up.

"She will live?" Magdala asked.

"It only brushed her. Don't let her walk for a while. Keep her foot up."

"She's not mine. Can't stay with me. Don't you have a place for her?"

"Not here," the nun said. She looked furtively at the night priest, then lowered her voice. "Miss Magdala, you have been down close to the meeting of the Colorado and the Gila rivers?"

Magdala shrugged.

"There's a woman there. Name of Mrs. Whitemorning. She has a house for orphans. But there's a thousand orphans in this city. I shouldn't even have told you. No reason for one child to get special treatment over all the rest. The Church wouldn't want me saying her name to you. But if *you* take her—well. Do you understand?"

"It's awful far to go," Magdala said, her eyes on the crucifix, the river of blood meandering lazily down Christ's left thigh. "For one child who's not mine."

"We don't have a bed to spare."

"Someone else can't take her?"

"We don't have a rider to spare either."

Magdala hesitated. "It's no place for a child to grow up," she said, after a moment.

"Nor is this," the nun whispered, almost pleadingly, and retreated into the dark innards of the church, letting Magdala follow at her own pace. By the time she got there, already the bullet had been yanked from the child's foot. Only the bandaging remained to be done. The nun allowed a capful of disinfectant to dribble across the wound, then wrapped a scrap of cloth three times around the entire foot.

"Change this once a day," she said. "Or else it'll get infected."

The child had refused to make any sound of pain while the nun worked, but tears glistened in the corners of her eyes now when she was handed to Magdala. She would not let her hurt foot brush the ground. Instead, she grabbed hold of Magdala's cane, her small fists just below Magdala's hardly larger ones, and tremulously hopped forward.

When they returned to the church sanctuary, the light was already paling with sunrise, ghosting in a colorless film through the windows. The night priest had fallen asleep on his thick-armed chair, his heels dug into the carpet, his mouth wide open. But the people who had slept in the pews were sitting up, singing the Lord's Prayer.

"For thine is the kingdom," echoed Magdala. "And the power. And the glory."

"How do you know this prayer?" the child said softly, clutching at the cane as if it belonged equally to them both. "Do you belong to the Church?"

"To the Deputy," said Magdala. "But it's all almost the same. For thine is"—and she hesitated on the threshold, to collect herself before she faced the morning—"the kingdom," she finished, decisively, and stepped down onto the road. In the half-light, she could see the child as a burden whose bearing might somehow purchase her salvation.

Until she found an excuse to leave the city, the child had to be hidden from the Deputy, and the Deputy had to be lied to. She came to him in the late afternoon, when the shadows of the casinos fell in long charcoal-colored columns across the roads. By then the heat was shoving its fists into all the hidden places and hollows in Las Vegas, the Hacienda not the least among them. The pink paint on the motel walls spread itself out wantonly for the setting sun.

She never got down from her horse in front of him unless it was afternoon, and this was going to happen. He would not have known what to think if she had dismounted and not gotten onto the bed, lying back on the crumpled sheets with her head on the thin, dispirited pillow, saying nothing, making no sound besides the soft hissing of fabric as she got undressed. When she was done, she would only be wearing the dingy, pale pink brassiere that she had not removed unless to wash for as long as she could remember. It was an elderly woman's garment, larger than she needed, the straps twisted on her lean shoulders so they wouldn't slip loose. The rest would come off: the pants that concealed most of her prosthetic, the worn-thin polyester underwear, the overlarge men's shirt.

She was always the one to initiate, ever since that first time late at night in the dregs of Vegas after she had watched him kill a man with his bare hands. The man died too fast, without putting up a fight, and she could see the Deputy's unsated fury in the curl of his fists and the set of his jaw, as if he were chewing with nothing in his mouth. For minutes he stood like a coiled spring over the dead man, his eyes roving the horizon for a substitute that never materialized.

After they buried the man, they camped out beneath the twisted frame of a long-dead car, close together in the dark, and a terror suddenly wracked her that she could only settle by reaching between the Deputy's legs, between the plates of aluminum that guarded him, and holding him in her fist. For a second he was still as she felt the length of him, and she thought he was angry or disgusted or simply uninterested, but then he angled his hips so she could reach more easily. Said in a low and slurred tone half-unrecognizable to her, "Turns you on, huh? The violence." *Yes*, she said, though it didn't. She was remembering being eleven years old and lying on a hammock in a dark bank vault, listening as men discharged their rage and loathing and sadness into the women of Caput Lupinum. "They're safe, afterwards," Alma had whispered to her once. "Just stay out of their way before."

It was not really true, what Alma had said, but sometimes, afterwards, the Deputy's head stayed on her thigh for a while, and she thought she could have hurt him if she wanted to, and she felt, for a second, that he was more vulnerable than she was.

As shadows fell across the wall, she said, "The job's done."

He lifted his eyes to meet hers.

"All of them dead?"

"Yes."

"Anyone see you?"

"No one," she lied.

"Where's your trophy?"

She had known the question was coming. "Didn't take one."

"Didn't take one," he repeated. He lifted his head and looked at her with something between contempt and fear. She could see that he was weighing whether to press the issue, deciding whether it would weaken him somehow to admit aloud that she had disobeyed him. Some delicate stab of retribution was in store; if not now, then later. After a moment, he got up. She hoped he was forgetting it for now. She followed his lead and began to get dressed, watching him surreptitiously. It was almost dark outside.

"I got a new job for you," he said.

She pulled her shirt on over her head. His tone made her suspicious. "What?"

"I want you to steal the feet of Saint Elkhanah."

Magdala froze, only for a second, then gathered her hair and combed through it with her fingers, a pin in her mouth to excuse her silence.

"You heard me?" he insisted.

"You wanna steal some old huckster's bones," she said with feigned disinterest.

"The Church has been trying to tell me what my business is. First it's, 'Well, we can't pay you if he's decapitated and it's only the body.' Then it's, 'Gotta take a cleaning fee out if you do it on the Strip in one of our places.' They think I don't see how the lasso's tightening. Pretty soon, they'll be expecting me in a black dress on time for mass. But you and me, we're gonna remind them of the reality of their situation."

"You know they're powerless," she said. "The bones, I mean."

"Don't shock me." He grinned with his metal teeth.

"So why Elkhanah's feet?" She knew why, and he knew she did. He never forgot any morsel of information that might be used against someone. She was only surprised he had waited so long to play such an easy hand.

"They're the biggest moneymaker in town," he said. "Always have been. I get ahold of their most precious asset, I might as well be the first pope of the Holy Church of Las Vegas."

"You think they won't just kill you? Those bones are worth more to them than you are."

"Oh, but Magdala," he said, "who are they gonna send to do that job? Not you, surely."

"You think in the whole Mojave there's not one other half-decent killer?"

"I have my doubts," he said. "Having killed most of them. But you can find out for me. You're gonna be the one to get those bones, it's gonna be you they go looking for. And I know you'll keep them safe and sound for me. You'll even take the fall for me because I'll kill your foundling if you don't."

A chill passed through her. "What do you know about that?" she demanded.

Though she couldn't see him, she could feel he was grinning. "You know, I never pegged you as real maternal," he said. "It'd be almost sweet, if it weren't so stupid."

It would not be hard to steal the bones because she was not going to try to go unseen. A couple of guards would stand in her way, but they would only be the same old Vegas thugs who showed their bellies the second they thought they were being inconvenienced. The relics were not well-protected; they didn't need to be. Anyone capable of stealing from the Holy Church of Las Vegas knew that no pile of bones or lock of hair was worth the heat that would rain down on them if they stayed within a hundred miles of the Strip. Somehow the Deputy thought she didn't know.

"When the job's done, you ride to our place off exit 143, go inside so no one can see you and wait for me there," he'd ordered her. "I wanna see those bones for myself." She'd nodded her assent. But she had no intention of stopping in the hollowed-out corpse of Big Sensations Adult Video, their customary meeting spot, nor of letting the Deputy see the bones for himself. She was saying goodbye to Las Vegas that night, and so was the child.

The child was small enough to fit across the horse's neck in front of the saddle horn, her legs dangling on either side of the animal's broad chest. She made no sound while they rode. Magdala could feel, though not see, her watching their surroundings, stiffening at the disquiet of the Las Vegas silence, flinching once when someone screamed distantly.

"They're only angry, not murdered," Magdala said to her.

The child wouldn't say anything. At the front steps of the Sunlite, Magdala lowered her down from the saddle and stood her on the ground.

"Do you know what we're doing?" she said. There was no reply, so she went on. "We're robbing them," she said. "Not this one, the casino across the way. But there's guards in all these places just waiting to pick a fight with somebody smaller than them. They come anywhere close to you, you run and you hide. That make sense to you?"

The child managed, now, to say yes. Magdala looked sideways at her and thought she must understand she was not really being protected. Alone out here, she might be shot or found by men even worse than the ones who'd had her before. Magdala had contemplated letting the girl go inside with her, but that could have been worse and besides, the bones of Saint Elkhanah were not far from the door.

Outside of the casino, she cocked the big, showy gun the Deputy had lent her. He wanted her to get caught, she had understood. A spray of bullets into a casino wall like that, she could hardly expect to make a clean break. He intended for this to be the last and most spectacular thing she did for him. It was going to be that. Not on his terms, but it still would be.

She nudged the horse in the sides. The animal had gotten practiced at coming right up close to a door so she could strike the lock with her wooden cane. Most of the padlocks on Vegas doors were by now brittle, clanking a few times and then splitting cleanly. The first lock fell to the dirt in a plume of dust, followed by the second. She had figured there would be guards at this point, but there were none. The horse shifted to the side as the door creaked open. No one rushed out, no gunshot. She exhaled a short, sharp breath and rode inside.

Empty of pilgrims, the casino lobby was strange. All those dusty footprints mashed into the carpet and cheap tin *milagros* glinting off the clothes of the other relics. She made for the elevator. The mirrors caught her foot in the stirrup and the horse's lean, dark forelegs. She was close when she saw the lone guard huddled in the corner, holding his gun but not aiming at her. Incomprehensible that they could only have one man guarding such a collection of treasures. Magdala suspected she could shoot him once and he'd fall dead, and she would have time enough before someone else came.

She was close to the relic when the guard stood up and aimed his gun. She could only half-make out his face in the dark, but still she could see he was hardly more than a child. He had the sunken cheeks and deep-set eyes of someone who had been hungry his whole life. When he recognized her, he lowered his weapon, his face scrunching in confusion. She held a finger to her lips. She did not want to shoot him. He stayed quiet and she rode past him to the elevator, waiting for a phalanx of broad-shouldered men to come running out. Her heartbeat galloped through her chest into her fingertips. She dismounted before the glass case, grasping her cane in one hand and the horse's reins in the other. A whispered prayer of contrition snuck between her pursed lips before she could stop the old ritual words.

The bones looked the same as they had been the time before, when she had knelt and thought she would rise, like after a baptism, remade, all her old iniquities and pain forgotten. The Church did not let pilgrims touch Saint Elkhanah's feet with their hands. Lips were gentler. The soft, yellow gleam of the bones had not faded. Years of kisses had pressed a shallow divot into the flat tops of each foot, the right one maybe a little deeper. Magdala lowered her face. She remembered the bones smelling like something, feeling like something, but they didn't. They were as clean and featureless as plastic. The feet were nailed like the feet of crucified Christ to the platform. Magdala used a hammer to rip out the nails and grabbed the feet by their toes. The bones, strung together with white thread, rattled like snakes, like manacles. She stuffed them into her bag and tapped the horse to kneel so she could mount. The work was nearly over. Still no guards had come. She had a lump like nausea or tears at the back of her throat.

No one was on the street when she came out. The Vegas night was sooty and close, neon filtering mistily from the marquees at the other end of the street. Pilgrims would be tucked away in their hotel rooms or in the dregs of the city at their campfires by now, but the locals wouldn't sleep until dawn was closer; no doubt she was right now being watched by someone.

When the child emerged from an alleyway, hobbling on her hurt foot, Magdala swung her up onto the horse's neck and without a word they rode, the horse's long stride eating up the cracked pavement as they made for the dregs of Vegas. They ran incautiously down the middle of streets. The cast-iron statue of the first archbishop of Las Vegas passed blurrily through her sight; they were close to the walls surrounding the Strip. Still no one. Impossible good luck that still there was no one.

"You get what we're doing?" she said to the child.

"Yes," the child replied.

"You and I are both done for if we ever come back here."

"Where are we going?"

Magdala felt for the bones in the bag at her side, interlocking her fingers with the skeletal toes, steadying herself. "South," she said. "We're getting you a home. And me out of here."

The vultures in the garbage heaps were mean with hunger, lunging at the horse's neck and the child's hair. Magdala beat them off with the butt of her six-shooter, prodding the horse with her leg to keep him going. Once they were through the worst, she slowed down some, but she didn't let the horse walk. If he didn't know already, the Deputy would soon realize she was not going to keep their meeting, that she had betrayed him. She could only hope that he would not ascertain where she was going. The bones of Saint Elkhanah were rattling in their sack. The child sagged wearily on the horse's spine, her body sliding perilously to the side. "You keep awake," Magdala told her. "If you fall off, I'm not getting you back up." But she brought her arms closer around the child's sides to steady her.

The high desert was as she remembered. All the vegetation looking either hungry or glutted, plants with ribs and collarbones and heavy, pendulous bellies. She had been back out in the Mojave plenty of times since she'd first come to Vegas: when some runaway needed apprehending, or a job was too messy to be done in Vegas proper. But she had not gone farther out than a few miles. She had no need to.

Only ones who could survive out there for long were *them*, drinkers said sagely across their cups of prickly pear wine, and the *them* was anything that partook in the sheer, raw strangeness of it. Animal or demon or unnamable atmosphere. Magdala didn't know whether to count herself in that number. She remembered the heretic had said once she belonged to the desert. But the child plainly didn't. *Kinder,* the Deputy said, *to let some folk die.* He was always grinning when he said those words.

She had recollections of the people who were incorporated into the desert after they died, the selfhood faded out of them, their bodies become a kind of compost. By now some of those bodies had been part of the desert for so many years that they were no longer recognizable as hybrid things. They were only things, thorny-skinned and taller than any man Magdala had seen, leering with mouths accompanied by no eyes, no face at all, only a gaping hole that looked as though it wanted to suck you in. But they did not advance, and anyway she was going too fast to be stopped.

They were a few hours from the city when at last she let the horse breathe, sliding down his sweat-soaked withers and carrying the girl after her. She feared the animal might drop dead, but he managed to dig for groundwater before he collapsed into the mud that rose up, drinking in long, desperate swallows like she'd never heard from a horse. When he'd had his fill, she and the child knelt at the watering hole the horse had created to drink the muddy shallows that remained. The child recoiled from the taste of the groundwater, sticking her dirt-streaked tongue out. Magdala forestalled her complaints with a hard look.

"Do we have to keep going?" the child said.

Magdala glanced between the horse and the girl, seeing their exhaustion.

"No," she relented. "We'll stop a while. Have a fire to keep the animals off us."

The girl laid down while Magdala gingerly gathered branches from the plainest-looking tree she could find, an old, gnarled Joshua that seemed as if it had never been part animal or human. The branches smelled wrong when they burnt, and she realized it was flesh alongside wood that was burning. But the deed was done, so she let the kindling get down to coals, sucking in the poisonous air that rose, watching the smoke curl in pink tendrils that evaporated when the wind struck them. The old desert sounds half-soothed her: the howls and screams of far-away predation, the laments of mourning doves, the chirps of the lizards in their mating season. The sound of whistling was, for a while, indistinguishable from the rest.

Her eyelids were drooping when finally the thread of the lilting melody emerged, as if suddenly, prodding her awake. She blinked, rubbing the grit from her eyes and with it her weary complacence. The Deputy would be suicidal to follow her so far into the wilderness at night, but the Deputy had grafted armor to his own skin so that he felt impenetrable; he had pursued a two-bit murderer like Barabbas Knight for years when he'd had a mark on the man, and he would not be deterred by the prospect of going far out into the desert. There was a mocking sound in that whistled tune, she thought, and underneath, a wretched melancholy one. Quietly, she withdrew the pistol from her holster. The child was still sleeping to one side of her.

When a figure glistened among the Joshua trees a moment later, Magdala aimed and almost fired, hesitating only when she realized it was not the Deputy but a stranger. He was a white man with a face perfectly clean-shaven, unnervingly handsome, wearing a white Stetson and cowhide chaps and the most ornately embroidered boots she'd ever seen. He was the image of the man that every other man in Vegas was trying to resemble. She got to her feet and kept her gun trained on the stranger's head.

"You ain't gotta be *so* untrusting," the man said, his voice low and honeyed. He withdrew two antique six-shooters from twin holsters, twirled them ceremonially on his pointer fingers, and then replaced them. "I can't hurt ya."

He was close enough now that Magdala thought his voice should have woken the child, but neither the child nor the horse seemed aware of him. The horse stood with his head low, his eyes half-closed. The girl slept on. She was, she realized, the only one who could see him.

"You're not real," she said, but just the same, she reached down for a stone and tossed it. The rock passed straight through his body, thudding to the ground a few feet behind him.

"Oh, tenderfoot," he said. "You're breaking my heart."

As he strode closer, a dozen feet from the glowing coals of the campfire now, Magdala's finger itched on the trigger. She was afraid to wake the child and more reluctant still to waste a bullet on a figment of her imagination. But she kept her gun pointed. After a moment, feeling weariness set in, she lowered herself slowly to the ground. The cowboy remained a few feet away, bisected by the shadows the fire-light cast.

"Who are you?" she asked.

"Better question, who are *you*?" he countered. "I was settling right down into my immortal rest until you took a shine to my weary feet."

"You're not him," she said, loud and hard-edged enough that the child stirred in her sleep.

The cowboy smiled ghoulishly. "You know, you could at least spot me a corporeal form if you're gonna run me across the whole Remainder. Your body's nothing to write home about, nothing like what I had before, but it's better than . . ." He whipped his hands through the air. "*This,*" he concluded with disgust.

"You're not him," Magdala repeated, this time in a whisper, and her eyes fell to the sack containing the bones: meaningless, she would have said, in every way besides its usefulness as leverage. Saint Elkhanah was not a saint she venerated now; there were no saints she venerated now. As his spitting likeness whistled a cowboy ballad across the fire from her, she wanted to crush his bones to powder. She wanted to bury them in the mud-choked water that swirled in the arroyos come monsoon season. She wanted to toss them from a cliff. She wanted to kiss the toes and stand and be whole. And she refused to see the apparition, at least refused to look at him. But she thought, if he wasn't Saint Elkhanah Fleetfoot, who was he?

For days, she and the child rode southeast, keeping the black curve of the pilgrim highway to one side of them, stopping only for water or to empty their bladders or to pilfer a few hours of sleep in the afternoon shade cast haltingly by Joshua trees that were not only trees anymore. The ghostly figure in his cowboy boots and leather chaps trailed them at a distance, visible as a dot on the horizon whenever Magdala glanced over her shoulder. She did not mention him to the child. She was certain the child could not see him.

The way from the holy city to the house of Mrs. Whitemorning was long and monotonous, marked only by the lonely carcasses of motels and drive-thrus and gas stations. They kept a wide berth from these ruins; Magdala remembered the tricks they had played on Barabbas Knight and his posse. But the Mojave itself could not be avoided, and the desert was nothing if not one sprawling trick played at the expense of the traveler. Magdala had learned to see their surroundings without really seeing, but the child was big-eyed with wonder at every new effusion of strangeness. She was only distantly afraid of the stuffed men that traveled in strings or packs or alone, wearing the remnants of their old bodies like half-shed skins; Magdala soon realized she did not really know what they were.

"Could we . . . eat them?" she wondered on their second night, staring down a precipice at the crowds that shuffled restlessly across the plain below. Magdala shuddered. She had seen the stuffed men's prone bodies flung around by a dust storm before. It was tempting to think of collecting what remained after the winds died down: bodies packed with ample swollen lumps of vegetable-meat that would be lush and rain-saturated and taste faintly of prickly pear. But she had been seeing the child as a perfect innocent, spared the kinds of hungers that Magdala felt, and she recoiled at this showing of the girl's instincts for predation.

At her side, the ghost of Saint Elkhanah—always, at night, close to them—spat a black wad of chew down the cliff. It never landed. "She's a canny one," he said to Magdala. "How'd she guess your favorite food?"

"We'd get sick," Magdala said to the child, ignoring him.

"I'm so hungry," whispered the girl.

"I know," she said, remembering she had herself, as a child, gone days in the desert without a morsel of food passing between her lips. "Thing is, nothing out here is safe for eating."

"How come you didn't bring anything?"

Her first reaction to the question was contempt—at the child's softness, her unembarrassed expression of need, her failure to be afraid that such an expression would be met with cruelty or indifference. Guilt came quickly afterward, succeeded by a lash of anger. A half-decent guardian would have brought food reserves. But she never asked to be anyone's guardian. "I was in a hurry," Magdala said at last. "Wasn't really supposed to be leaving Vegas and had to be secretive. You'll have something to eat. Sometime soon."

The child was unappeased. "When?"

"When we get to Mrs. Whitemorning."

That half-sentence, by now, had become her refrain, and the girl's face revealed how weary she was of it. "But *when's* that?"

At least six days more, at the pace they were keeping. The child wouldn't make it. Magdala felt the absence of her own hunger like a gnawing presence, which was always superseded the moment she reached open country by the restless pining the desert stirred inside her, a hunger stronger than food-hunger. Her eyes fell across the half-vegetable forms of the unrooted, wandering creatures below. "I'll find you something," she said to the child. "Tomorrow. I promise. We'll scavenge from somewhere."

"You so sure that's wise?" taunted the ghost, spitting for emphasis.

Magdala said nothing. Though the child could not see nor hear the ghostly figure, she could still hear Magdala's replies to his provocations; already she had overheard Magdala mumbling to him on at least one occasion. But the ghost's questions had a way of lingering inside her head, and she only waited for the child to fall asleep before she said, "Why wouldn't it be?"

"Well, *I* had the impression you were running from somebody," he said, hands lifted in defense. "Seems to me that dilly-dallying by digging around in the trash heaps of civilization is a real slick way to get yourself caught."

"He could find us anywhere," said Magdala. "You know something about him?"

"I'm not telling you what to do," said the ghost. "Wouldn't dream of it. You, a real living person, and me only a revenant without so much as a layer of skin to his name. But I can tell you that I got here by underestimating just how small this big old wasteland can be when you got an outraged lawman on your back."

"He's no more a lawman than you are a saint."

"Be careful, tenderfoot. Wouldn't want to bring my wrath upon you. You're on shaky ground already, what with the thieving and all that horseback jostling of my sacred bones."

Her gaze returned, only for a moment, to his moonlit face. "You're not real."

The ghost grinned, showing teeth that were too blindingly white, whiter than any set of teeth Magdala had ever laid eyes on. "The worst part is, you don't know, do you? A haunting seems a fitting punishment for stealing a holy relic. Seems like the kind of thing that *should* happen to a reprobate like you. But then, bad men never get theirs, and maybe you're just bad enough to start outrunning consequences. If only you didn't have the girl-child tied to you."

"Don't say that," she said. She wouldn't look at him or the child. She was remembering her father, insane and bloody-mouthed at the end of the last journey he ever took, brimming with resentment for the burdensome child he had carried to his death.

They had only ridden for an hour in the morning when a squat compound materialized on the horizon. "You said," the girl insisted in a half-whisper, turning her head to fix her big, dark eyes on Magdala, and Magdala, turning her own head to see the ghost rambling on after them in the distance, said, "I know I did," and nudged the horse in the compound's direction.

The cluster of buildings seemed at some time recently to have been inhabited. A fence of ocotillo and twine had been put up; someone had gone to the trouble of climbing the twenty-foot-tall marquee sign at the edge of the complex and painting the word *NO* over the phrase *Mesquite Creek Premium Outlets* so that the sign now read *No Outlets*. Beneath, sun-faded lettering promised *Top Designer Brands*, *Athletic Wear*. At the fence line, Magdala hesitated to contemplate the hole torn through the ocotillo barrier, which might have been a carelessly made gate or a more sinister omen. She wondered if the Deputy had come looking for her here. She wondered if he'd seen the hole and assumed she'd made it.

The silence of the place was tense and conspicuous, a held breath. A man's body lay still disintegrating in front of a dust-fogged glass storefront that had once been someone's home. She could see furniture arranged inside, armchairs and low plastic benches and shelves filled with the inconsequential stuff of life. At the sight of the body, she resisted the impulse to cover the child's eyes, then felt a weary, confused resentment at feeling obligated to shelter the girl at all.

"No one here," she said once they'd traced the perimeter of the place.

"What happened to them?" asked the child.

"Don't know," said Magdala. "Same things that happen to everybody, probably. Something ate them or they turned on each other." Leaning over the horse's neck, she tugged on a door stuck closed by heat and disuse until it cracked open. The horse pinned his ears back and shuffled his feet, balking at the prospect of entry.

"Does that mean it's not safe?" the child asked.

"Means he's temperamental and only half-broke," said Magdala. She dismounted, and then the girl slid down heavily into her arms, wincing as her hurt foot collided with Magdala's hip. While Magdala hitched the horse to a rust-eaten bike rack, the child stood still, her lips pursed, her eyes wide but not yet tear-filled, and Magdala tried not to see. She hadn't changed the child's bandage since they'd left the city; bandages were something else she'd neglected to carry. She was afraid to think how the bullet wound looked now.

They entered the dusty sepulcher of the store, the child's eyes on her as Magdala maneuvered through a jumble of furniture, poking at a bundle of wrinkled clothes and then an assemblage of shoeboxes with the end of her cane. "Best not to reach with your hands into things you can't see," she advised the child. "Could be snakes, or insects."

"What are we looking for?" said the child.

"Something edible," Magdala said with a shrug. "They might have kept food here."

"Like, what kind of food?"

"Something preserved, most like. Something in a can or a tin or a jar."

"What if they didn't?"

"Then they didn't." She crouched on her good leg to examine the lower shelves.

"I found something," the child said.

Magdala stood and glanced across the store. The child had a big-eyed plastic doll in her hands, its body scarred by pink crayon and bleached to a peculiar color by sun exposure. She tugged on the doll's leg and the doll emitted a harsh, hoarse-sounding cry like—but not like—a real infant's. At the sight of this wonder, Magdala forgot for a moment the Deputy on their trail, the saint lingering even closer, the corpse in front of the store. She crossed the room and watched as the child tugged on the doll's leg again, this time eliciting a curdled mewling that might once have been baby talk.

"How does it work?" she said, looking wide-eyed at Magdala.

Magdala shook her head. "Do it again," she said.

The girl complied. They both stood there listening, enthralled, and then the child suddenly giggled. Magdala realized she had never heard the girl laugh before.

"It's not like a real baby," the child said.

"Not like a real anything," Magdala agreed.

The child began lowering the doll to the floor. Then she glanced back at Magdala. "Can I keep it?" she said. "I never had anything like it."

"As long as you keep it quiet when we're outside," said Magdala, harsher than she needed to, and returned to digging through the shelves. It was not long before she found a collection of jars, all holding fermented vegetables of an indeterminate reddish color.

"Here," she said. "Easy." She wrestled the lid of one jar open. "This one's good," she said, choking back a spike of nausea at the heady scent of the fermented vegetation. She never could stomach ordinary food once she got out into the desert.

"Do I have to eat that?" the child said with a kind of dismay, staring into the murky depths of the jar.

"It won't hurt you."

Gingerly, the child reached for one of the vegetables and held it in the palm of her hand. Her tongue darted out questioningly, drew back. "I don't like it," she said.

"It's this or nothing."

"But I'm so *hungry*."

"Then you've got to eat it."

"Why didn't you bring real food for me?"

Magdala, losing her patience, pushed the jar into the child's hands and hobbled back to the door. Outside she stood still for a moment, angry with the girl for her frailty, with herself for momentarily forgetting they were fugitives, and with the ghost for slipping the unthinkable life-nourishing thought into her head that she should abandon the child.

It was several minutes before the girl emerged, clutching the half-emptied jar but not the doll. "Magdala," she said, and Magdala could not remember the last time anyone had addressed her so gently; perhaps not since the heretic walked out of Vegas five years ago. She came stumbling to Magdala's side, holding the jar out. "Do you want some?"

Magdala accepted, swallowing around her nausea. They stood together and finished the jar in companionable silence. Across the courtyard, the saint's ghost stood motionless between a dead Coke machine and a small mechanical bucking bronco. He was waiting, she thought, for a reversal of fortune; for something to go wrong; to be able to say he'd told her so. "Let's get out of here," she said to the child as soon as the jar was empty. "Sooner we can get you to Mrs. Whitemorning, the better."

"Magdala," the child said, "who *is* Mrs. Whitemorning?"

"She takes care of orphans," said Magdala, feeling the inadequacy of this explanation but having none better.

"Is she kind?"

She could not force a lie. "She'll take good care of you."

The child was quiet, contemplating. "Magdala," she said, a little later. "Where are you gonna go? When I go to Mrs. Whitemorning."

The question had somehow not occurred to her. Beyond ferrying the child to a safe home and getting away from the Deputy, there had been no plan. In five years, she had not thought beyond following the Deputy's orders or spitefully eliding them. She could never return to Las Vegas. Certainly she would not be welcome with Mrs. Whitemorning. She thought with absurd longing of throwing herself upon the mercy of the cactus-sitters. But the thought of showing herself to them as she was now was more unbearable than the thought of wandering a lifetime alone in the desert. Whenever she thought of them, she thought of the mule on the ground with gouges from her father's fingernails in his flesh. The soft cries the mule uttered as they walked away from him.

"I don't know," she confessed, and across the miles, the weight of it settled on her: that after the child was gone, it would be her and the desert and the saint's bones and the low hum of the Deputy's motorcycle always in her ears even when he was nowhere near her.

They rode five more days before at last they came to the house of Mrs. Whitemorning. Saddle-sore and impatient, the child squirmed on the horse's neck as Magdala dismounted outside the old farmhouse and stood absorbing the sight of it. The house was just the same, the roof half-collapsed and the clapboard walls faded to the exact shade of blowing dust. But the creosote bush around the door had grown tall and wild since she'd gone, reaching with puff-shaped blossoms nearly to the eaves of the roof; to the side of the house, a pile of junk had amassed: broken tricycles, a much-abused armchair, a crib with bent bars.

Inescapably, she thought of the night she'd run from Mrs. Whitemorning, a pilfered six-shooter tucked into her waistband and little else; no food reserves or real plan then either. The other children had slept soundly as she stole out the door. She had felt nothing for them then, no regret at leaving them, only terror that her half-formed plan would not work, and the heretic would get ahold of the gun or else simply laugh in her face when she demanded he go with her. She had given even less thought to whether Mrs. Whitemorning would be angry, or worried, or grieved. She had never seen Mrs. Whitemorning have any of those feelings.

"You'll have to help out here," she explained to the girl as she hitched the horse to the trunk of a mesquite. "Everybody does. But there'll always be enough for you to eat, somewhere to lay your head, if it's the same for you as it was for me."

"You were *here*?" the child asked as Magdala helped her dismount. "How come you left?"

"It's a long story," said Magdala. And for a second, only a second, she wondered how the girl would leave Mrs.

Whitemorning, if she ever left Mrs. Whitemorning at all. Then she knocked on the door.

No one answered. Magdala knocked again, shifting impatiently on her cane. She wondered if Mrs. Whitemorning would ask how she'd lost the leg. What she had done between leaving here and coming back. Who she was now.

The child peeked through the dirty glass of the window to the left of the door, cupping her hands in front of her eyes. "I don't see anyone," she said.

Magdala tried the door. She was taken aback when it opened. She had never known Mrs. Whitemorning to keep the door unlocked when anyone was inside; not, in this little-traveled land, for fear of intruders so much as for the inevitability that someone in the house was desert sick enough to wander in their sleep.

She stepped across the threshold, feeling the wrongness of the house in her body as something unnamable but too familiar. The girl followed, limping in her shadow. The living room was the same inside, give or take a chair; the old upright piano stood demurely in one corner, the sagging, pillowless sofa dominated a wall across from it. But she could see from the thin sheen of dust on the surfaces that no one had been here in a few weeks or months. It was so like *No Outlets* that she half-expected to see a decaying body on the sun-faded Oriental rug.

"Where did they go?" asked the child.

"I don't know," Magdala said. "The nun at that church thought she was still here."

The kitchen was in the same neglected state, as was the bathroom. When the girl made for the staircase, Magdala reluctantly followed, wincing as her wooden prosthetic creakily bore the weight of climbing.

Upstairs, the walls in the hallway were blood-streaked. Mechanically, without thought, Magdala crossed herself and the child did too.

"Did they die?" the girl said, her voice shaky.

Magdala hushed her. From one of the bedrooms, she could hear a low series of thuds she had not heard a moment before. She did not have time to form the words *go downstairs* before the creature emerged from the bedroom at the end of the hall. It had too many legs and what appeared to be the trunk of a dog woven into the motley fabric of its body, but its head was still recognizably human, ears sticking pluckily out to the sides and pupilless eyes rolling in their sockets. As it came lumbering across the hallway toward them, she could at first only think numbly that she had always felt so safe within these walls, as if the desert could not get in. And then she cocked her pistol and fired. The creature gamely absorbed the bullet, flinching back and then moving forward again.

Behind her, absurdly, the girl began softly to sing. Magdala fired another shot. "What do you think you're doing?" she demanded.

The singing ceased. "Never mind," the girl stammered. "Never mind. It's only—"

Glancing back over her shoulder at the child, incredulous, Magdala stumbled. She fell down the stairs, bringing the girl with her. They did not stop falling until they landed in a bundle on the floor below, the bones of Saint Elkhanah clanking loudly in their sack all the way down. For a moment, the creature stood in the dark hallway above them, and Magdala thought the two shots she'd fired must have been enough to deter it. Then, gracelessly, it began clambering down the stairs toward them. "Come on," Magdala shouted. "Come on!" And they both crawled out of the house to the flat land outside. The creature followed, breathing in labored gasps as it heaved its overlarge body through the cluttered house and then out the door, into the dirt. It was not looking at them anymore, but at the horse. Magdala was relieved for a second before her panic deepened. She could not reach the tree where she'd hitched the horse before the creature did; the horse was still bound when the stuffed man came upon him.

The horse tossed his large, bruise-colored head and reared as the stuffed man grasped at his neck. It was trying to eat the horse, she thought. It was dead but still raving. Bound securely to the post, the horse kicked and wrenched but could not maneuver his powerful hindlegs where he wanted them. His screams were raspy, desperate sounds like she had never heard him make. "You hide," Magdala said to the child. "Hide somewhere good." She got to her feet and staggered closer to the creature, firing her gun until the chamber was empty. Somewhere in that blur of smoke and screaming, the horse tore loose from the hitching post and fled. The stuffed man, soundless and expressionless even while bleeding profusely, turned on her; only then could she see the horse's blood slicked on its mouth.

The creature reached out with its too-many hands, and Magdala reeled back, landing hard. For a blinding second, she could not breathe or think; she emerged from the shock of the fall to fumble for her gun and find it out of reach. She retrieved her cane just in time for the creature to reach her. The creature's lips parted in a miserable, long-toothed grimace, and she jammed the cane inside its mouth. It mewled around the stick, spat blood onto the sand and reeled back. Magdala aimed for its mouth again, but she missed and instead impaled the creature's head. She persisted, striking blindly. When at last its body sagged to the side, hers did too.

"Well, goddamn," said the ghost. "That was almost worthy of being canonizable, wasn't it?"

"Leave me alone," gasped Magdala, opening one eye to see the apparition leaning against the spiny back of the dead creature.

"Took your horse though. A true Vegas saint would've kept her mount."

Magdala absorbed only then that the horse had gone. Her lips parted, but she made no sound as her eyes followed an imaginary trajectory through the flat, colorless land. She could not see the animal. Assuredly he would not come back. Desert horses could never be fully domesticated. She was only lucky something like this had never happened earlier. She had not loved the horse and the horse had not loved her, but she felt as bereft without him as if she'd had a second amputation. "Where did it come from?" she whispered, her eyes falling to the collapsed figure of the stuffed man. "How did it get inside?"

"Don't you recognize it?" the saint said instead. "An arm here, a finger there, here an eye. You want to know where everyone went, there's your answer."

Her indignant reply was crushed when she saw the truth in his words. She knew even the patchwork of clothes the creature's body parts wore. Mrs. Whitemorning's own robes were there, although almost nothing else of her.

"It was almost human," the saint went on. "Mostly made of human. Although I suppose murder is nothing new to you. The murder of children? Now there's something, maybe."

"It's not human," Magdala said, but she wasn't certain. She grasped her cane, the end now slicked with the creature's thin, whitish blood, and made her way back to the house. The child was hiding inside a kitchen cabinet, her knees to her chest. When she came out, she threw her arms around Magdala, and Magdala sat in her spindly, hesitating embrace and did not feel it.

"Why did you do that?" she said to the child, after a while. "Sing to it, I mean."

The child fidgeted with the ends of her braid. "You remember how all those men were coyotes?"

"Yes."

"Well, I sang to them and . . . *that* happened. My papa always said I was saint-touched, but I didn't know until then if it was true. And I didn't know until then that the singing would do it. I didn't even *try*. Just, they told me to sing for them and I did and they became, you know, animals. I thought it might work again. I wanted to help."

Magdala's instinctive disbelief in the claims of any backwater pilgrim to holy power was tempered only by the indisputable fact that someone or something had undeniably made coyotes from men in that Paradise bar basement. "Touched by what saint?" she asked, eyes narrowed. In her five years in Vegas, she had met devotees of Saint Antonio supposed to share in his powers of foresight and devotees of Saint Elena supposed to share in her powers of healing and an unbearably great number of devotees of Saint Elkhanah supposed to share in his powers of incredible speed, but she had never met anyone who professed to transform men into coyotes.

"Saint Araceli," the girl said. "My namesake."

It occurred to her, only now, that she had never asked the child's name. That she knew nothing of her traveling companion, not even what kind of pilgrim the girl had been

or where she'd come from. She had been seeing the child
as a kind of moral cargo. "I don't know that one," she said.

"She could transform things. That's what my papa
would say. We had her whole hagiography in a pamphlet
but they took it."

"Transform what things?"

The girl shrugged. "Animals. Maybe other things. She
did a lot of miracles. Made a snake into a stick and a demon
into a javelina."

"And you thought you'd make a stuffed man into something that couldn't hurt us."

"I wish it had worked. I don't know if it was only one
time. If I can't do it anymore."

"You should've told me," Magdala said, but the admonishment was a hollow one; she had not wanted the girl to
tell her anything.

They stayed that night in the empty house. In the
bathroom, Magdala found an old and dust-glossed roll of
bandages, a half-emptied bottle of rubbing alcohol. "Long
overdue," she said, holding them up to show the child.
Obediently, but with plain displeasure, Araceli climbed
onto the sofa and unwrapped her dirty bandage, exposing a
festering wound beneath.

Magdala sucked breath in through her teeth. "Does it
hurt you much?" she asked.

The child shook her head. She was quiet as Magdala
pressed alcohol on the wound and rebandaged it. Magdala
saw her stiff upper lip, the stubborn look of concentration
on her face, and she thought with a dull pang of recognition that the girl was becoming just as she herself had
been at that age. Not a real child, but a little ghost trying
to survive inside the body of a child without ever making a
sound.

After they'd pillaged Mrs. Whitemorning's kitchen, Araceli fell asleep on the sofa and Magdala went out to bury the stuffed man's body. She could not explain what compelled her to do it. Only, when she looked on the creature's slumped form, she saw not only the whole but the parts, the limbs and appendages of the people that the desert had hollowed out and stuffed with itself. She did not want them to go unburied. The steady rhythm of her shovel hitting the ground braced against the eerie, mournful melody of Saint Elkhanah's whistling. He had returned almost as soon as she went outside, as if deterred by the walls of Mrs. Whitemorning's house.

"What do you want?" she said to him, when she could stand his song no longer.

"You know, I *told* you," said the ghost, materializing before the half-dug grave. "I did tell you."

"I'll bury you in this very grave," she said. "Never mind my leverage."

"And then I guess your troubles would be all at an end."

She flinched. "This was supposed to make up for . . . the rest," she said. "For my papa and Alma and Mateo and Rosy and Dulcinea, and for the heretic, and for all the rest."

"Oh, tenderfoot," the saint said. "I can tell you firsthand that blood won't wash. Not with one measly orphan trafficked out of Vegas. But I understand the impulse. Used to do what I would call guilt-trip rescues. No reward money. Not even a stolen kiss or three from the hostage. Just me and my good deeds, all stacked up like coins paying my way into heaven. And yet here I am, stone-cold dead, making conversation with the dourest little hired gun in the Remainder. So I guess it really don't amount to anything."

"They sainted you."

"And a good gig sainting is, if you can get it. And keep it." He looked contemptuously at the sack that held his bones, which sat at her feet, safe from Araceli's possible curiosity.

"I'm not sorry," said Magdala. "That I stole your bones. If they even were really yours."

"You know," the ghost said, "what you really would do, if you wanted the blood off your hands, is let me take over things here."

Magdala looked at him, uncomprehending.

"You're not cut out for this life," he said. "Still flinch at what needs to be done. A decent shot, not a great one. And much too sentimental. If I only had your years, I can tell you now, I'd make better use of them."

He was not half-wrong, Magdala thought. "What do you mean, my years?" she asked.

"It's easy," he said. "It's easier than anything. Just close your eyes."

She didn't, but still she felt his proximity like a millstone around her neck; he was, she realized, trying not only to get inside her head, but her body too. For a dizzying second, it was he who manipulated her limbs. She buckled under a wave of nausea and then her arms became hers again.

"Not everyone has the chance to carry a saint through his afterlife," the ghost said. "But there's a likeness between us, I can tell it. An affinity. Enough that we could share one body between the two of us. And wouldn't you be the most pious little pilgrim if you did that? Wouldn't you be a living martyr? Think of it."

"I have a job to do," she said, as much to herself as to him. "I'm not finished yet."

"Easier, if I were the one to do it," he said. "Just think on it, tenderfoot. Much easier if you were to just let me drive."

She was so weary then that she almost relinquished herself to him. With her fists clenched around the shovel and her weight on her good leg, she hung onto herself and did not let go. It was barely enough to keep him out.

After that, he never ceased trying to get inside. It was all she could do to keep her head; it was impossible to keep her body entirely. They left Mrs. Whitemorning's house the next day, although it was undoubtedly the best shelter they'd find for miles, with no destination and no intention but to stay in motion. As they progressed through the desert, the ghost chose their direction, Magdala trailing him and Araceli trailing her. He rarely spoke now, communicating instead through her nerves and her limbs, becoming her. She followed his silent orders, heedless of the confusion and dismay on Araceli's face. For hours on the first day, the girl tagged faithfully along, limping on a walking stick she'd recovered from Mrs. Whitemorning's house. Only in the depths of the afternoon heat did she protest.

"Magdala," she said, "please, can't we rest?"

Magdala braced against the force of the saint and made herself stop. But as soon as she did, Elkhanah began again to wheedle his way in. "Come on, girl," he said. "Let me drive us."

"No," she said to Araceli. "Not yet."

"Please, Magdala, I'm so tired. My foot hurts every step."

"She has to stop," Magdala said to the ghost. "Can't you see she's suffering?"

"Whom are you *talking* to?" said Araceli plaintively, and Magdala realized only then that she'd spoken aloud.

"Not as much as she'll be suffering if you both become dry bones in the middle of the desert. Running a perfectly good—well, perfectly *living*—body into the ground. I told you, if you can't handle it—"

"It's not safe," she said to the child. And she began walking again, guessing rightly that no bullet wound could surmount the child's terror of being left alone. Araceli limped after her.

The girl protested only once more, late at night on the second day. "I won't go," she cried, and Magdala looked back to see her face tear-streaked and defiant, her walking stick stuck in the dirt like a flagpole. "I don't care if you leave me," she said. "I don't care. You're not my mama or my family. You can wander off on your own without me."

Magdala was paralyzed. The ghost pulled at her insides, and the thought came unbidden, *Quicker without her. You would* survive *without her.* She pushed him back out and saw, a second too late, the abject horror on the child's face.

"Who was I?" she said. "Was I him?"

"I don't know," Araceli said. Her eyes were on the sack of bones; on the dirt; anywhere but on Magdala's face. "Who were you?"

"You can't *do* that," Magdala said to him, but the ghost had, for the moment, receded. She was almost frightened by the loss of him. If she did not have the choice of relinquishing herself to the ghost, if it was her and her alone who had to keep going, then anything that happened now was her fault.

"Can we rest?" asked Araceli.

"Yes," she said. "Yes. Let's sleep." And they managed several hours without the ghost returning.

There were not many such reprieves. Across the days, they fell deep into the Sonoran, passing in the darkness of night a wind-torn signpost welcoming them to the state of Arizona. The desert here was brimming with vicious, strange, inhuman life: nests and egg sacs and hives that hung pendulously from the paloverde trees so the whole landscape was cobwebbed, pulsing, horrifically vibrant. Big, vivid berries in nauseous colors sat heavily on barrel cactuses like tumors. The first time Magdala picked and ate them, Araceli balked: "I thought you said these would make us sick," she said.

"We're sick already," said Magdala. "It doesn't matter." And she found that eating the desert fruits softened the ghost's hold on her, although they gave her a distant, unsteady sensation, as if she was just looking at a picture of herself walking. Araceli, for her part, seemed to be one of those people—lucky or luckless—who was immune.

Through those days, she told herself the saint's hijacking of her leg and her hand on the cane were meaningless; that she was walking onward because she wanted to; that she would stop as soon as she found a safe home for the child. But she was becoming certain she was not going to find one, that there was nowhere safe in the Remainder that would welcome the kind of creature she had become.

She thought a hundred times of going to the cactus-sitters and a hundred times forced herself to imagine what they would think if she came stumbling into their camp with a ghost whispering in her ear and a child suffering with a bullet wound she herself had made, and no mule in sight.

It came to feel like she was overlooking a gift of unimaginable generosity by refusing the saint entry into herself.

Was he not merely a better version of her, more inured and less gutless? If he were her, she would already have shot the Deputy and hung him out as a warning to all her enemies. She would already have broken another desert horse to the saddle. She would already have delivered the child back to wherever the child belonged and ridden on alone, a cowboy ballad on her lips.

When she came to a wolf's skull propped on a wooden stake, she thought she was only seeing things. She stumbled and caught herself and realized she was holding onto an old garage door refashioned into a gate, and for a second, she was a child awkwardly bundled in her father's arms. She closed her eyes and then opened them. The gate and the wolf's skull remained.

"Here we are," said the saint.

"No," Magdala mumbled. She was halfway sure none of it was real.

"Don't you remember this? Caput Lupinum."

"I don't want to be here."

"Then don't be," he said. "Close your eyes. Come on, now, just close your eyes; quit resisting. You won't see it."

"Not yet," she mumbled. The town was spread out beneath her, just the same: the buffet, the *Savings & Loans* sign, the bank. Beyond, the houses arranged on cul-de-sacs, their cheerful primary colors sun-bleached to obscurity. She could hardly believe it all still existed.

"Magdala," Araceli said. "Where are we?"

"Please," she whispered as if the saint's ghost could make it all disappear.

"You know what you have to do if you don't want to see it."

Magdala faced the bank lobby, empty still, but now cobweb-crossed and bat-infested. "No," she protested.

"Magdala, let's stop," said Araceli.

"You could go in there and lie down and when you stand up, you'd be me," said the saint, nodding to the bank.

"No," Magdala said to them both, so firmly that the sound echoed in the squat structures surrounding them. She kept walking, jabbing at the dirt viciously with her cane.

On the steps to the larder, she saw through the dirty glass door a moving figure. Dulcinea, it occurred to her. The vision frightened her. She thought she might see Oscar next, stuffed and reanimated. Or, worse, Rawley; not as he had been in Caput Lupinum, but as he had revealed himself to be on the pilgrim highway: cruel and hungry. Her vision blurred; she staggered backward as the figure wearing Dulcinea's delicate features moved closer. It was not fair, she thought, that Dulcinea's ghost was here. She was the only one who did not deserve to haunt Caput Lupinum.

"Make it go away," Magdala said to the saint. But he had vanished. In his absence, she was not him but herself, only not herself as she was now. She was eleven years old; she was wearing a loose, white dress borrowed from a woman fully grown; she was eating scraps of meat the men did not want; lowering herself to a vinyl floor to be branded; letting Rawley's hand stay on her knee because she wanted not to be troublesome.

As she stood reeling, the door to the larder opened, and there stood Dulcinea: not fifteen, but a decade older, wearing denim and pointing a six-shooter.

"Magdala?" she said, lowering her gun.

"You're not here and neither am I," whispered Magdala. She blinked, trying to make the apparition in front of her disappear just as Elkhanah had disappeared. "Don't you try to tell me otherwise."

"Please," Araceli said to the ghost of Dulcinea. She came up alongside Magdala and curled her fingers around Magdala's cane to steady them both. "Can you help us? Magdala's sick."

In the larder, Dulcinea had made a home for herself from the wreckage of Caput Lupinum. Magdala recognized most of the furniture posed between the empty shelves that formed makeshift walls for the makeshift living room. Amid the tableau of half-familiar things, she stood lost until Dulcinea came to her side and took her arm. The ghost of the saint had not returned yet, but she was afraid he would soon.

Dulcinea poured well water for them and settled Magdala down onto her own tidily made-up mattress without seeming to think of the filth on Magdala's clothes and skin. Then she tended to Araceli; Magdala watched through heavy-lidded eyes as Dulcinea unwrapped the child's bandages, winced at what she found and began slowly the work of re-dressing the wound.

"How did you come to travel together?" she asked the child.

"My papa died," said Araceli. Her voice was flat, soft. "Or got killed. Magdala said she was going to take me to an orphanage."

"Got killed by whom?" Dulcinea suspected her, Magdala thought.

"Bad men. They had tattoos on their necks," said the child. "Like yours, only not a name, just a shape. I don't know who they were."

"I do," said Dulcinea, grimly. "Were you on the pilgrim highway?"

The child nodded.

"And what about this orphanage? Are you going there now?"

"It was empty. We almost died. There was . . . something in there."

"Like a monster?"

"Like a monster."

Dulcinea crossed the room to the mattress and crouched low beside Magdala. Up close, her face was the same beneath the cracks and wind-chapping; only she had a scar threading across her temple, disappearing beneath her hairline. "You lucid?" she said.

"How do I know you're real?" said Magdala.

"Why wouldn't I be?"

She clung to Dulcinea's sleeve as if she were still a child of eleven, taking the measure of the woman's reality through the rough sensation of fabric between her fingers. "I never thought I would see you again," she said. "I thought you might be dead."

"I thought you might be dead, too," Dulcinea admitted. She rested the back of her hand on Magdala's forehead. "You're feverish," she concluded. "Is it just desert fruits? I remember how sick you got, all those years back."

"She sees a ghost," said Araceli.

Dulcinea narrowed her eyes. "What kind of a ghost?" she asked.

Magdala had no time to protest before Araceli said, "The ghost whose bones she has," and carried the sack across the room to Dulcinea. Araceli let go too soon, Dulcinea didn't catch it, and Saint Elkhanah's bones spilled out onto the floor like a clumsy work of divination.

Magdala sat up and hurriedly gathered the fragments of the pilfered relic, shoving them down the mouth of the sack as if by making them disappear, she could make Dulcinea forget what she'd seen. Dulcinea's mouth was open, her eyes big.

"Elkhanah's feet," she said, and it was not a question but a certainty.

The ghost was there again, standing in the doorway with one boot propped against the frame. "You gonna tell her?" he said. "The whole miserable story? That you're a little pilgrim no longer but a downright iconoclast?"

Magdala's eyes leapt from the apparition to Dulcinea and back again.

"I can't explain," she said. "Please, don't make me."

For three days they stayed in Caput Lupinum, shadowing Dulcinea through the quiet rhythms of her hermit existence. She had a goat and a brood of quail; in the shade of the larder's roof, she was growing squash and melon and cactus. She had formed a complete life for herself.

She did not begrudge her guests their filthiness, nor their weakness, nor their secrets. She did not ask why Magdala had stolen the saint's bones. She seemed not to care what the answer was. It was only on the third night after Araceli had gone to sleep, as they sat on the steps to the larder with their eyes on the stars, that Magdala feared she would ask the question again. But instead she said, "I know you don't want to tell me what's become of you. Even so, I want to tell you what happened to me after we left you outside Phoenix."

"I was so afraid you would die if we left you alone, but I was more afraid of what Rawley would do to you. That's why I told him I was willing to go if you didn't have to come, that I would make it easy. We left in the middle of the night.

"I was two years with Rawley before he got sick of me. I was already too old for him when we started, and by the time we were finished, he was repulsed by even looking at me. He was mostly using me for barter by then. We were nomads, traveling the pilgrim highway but not *to* anywhere. I got to know every stopover town on the road. Went back to Alabaster three times and got my fortune told by that street preacher, remember him? The one who said you were a hero from a ballad of twenty verses. He never said anything like that about me. Saw a lot of the country. Met a lot of people. I never made it all the way up to Las Vegas. I didn't want to face any saints anyway.

"I wasn't really a captive. I could have run away. But I always thought, where would I go? And the answer was nowhere. I had no home and neither did he. That kept us together until he was drunk and cantankerous one night and chased me off. After that, I was wandering alone. So lonely and so desperate that I thought of going back to him, though I never did. One day, I scraped together enough money to travel with a trail guide leading a group of pilgrims back south from the holy city. I pretended I'd come from there too, had a whole lie about Saint Rosalinda the Comforter and a bellyache that I dreamed up from Alma's old bedtime hagiographies. Had a fake name too. Of course, Dulcinea's not even my real one. Rawley gave it to me a long time ago. It's just from a story. It's all from a story.

"It was so nice to be with other people again, even strangers, and somewhere along the way, I decided I was gonna go back to Caput Lupinum. It was the only thing like a home I'd ever had. I thought, I'll just tell them Rawley made me go with him, that Oscar's dying had nothing to do with me, and they'll believe it because it was gunshot he died of and not poison, and Rawley was the one who brought me to Caput Lupinum in the first place. I was all ready to accept whatever kind of punishment they had for me, to grovel and beg, to get a third brand on my neck. But the town was empty. Wiped. It had been scavenged to hell and back—not all the houses, lucky for me, but anything easy to access—and everyone was gone.

"It took me a while to figure out what happened to them. In the meantime, I just hid in the bank vault. I had the complete run of the town, and I still went back to that prison. Like burying myself alive. For a month or so I must have slept in there. I caught mice and lizards and ate whatever was left in the larder; pinto beans, mostly, since I guess those were too heavy to be worth carrying.

"It was a while before I got up the courage to go in the blue house and see what happened to Oscar in the end. His body wasn't there. I don't know precisely what happened to Caput Lupinum. I think probably the men all cut their losses after they found Oscar murdered. No one wily or forward-thinking enough to succeed him. Some of them probably just went their separate ways. Others, I know, formed some kind of posse up near Vegas. Once I determined they were gone for good, I realized this town was more mine than anyone else's and so I decided to stay. It's been seven years now.

"I want to tell you that for most of that time, I was angry at everyone, including myself. At Oscar and Rawley, at your father, at Mateo, and even at Alma. At my own parents, at every mercenary fuck who ever took part in the buying and selling of me. Practically the only one I wasn't angry at, Magdala, was you. I thought, everything that's happened to me before and after that doomed half-pilgrimage has some meaning if I managed to save your life. And I did. I see that I did. I don't know what you've done, I don't know how you've suffered, but you're here and you're living and I'm thankful for it."

"You shouldn't be," Magdala said. "I didn't end up how you thought."

"You can't tell her, tenderfoot," said Elkhanah's ghost. "You'll break her heart."

Magdala did not look at him. She reached for Dulcinea's hand and Dulcinea took it. In a voice at first shaky and then assured, she admitted everything. Dulcinea listened. Her heart did not break.

"Well," asked Dulcinea, when she was finished, "is the ghost still with you?"

Magdala glanced behind her at the larder door. She nodded.

"Have you tried to exorcise him?"

"Only by telling him to leave."

"What if you buried his feet?"

"I can't," said Magdala. In the desert, feeling the ghost slip inside and out of her head, she had thought many times of abandoning the sack of bones. But she could never make herself do it. Not only because they were her leverage, her hope of surviving the Deputy if ever he found her, but because some idiotic and devout portion of her still believed they were imbued with power and that somehow, sometime, it was a power she might lay claim to if she only kept possession of them. *There's a likeness between us*, the ghost had said to her that night in Mrs. Whitemorning's house.

"Might not matter, anyhow," Dulcinea admitted. "I heard a story on the road once of a man haunted by his dead wife. Turns out he'd kept a lock of her hair, sentimental-like. He tried burying it to see if that put her to rest, but the haunting stuck until he brought the hair to the Church and got an exorcism. Could you . . . try—"

"I don't think they'd be amenable," said Magdala. "Being that I'm haunted because I stole a relic from them."

"What about someone else, then?" she said. "Those cactus-sitting hermits we met way back on pilgrimage. They're holy enough. They got no Church affiliation. They would help you."

"I can't go back there," said Magdala, quickly.

"Why not?"

"They saw me how I was before," she said. She would have thought Dulcinea, of all people, would understand why she was too ashamed to consider going back. "What'll they see now when they look at me?"

"And so what?"

"What do you mean?"

"It wasn't just you they sheltered all those years back. It was a bunch of outlaws. Marks on their necks and everything. And they did it no question. You kidnapped that heretic, and he didn't bear a grudge over it. You think none of them would exorcise your troublesome saint if you asked sincerely?"

She had not considered that it was not only herself, but Rawley and Mateo and her father whom the cactus-sitters had welcomed. She thought of the cactus-sitter with the mule's lead in their hand, their look gentle as they said they knew she would come back. She thought of the heretic kneeling at the shrine of Saint Elkhanah, rising alongside her still-clubfooted self, holding her arm to steady her as she crumpled. And she longed for the child she had been with all of them.

"But what if they're gone?" she said to Dulcinea. It seemed impossible that the cactus-sitters' community had survived when nothing without armor ever did. "Everything's been emptied out. Seen more ghost towns than living ones, coming back from Vegas."

Dulcinea shrugged. "Then you come back here," she said. "And we'll survive your saint and your Deputy and the rest of it."

Dulcinea sent them back into the desert with two canteens of water, three precious bullets and a page torn from a road atlas with the pilgrim highway still outlined in Oscar's shaky hand. At the edge of Caput Lupinum, she embraced them both.

"I meant it when I said you should come back if it goes south," she told Magdala.

"I know," said Magdala, and she could see from Dulcinea's face that Dulcinea did mean it. With a sudden thoughtless urgency, she embraced Dulcinea again, hanging on for as long as she could. Then she left the place. As she walked past the wolf's skull on its wooden post, she knocked it into the dirt. "You should rename your town," she said over her shoulder, and then they were off, Araceli moving eagerly ahead into the dusk and Magdala tailing her. The ghost resumed trailing them, always visible on the horizon.

Magdala kept her eyes forward; she did not listen when his song stole into her ears. But at daybreak, while Araceli slept in the shade of a solitary mesquite, he came upon Magdala again. In Caput Lupinum, where there were walls and ceilings and Dulcinea, he had been diminished. He had lingered in her periphery; he had not tried to get inside. But in the open desert, he was unhindered. As Magdala looked anywhere but at him, he settled himself down with a sigh and held his palms to a fire that could not warm them.

"Engine smoke on the wind tonight," he said. "Would make me nervy, if I were you."

She didn't answer him. Dulcinea had said she should try not answering him.

"I know you're thinking you outfoxed him. You're thinking, he won't trouble to chase me and this battered old relic all the way down deep into the Sonoran. You're thinking, no better time to retrace my old childhood pilgrimage from back when I was beloved and pious and still two-footed."

At her silence, he edged closer, sitting halfway in the fire. "I ever tell you how the Deputy became the Deputy? I think it's a real instructive story. I know folk like to say that the Deputy came from the desert, from the berserkers, but cross my heart, he came from Vegas. Born and raised. Any appetite for slaughter he got, he cultivated right there in that city. But I'm getting off track here. Around the time the Deputy came of age there was a bishop who had himself a daughter. Being as she was a bastard, like any daughter of a bishop must be, he kept real quiet about her. But he had a pathetic kind of fatherly fondness for the young lady. Well, the Deputy ferreted out who she was, no ordinary Vegas nun but real Church royalty, and he took a shine to this woman, a shine in the way that only he could, which is to say, he decided she would serve his purposes. You wouldn't know anything about that, would you, tenderfoot?"

She stole a glance at him.

"He was no instrument of the Church then, but its sworn enemy. Of course, the young lady didn't know anything of that. Her father kept her ignorant. Innocent. She thought she was in love. He didn't look then how he looks now. He was a real handsome fellow, devilish smile, had a way of making you think you should confide in him. When he kidnapped her, she thought it was an elopement. She didn't know she was just currency to him. He carried her way out into the desert and hid her away, then ransomed her back to the bishop for a whole heap of the Church's dirty laundry. The bishop couldn't squeal on him because the daughter's very existence was supposed to be a secret. So for the low price of one fool woman, the Deputy bought himself a lifetime of leverage. He knew which relics were fakes, whose pockets had been getting wrongfully fattened, which shocking tragedies were well-planned inside jobs. And with his passel of secrets, he went to the archbishop—the very same one you met in the Sunlite a few years back—and he said, 'You make me sheriff of this town.' The archbishop was too sly for that. 'There's no pope here,' he said. 'No sheriff either. But I'll make you deputy, and you do what you want so long as sometimes it's jobs for us.' Your Deputy's been riding on that deal ever since."

"And so what?" said Magdala.

"So," said the saint, triumphantly, "he's got no need for saints' bones. Awful suspect that he wanted you to steal them, don't you think?"

"Leave me be," Magdala said.

"Would be satisfying for him to nail your heretic. A fitting punishment for his wayward lieutenant."

She said nothing, wanting to wake Araceli so she would not be alone, but seeing the soft slack on the child's face, wanting more to preserve what little peace she had.

"Would be a real pity if you were all the time just leading the Deputy right to your heretic and the rest of those peaceable old hermits," said the ghost. "Blood on your hands like that don't wash clean with a hundred smuggled orphans."

"He's not gonna find me," Magdala said.

"When he does," the saint said, "you're gonna be sorry you didn't let me inside a long time before."

The farther west they got, the lonelier the landscape became. Apart from the throngs of stuffed men, there was nothing. No settlements, no pilgrims, not even much vegetation. On the end of the third day, they came to an RV. Perched on the horizon, battered and lonesome, it had the look of a skeleton just picked clean.

"Pilgrims used to drive that kind of thing," said Magdala, squinting from underneath her hand at the hulking shape. She was thinking not only of the west Texas pilgrims, but all their reserves: their unused sacks of flour and salt, their sarsaparilla in its gleaming purple bottles, their jars of mangoes. She and Araceli had not exhausted the reserves from Caput Lupinum yet, but they would soon, likely before they reached the cactus-sitters.

"Do you think there's someone in there now?" the child said.

"No signs of life," said Magdala. Like Mrs. Whitemorning's house, she thought but did not say. Wiser, she thought, to go on ahead and nowhere near it. Only, there was a half-decent chance that without more food reserves, Araceli would go hungry. Slowly, she approached the hulking body of the trailer. A plastic stop was wedged beneath one of the front tires, plastered in a layer of dirt and wind-flung garbage. The windows were obscured by a set of dull curtains; one had been pierced by a rock, leaving behind a perfect spiderweb of shattered glass. Through the windshield, she could see the scattered detritus of a pilgrim existence. She recognized among the brittle papers piled on the dashboard some of the pamphlets that used to circulate among the west Texans ten years ago. There was a crucifix hanging from the rearview mirror, a prayer shawl draped over the back of the passenger seat. She came around to the side of the RV and tried the door, found it unlocked. A shudder passed through her body as she ascended the steps into the small, closed space.

"It's safe," she called out to Araceli. "Empty."

While the child thumped up the steps behind her, Magdala stepped into the cab, then maneuvered awkwardly into the living quarters. There, she stopped, because she had found the occupants: a whole family of them, or at least part of one. Two of the skeletons lay side-by-side on the bed, their skulls beaming patiently up at the ceiling. A third was splayed across the floor beside them. It was missing a leg from the knee down; she wondered if that had been its pre-mortem condition.

"When do you think they died?" whispered Araceli.

"Not recently," Magdala answered. "So whatever troubles they got into, you don't have to worry those troubles will come for us next."

Araceli's eyes were on the children's skeletons crowded on the bed. "Look at their feet," she said, getting closer. She lifted the bent foot of one and the bones came apart.

"Clubfooted," said Magdala as the child startled momentarily back. "Guessing that's why they went on pilgrimage."

"To be healed?"

"By Saint Elkhanah, like as not," said Magdala ruefully, shifting on her cane and returning to the cab of the RV. She dropped numbly into the passenger seat and let her eyes wander to the pamphlets littered across the dashboard. Sure enough, Saint Elkhanah appeared on the front of more than one.

"Did you ever do it?" asked Araceli, still rummaging around the living quarters.

"Get healed?" she said.

"Go on pilgrimage."

"Yes," Magdala confessed.

"Were you born without a leg?"

Magdala was startled by the question. "No," she said. "I had a clubfoot."

"Why did—then—"

Magdala's eyes were on an oversaturated print of Saint Elkhanah astride a rearing gold mustang as she fumbled for an answer she could give the child. Four years ago, the Deputy had looked at the black, swollen lump of flesh that was her clubfoot, fresh from fifteen miles without rest through the desert, and said the foot would need to be amputated, and she had believed him. Cut it off, then, she had said. She had bitten down on a piece of rag and not cried when he strangled her calf with a length of rope and brought a dirty hatchet down across her ankle. She had not cried when the stub got infected, and the nuns in a church basement whispered grimly that they would have to remove her leg past the knee if she was going to survive. She had not cried when she hobbled back to the Hacienda with the support of the juniper stick, her leg gone from the mid-thigh, and the Deputy laughed because she was a real, true cripple now, wasn't she?

"It was making me sick," she said. "It's better that it's gone."

"Do you pray you'll have your leg back someday? Like if you did another pilgrimage?"

Magdala hesitated, only for a moment. "I guess I still think things would be easier if I had both my two legs," she said. "But I found other ways of being." She felt shy, suddenly. "Besides," she added, "the horse wouldn't be accustomed to the weight."

Araceli said nothing, and she wondered what the child was thinking, if she was deciding whether to point out that Magdala no longer had a horse. Then came, suddenly, a small sound of dismay. "Magdala," the child said. She was staring through the door to the bathroom.

Magdala stumbled over to her. The bathroom was the only part of the RV she hadn't checked for signs of life. The figure inside was half-submerged in the toilet, easily mistaken for dead, but after a second, she saw a breath inflate its trunk and realized it was alive, or something like it. It was an old man wearing a shapeless cloak. He was bending at the waist to rise, emitting soft sounds like gurgling. He was not moving right; he was desert sick as her own father had been once, long ago. He managed to stand, whipping around to face them, his arms reaching out from his cloak like the legs of a spider.

When the girl began singing, Magdala felt the same panicked itch to silence her that she had felt in Mrs. Whitemorning's house, the same throb half of terror and half of impatience. But when she reached for her pistol, Araceli's hand shot out—to restrain her or to restrain the man, she couldn't know which—and she stopped. The man hesitated before the girl's open palm as if it were a barrier impassable, his eyes whirling in his head and his arms still at his sides.

The girl kept singing, her soft fluting voice flung from one wall to another in the close space of the RV, and all at once the man began to change. His transformation was like paper catching fire, a slow slide and then a sudden crumpling: he was a man, or mostly one, and then his arms were lengthening, unspooling, getting narrower but also stronger; he was sprouting a tail, his haunches becoming broad hindquarters, his head lengthening as his eyes slid to either side, his hair flattening into a black thatch that fell across a furred neck, and there stood a small gray mule with a cloak lying in shreds at its hooves, his hindquarters brushing the sides of the narrow doorway.

Magdala stared at the mule's docile, dark eyes, looking for any trace of the creature he had been formerly. "They told me I'd bring a mule back to them," she said. "Ten years ago, they knew already." She could not but believe, with a desperate, hungry hopefulness, that the miracle meant something.

Beside her, Araceli was frozen. "What if he's still hungry?" she asked.

Magdala extended an open palm to the animal, letting him huff a soft breath onto her skin. "Doesn't seem to be," she replied.

The girl reached out her own hand. The mule lowered his face into the cup of her palm and rested it there for a moment.

"Did I kill him?" said Araceli softly. "The thing that he was before?"

Magdala traced her hand down the mule's face. "How the desert is now, dead-looking things aren't dead and living things aren't always alive," she said. "That man was dead in every way that mattered. And now he's brought back to a kind of life."

"Is he still . . . in there?"

Magdala thought of her father, beaming and sickly with a mouthful of mule's flesh; she thought of the saint pushing at her thoughts until his own thoughts got in. She could not answer the question. "I don't know," she admitted.

As they led the mule out of the RV, the cloak wrapped around his neck as a makeshift lead, Magdala's eyes were drawn unavoidably to the ghost on the horizon. He was not looking at them; he was not trying to get inside her head. Instead, he was watching the flatlands beyond, his hand shielding his eyes as if the sun could still trouble him. His gaze followed something.

For five nights and five days more they walked, swallowing down the distance to the camp of the cactus-sitters. Across those miles, they accustomed the mule slowly to the weight of them and to their closeness, first only walking beside him with a hand on his shoulder, then sitting on his back as he grazed or rested, then riding. They passed the hours reciting hagiographies, reciting half-remembered stories that had the larger-than-life vibrancy of tales told by one child to another. In the shriveled landscape, the lives of the saints and all their tallied miracles were as improbable as they were nourishing.

All the while, Magdala did not let herself look back; she forced herself, as much as she could, to sleep and to eat. When they rested, she tied her foot to a tree so she would not wander. And she did not answer Saint Elkhanah's grandiose and rambling speeches, nor his threats, nor his honeyed assurances that she would be stronger and better if only she let him drive the worn-down body that, really, belonged to them both, when she thought about it.

They were within sight of the saguaro forest when the Deputy caught up to them. The hum of the motorcycle's engine was still soft, still faraway, when her ears caught it. Down the long slope of a hill, riding parallel to them on a black strip of an old state highway, he was only a silhouette. She thought he must know where she was, he must want her to know that he was here, but he did not want to confront her yet.

"I promised you," said the saint, picking his way lazily across an outcropping of boulders. "He always finds who he's looking for."

Magdala led the mule to one of the rocks and slipped down from his back. Araceli made to follow, but Magdala stopped her. "Listen to me," she said. "I want you to kick that mule in the sides until he runs and hang onto his neck and don't let go or let him stop until you come to someone straddling a cactus. They'll help you."

"What about you?"

"I gotta stay here."

"Magdala, why?"

"That man who's been chasing me has found us now. I don't want him finding you."

Araceli glanced anxiously across the horizon. "I could try to sing him into something else," she said. "I could help you."

Magdala heard in the child's soft, trembling voice her own impotent pleas, just as desperate and as frightened, to a father far from being able to hear them. "You got no responsibility here," she said, taking the girl's arm and setting it on the mule's neck. "Please understand me. Nothing that happens after this has anything to do with you. Do you understand that?"

Araceli slowly nodded.

"Good," Magdala said. She lifted her hand, hesitated only for a second, then slapped the mule's flanks with enough force that he bolted.

In the plume of dust lifted by Araceli's exit, she cocked her pistol and aimed it. She could not hope to strike the Deputy from such a distance, but she wanted him to know she was not the rider fleeing; if he wanted her, he would have to come to her. She fired a shot that sank into the ground twenty yards or so away from him. She saw him bring the motorcycle to a sudden halt, saw him dismount and step away from the road to scan the distance.

"A mighty stupid fight for *you* to pick, tenderfoot," Saint Elkhanah said. "But then, that's why I like you. Let me get inside. Just let me get inside. You'll hardly know the difference."

She fired another shot, this time into the air, so he could have no doubt about where the first shot had come from. She had only one bullet left in the chamber. She could not spare another.

"I should've known all along you were a born martyr," the saint said with loathing.

Magdala unlaced the straps of the sack holding the saint's bones. She removed one foot, the bones all rattling, held it aloft for a moment, then tossed it into a creosote bush where it could not be easily seen. The ghost raged then: she felt him at her periphery like a headache.

"I'm not getting martyred," she said. Leaning heavily on her cane, she made her way down the slope toward the Deputy.

She was still thirty paces away when the Deputy lifted his six-shooter. Slowly she edged closer, the too-light sack perched on her shoulder, the ghost trailing after her. She prayed in an unceasing, soundless stream that Araceli had reached the cactus-sitters, that the Deputy had not seen her. When she was close enough to see the look on his face, she stopped short.

The Deputy was thinner now; he had the hollow look of an animal half-starved. He was dirtier, too. He had a scar, fresh-looking, across his left eye that left him permanently squinting. Beneath the purplish crust of the unhealed wound, he looked at Magdala.

"Been a long way through a wasteland to see you," he said.

"You didn't have to come," she said.

"Well, you know me. I keep my appointments." He cocked the gun. "You of all people should've known that."

Magdala threw the sack of bones to the ground between them. They clanked and rattled; she thought she heard one splinter. "I don't have them all with me," she said. "That's half. You'll get the other foot when we come to an agreement."

"Tough talk," the Deputy said, laughing in that hard, hoarse way that did not ever seem to mean he was amused. "If I were in the mood to bargain, I'd probably cut you a half-decent one. But I thought you'd know it's not about the relic now."

Magdala froze as she absorbed what he'd said, her eyes moving from the bag of bones in the dirt to the man standing across from her. She could hear, over her shoulder, the saint's splitting laughter. Elkhanah had known, she thought. He had known and he had even told her and she had not believed him.

"You don't want them at *all*?" she said.

The Deputy came closer, nudged the sack with the toe of his boot. "Well, you know me, Magdala. I never was a pious man, and the business these days is in the living, not the dead. Damn sensible, you ask me. No one ever got anywhere kissing dry bones. Why not try sucking what you want out of someone who's still got blood in their veins? And that's you. At least, that's what they're sayin'. You know, you're a goddamned folk hero back in Las Vegas."

"You're lying."

"Wish that I was." His eyes were on her cane as she edged slowly back. He began to follow, matching her measured pace. His gun was not aimed at her. She thought there was a small chance he would miss if he fired once she'd already started running, as slow and as painstaking as the run would have to be. "First eighty-five times I had to hear the legend of you—goddamned *you*—around some would-be heretic's soapbox, I thought to myself, there must be another one-legged woman running around carrying out the holy vengeance of the Church of Las Vegas, 'cause this living saint surely can't be the yellow-bellied bitch I'm thinkin' of." He lifted the gun and aimed at her chest then. "And then you fucked over the Church and skipped town, and they pivoted right to calling you a righteous outlaw. A democratizer. Carrying the saints to the far corners of the Remainder. Would you believe it?"

She realized with a dull shock of recognition that he wasn't lying. She thought of the street preacher in Alabaster. *A ballad of twenty verses,* he had said. "So you came to canonize me," she said.

"Canonize you. I like that." He paused a moment, contemplative, then fired his six-shooter. The bullet struck Magdala in her leg above the wood prosthetic and she buckled from the suddenness of the pain, landing on her back. She could not catch her breath enough to get up; she could not, through the wall of pain, even reach for her holster. She heard herself breathe the word *please*, although she knew he would feel no mercy, no matter what came out of her mouth. The Deputy's footsteps fell heavily as he closed the distance between them. He stopped when the toes of his boots pushed into the top of her head, then leaned over and held the six-shooter to her forehead.

Magdala met his eyes and held them. For a second, so quick as to be almost indiscernible, his face changed: his snarling features contorted into the polished, pale ones of Elkhanah Fleetfoot. The Deputy recoiled, stepped back. Then he was himself again.

"It's not me that has the likeness with him, really," she realized aloud.

"What the fuck are you talking about?"

"It's you and he who are the same, not him and me."

"I'll kill you," he said. Then he changed again; he was, for a moment, fully Elkhanah: His laughter came hoarse and desperate and agonized. "Oh, tenderfoot," he said. "Oh, tenderfoot, you're in it now." Then he was both men at once, his features twisting and melting into each other, mismatched teeth and cheekbones protruding out from the skull that belonged fully to neither of them.

Her impulse then, as strange as it was overpowering, was to comfort them. She could feel that they were not going to survive their combination. "A pelican of the wilderness," she murmured. "An owl of the desert. To hear the groaning of the prisoner. To loose those that are appointed to death."

The men dug the barrel of the gun into her forehead.

"To hear the groaning of the prisoner," she repeated. She reached out and her fingers brushed their mottled cheek. "To loose those that are appointed to death."

A gunshot pierced the quiet. They fell dead. Magdala laid perfectly still.

Magdala could not see who had fired the shot, but before the smoke dissipated, a crowd of cactus-sitters descended on the hillside, their robes fluttering across Magdala's eyeline like the wings of doves. They wrapped Magdala's blood-soaked thigh in gauze and carried her to their camp on a stretcher, weaving around three-century-old saguaro giants. Through a haze of exhaustion and pain and gratitude, she watched them slowly process across the desert, feeling eleven years old, feeling unhistoried.

When they came to the middle of the camp, they lowered the stretcher to the earth and left her there for a moment to speak urgently among themselves. Magdala could not comprehend their words, only their tone. Something was wrong, she thought; they were not panicked, but they were unsettled. After a few minutes, a small, and deeply hunched old man emerged from the crowd. His face cracked open radiantly into a smile when he saw her. She recognized him at once as Renato, the man who had ten years ago cooked for them and given them lodging.

"Little pilgrim," he said, although she was now taller than he was. He crouched and presented Magdala with a plastic bottle full of silt-colored water. She rose onto her elbows and drank deeply. It was impossible that he remembered her, she thought. She was unrecognizable.

"I sent a child here," she said. "Is she here? Did she make it? She was riding a mule."

She had barely finished speaking when Araceli emerged from one of the tents. The child's embrace was crushing, desperate. Magdala inhaled the girl's dusty, road-weary scent, felt in the force of her grasp what they had both suffered. Around them, the cactus-sitters murmured to each other.

"They didn't want to help you," Araceli whispered.

"That's not entirely the truth of it," said Renato. "It's complicated. There has been, for reasons understandable, a transgression committed. A very serious one."

Magdala felt the force of the admonishment without even knowing what it was for. Somehow, she thought, they had ascertained her many crimes and they had decided they could not extend mercy to her. "I didn't want to take the bones," she whispered.

"Oh, child," Renato said gently. "It is not your transgression, but Arturo's."

It was not easy to pry the heretic's whereabouts out of the cactus-sitters. "I have to see him," she told Renato.

He was calm but unwavering. "Arturo is outcast," he said. "He is not to be spoken to."

"I'm not a cactus-sitter," Magdala said.

"But he was."

"He would want to see me. He shot that man for me."

"Child," he said, half-pitying, "for that reason, you are the last one he would want to see." But Renato's stubbornness did not outlast hers, and it was not long afterwards that he agreed, reluctantly, to point her to the empty, wind-torn place beyond the saguaro forest where Arturo had sent himself into exile.

The heretic would not speak at first. He refused even to look at Magdala. He had prostrated himself on the dirt, facing nothing. His fingers were clasped across the crown of his head. He did not reply when Magdala spoke to him. She might as well have spoken to the wind. The last time she had seen him do this, she had held a gun to his head and forced him to stand and to acknowledge her. Now she could only move a little closer.

"He wasn't still a man all the way," she said to him. "He was . . . something else."

He said nothing.

"More to the point," she went on, "he would've killed me. He already killed who knows how many other people. Innocent people. Children. And Barabbas Knight, not that anyone's crying for him. He would have killed more. You know that."

He still would not speak. She could see he was trembling.

She tried pleading with him: "Just show me your face. I can't believe it's you for real 'til I've seen."

At last, the heretic lifted his head, curling his fingers. He had the weary, unpleased look he had worn when she had wound a lasso around his neck and dragged him through the desert. His face was so much older, she thought; or

maybe she had just forgotten how old he looked before. She
had done everything she could to avoid looking anyone in
the eye back then, especially the heretic. Beneath a sparse
thatch of white hair, the brand on his forehead was a little
faded.

"Do you remember me?" she asked.

The heretic made a face, dismissing the question.

"Forgot me?"

"I have not been permitted to do that," he said.

She pursed her lips to hold her next question inside,
but still it escaped. "Do you regret firing that shot?" The
wounded spike in her voice was audible; and he heard it,
and he saw that she too heard it, and he relented a little,
sliding upright so they could face one another.

He said, "It would be right for me to regret it, but I can
only manage to feel guilty."

"What's the difference?"

"I don't wish I had not done it. Of course, I had to do it.
I only wish the cost had not been a life lost by a gun that I
fired."

"Well, I'm grateful to you," said Magdala. The heretic
lowered his head. They were quiet for a moment. She said,
"Did you bury him?"

"No," said the heretic incredulously, as if such an idea
was so foreign to him that he could not fully understand it.
"Should I have buried him? Would that mean anything,
after the way I took his life?"

"Make certain he's dead."

The heretic coughed, suppressing what might have been
a laugh. "A shot to the head was not enough?"

"You know as well as anyone that nothing's really good
enough in the Sonoran."

He considered. "Do you think that he's still living?"

"Maybe not living. But something." She didn't know how to explain what had happened between the Deputy and Elkhanah as they held her at gunpoint. Slowly, he got to his feet. She led him back through the camp of the cactus-sitters.

Renato insisted that no one go into the desert at night. Too many dangers, he said. Animal dangers, vegetable ones. If Magdala and the heretic were to encounter any trouble, the cactus-sitters might not be capable of rescuing them.

"If we wait, he'll be the trouble," was all that Magdala said as she swung astride the mule. The animal was her property—or at least belonged more to her and to Araceli than to anyone else—and she was not a cactus-sitter, so the cactus-sitters could not strictly forbid the expedition. Only the hard, piercing look Renato gave to the heretic as they rode past the cactus-sitters' tents made Magdala hesitate. It was a look which promised that his disobedience would not be soon forgotten.

"You aren't one of them, are you?" she said to the heretic as they made for the west. The heretic walked beside the mule's shoulder, eyes on the soil.

"A cactus-sitter? Not any longer. I have broken the code by which they live, and that is a serious thing for them."

"But you were one before? You meditated on a cactus?"

He was almost laughing. "When I left Las Vegas, I was hopeful," he said. "That sounds strange, after what we experienced, but I was. And I wanted to be with other people. I wanted to show and be shown mercy. The cactus-sitters— and they do not call themselves that, you know—are merciful, but they are also exacting. I did meditate on a cactus. I endured the physical ills that come with it. I lived by their code. Until a few days ago."

She was afraid to ask: "Would you have been a cactus-sitter until you died if not for me?"

"It doesn't matter anymore. They will not accept a murderer into their order."

"But *would* you have?"

"I don't know," he said, with reluctance. "But I cannot be one now."

They had no trouble finding the place where the thing that was neither entirely the Deputy nor Saint Elkhanah had been shot. The air thickened as they drew closer and began to stink in the heady, too-sweet desert way that Magdala knew well. Startling vegetable growth came with the smell. Although she had seen men sprout into cactuses and fuse with inhuman things in their postmortem existences, she had not seen a corpse blossom into a whole otherworldly landscape.

Abruptly, the land was not barren, but flourishing grotesquely. A carpet of reddish-black undergrowth advanced tide-like to the top of the hillside. The mule's ears flicked anxiously backward as they descended through the tangle of weeds; after his hooves first brushed the leaves, he lifted his feet too high when he stepped, avoiding contact. Magdala prodded him onward, keeping a two-fisted grasp on the animal's mane. His breathing felt rapid and shallow beneath her. She could hear, as if from a great distance, the sound of whistling.

If the heretic was unsettled by the plant growth, he did not show it. On the border between the pale dirt and the dark vegetation, he stepped forward, not slowing or hesitating.

The weeds got denser and higher as they went on, first hitting the mule's ankles, then his flanks, then his shoulders. The heretic whacked branches aside with his walking stick, but the mule shied at the feeling of the leaves against his face, tossing his head and shifting uneasily from side to side. Magdala at last had to dismount and limp along.

"Never seen a death do this," she said to the heretic, who had been silent as they waded deeper into the forest of brush.

"We're close to him," said the heretic.

Magdala did not ask how he knew. The growth now extended past their heads. The confined feeling of walking inside of it was nauseating to Magdala. Her hands kept clutching at the branches to hollow out a little territory which was only hers, and the branches kept clustering in narrow, elaborate serpentines around one another and around her. There was something sentient in them, something hungry. The same fear rose in her that must have risen in the mule, and she felt again the sensation of something—the saint, she thought, or maybe now the desert itself—wanting to get inside.

"Here," said the heretic definitively. She thought, how does he know, why does he know, but she did not question him. He knelt and dug into the vegetation with her walking stick, fracturing branches and vines, exposing naked white soil that had the look of salt and a single sprout in a full, lush color that was foreign to Magdala as a desert child. He dug with his fingers into the dirt surrounding the sprout and brought up its roots, which trailed like gray hairs or telephone wires from the earth. Their reach seemed unending.

He pulled until he held the sprout above his head, then pulled some more. The sprout was connected to the rest, the black tendrils and the white dirt and the botanical odor of the wind. At the bottom of its roots was Saint Elkhanah's single skeletal foot. It emerged from the soil with a sudden burst, the bones of the toes clattering noisily together, and at once the whispers were silenced; they were, Magdala thought, just bones.

"It's not him," the heretic said, bewildered.

Her confession came seamlessly then. "I stole the bones of Saint Elkhanah from the Church," said Magdala. "I carried them all through the desert. And . . . something happened when I gave them back to the Deputy." She could not grasp what kind of hybrid thing they had become, the dead man and the living one, except that Elkhanah had at last found a life he could crawl inside and it had not been hers.

There was laughter on the heretic's face as he examined the bones; there was not condemnation. "And why did you do that?" he asked.

She explained the entire thing, the theft and the flight and the five years preceding, as they crossed back through the undergrowth. As they retraced their path, the vegetation underfoot began to wither and shrink; at the edges, the weeds were curling up into themselves, turning from hungry creeping things into delicate, lace-like ashes. At the crest of the hill, the heretic lowered himself to his knees and began, almost frantically, to dig.

"Where is the other one?" he asked. "You said you stole them both."

Magdala nodded. "I can get it," she said, hesitatingly. "If you want."

She dreaded the return to that hillside. If the other saint's foot had sprouted an entire forest, the one she had abandoned in the creosote bush might have done anything. But it was worse to think what might happen if the saint's bones were left unburied, so she mounted the mule and rode the short distance to the place where she'd hidden

Saint Elkhanah's second foot. She released a held breath when she saw the mundane look of the brush, first relieved and then fearful that someone or something had carried off the relic's other half. She dismounted and crawled into the brush. There in the depths was the single skeletal foot, looking as ordinary as any set of sun-bleached desert bones. On impulse, she glanced over her shoulder, half-expecting to see the ghost, resurrected and Stetson-wearing, taunting her. But he was not there. The wind moved softly through the brush, stirring up its herby, deep odor; the bones lay still.

She and the heretic buried the feet together. When they were finished, Magdala rose to her foot and extended her juniper stick to the heretic so he, too, could pull himself upright.

"I can't," he said softly, half-apologetically.

"Why?"

The heretic settled himself cross-legged before the grave. "This is something I must do," he said. "Please, do not take this from me."

Renato did not refuse when Magdala asked to plead the heretic's case, though his thin-lipped look of disapproval was plain enough. "The abbot has heard it already," he said. "Has heard the shots he fired, too. We are still not even certain where he got a weapon."

Magdala decided it was wiser to leave that question unanswered; it could only be her old revolver, her parting gift to him, that he had fired. She felt certain of it. "He'll die out there in the desert," she said.

"What makes you think he wants to live?" Renato asked. Magdala said nothing. She was almost certain that he did not. Still, she stood before a row of saguaros and waited as Renato lowered a white-haired, deeply sunburnt figure from their perch. With concerted effort, the hermit lowered themselves arduously to the ground. It was only when they settled in the dirt that Magdala recognized their face; remembered them younger, broader-shouldered, sitting across the fire from her father and handing a mule's lead to her.

"Magdala," they said tenderly. "You have come back to us."

Magdala did not ask if they knew all that she had done, the pilgrimages and un-pilgrimages and crossings through dark places. She had realized somewhere between leaving Caput Lupinum and the unearthing of Saint Elkhanah's foot that she did not need the cactus-sitters' absolution.

"I brought you a mule," she said.

"And a fine one, too," they said.

She hesitated then, gathering her nerve. "I'm here on Arturo's behalf," she said. "As his advocate."

The abbot nodded as if they had known already. "And what are you advocating for?"

"It wasn't murder, what he did. Or if it was, it can be repented. Don't let him be cast out always. Let him back in. I don't know what'll happen to him if he stays out there."

The abbot said nothing for a moment. The wind creaked in the old saguaros and some of the stylites shifted slightly on their perches. "He is where he should be," they said, at last.

"He's alone in the desert," Magdala said. "He'll die."

"Just as you found him."

"What do you know about any of that?"

"He told me," they said. "He spoke often of you, when first he came here. He said you saved his life."

"Did he say what else I did to him?"

"He did," they said. "And he told me what he did to you. Or rather," they amended, "what he could not do."

"I don't hold it against him," Magdala said. "He didn't heal my clubfoot, but he saved my life. He deserves to be here."

The abbot leaned back slightly, their frail body swaying as the wind passed through them. "It is not a question of deserving," they said. "Arturo's work is not here. Not with us."

"Where, then?" said Magdala.

"That is a question," they said, "for you, as much as him, to answer."

Magdala went every day to see the heretic. Sometimes Araceli came too, clutching a basket of broiled prickly pear or grilled lizard that one cactus-sitter or another had smuggled out of the camp. Sometimes Magdala came alone with only a canteen of groundwater that she had dug herself, not wanting to impose on the cactus-sitters. On the first two days, the heretic had to be made to drink; she forced open his mouth and wasted half the bottle getting a few sips down his throat. The third day, he held the bottle in his own hands and looked scornfully in Magdala's direction, but not at her face, as he drank. The fourth day, he accepted food, but only a little.

The fifth day, the heretic agreed to stretch his legs, and when he stood, she saw that where he had buried the bones, a sprout was growing. The color of the plant looked stark and improbable against the cautious palette of the surrounding landscape. If Magdala had not known its real origins, she would have thought it had come from someplace else, someplace still exploding with the kind of life that did not come even after death in the Sonoran.

The sixth day, the sprout had lengthened into a vine, small eager leaves forming.

The seventh day, seedlings were sprinkled across the desert floor, their leaves dripping not with the poisonous-smelling fluids of the dead, but with spontaneous effusions of water, pure and colorless and bright.

The eighth day, the heretic was surrounded by a dense thatch of young growth, all vivid, all incomprehensible, and the first sapling had begun to sprout a firm, green fruit. And Magdala realized that what he was doing was the same thing he had done in the shed with Jeroboam's snakebite, and what he was healing now was not a single wound on a human body, but a wound in the landscape, a lesion or scar or bruise that would have blighted the desert forever if he had not been permitted his bewildering gift.

The ninth day, Araceli came to see what he had done, and she could not be made to keep a secret; she flew back to the cactus-sitters and informed them, anyone who would listen, that Arturo had made a sanctuary in the desert.

"They will not come," said the heretic. "They will not want to see it."

He was right: Some of the cactus-sitters came, but none stayed, and they looked with fear and suspicion on the abomination that was a lush field of melons in the middle of the Sonoran. Magdala could not begrudge them their disquiet. She, too, was chilled by the speed of the growth, the weariness on the heretic's face as he worked his ongoing miracle, the intimacy between the withered body of the man and the voluptuous body of the landscape. She was afraid he might die when he finished. But when she came to him on the tenth day, he took hold of her cane for support and got slowly to his feet.

"Where are we going?" he asked her.

She did not hesitate. "Someone said it's my work to carry the saints to the far corners of the Remainder."

They followed the sunset into the west, the heretic leaning on a walking stick, Magdala with Araceli astride the mule. On the horizon, roving clusters of stuffed men crept inexorably toward the end of the world. Empty mesquite pods rattled, dry leaves hissed, the wind rasped through the dead branches of the paloverde trees. But everywhere behind them, a carpet of budding melon sprouts followed.

Acknowledgments

Thanks to Laura Cameron, for first believing in this book and for helping me to transform *Desert Creatures* from a quest romance to a novel.

To Sarah Guan, for helping me to fully realize both the Remainder and my heretic.

To Sarah again, along with Martin Cahill, Cassandra Farrin, Viengsamai Fetters, Kasie Griffitts, Dana Li, Kelsy Thompson, and the entire team at Erewhon for bringing *Desert Creatures* into the world.

To Ronan Sadler, for insights on portraying disability.

To Jerrold Hogle, for teaching me to rewrite.

To my theology professors at Seattle Pacific University, for teaching me to read the prophets.

To Craig Childs, for his book *The Secret Knowledge of Water*, an invaluable resource on death and survival in American deserts; Henri Nouwen, for his many writings on the desert fathers and mothers that inspired my cactus-sitters; and James S. Griffith, for *A Spiritual Geography of the Pimería Alta*, which deeply enriched my understanding of holy places and practices in the Southwest.

To all those who maintain the Santa Cruz River Park's running trail in Tucson, Arizona, where most of this book was mentally written before it was on the page.

And finally to Joe, for reading a dozen drafts of the same scenes. And for everything else.

Reading Guide

EREWHON

About the Author

© Caroline King

Kay Chronister is a finalist for the Shirley Jackson and World Fantasy Awards for her short fiction, which has appeared in *Strange Horizons*, *Clarkesworld*, *Beneath Ceaseless Skies*, *The Dark*, and elsewhere. Her first collection, *Thin Places*, was published by Undertow Publications in 2020. Originally from Washington State, she has spent time in Virginia, Cambodia, and Arizona. She now lives in the Philadelphia area with her dogs and her husband. *Desert Creatures* is her first novel.

Discussion Questions for
Desert Creatures

These suggested questions are to spark conversation and enhance your reading of *Desert Creatures*.

1. How do you interpret the novel's title, *Desert Creatures*? What does it mean to be a "desert creature" in this book? If you were to create a film or TV adaptation of this book, what alternative titles might you suggest?

2. Throughout *Desert Creatures*, characters fear the desert "getting inside of them." What might the threat of desert sickness symbolize? Why do you think some characters seem to be more vulnerable to desert sickness than others?

3. The cactus-sitters are based on a real tradition of early Christian hermits called stylites, who spent their lives meditating on pillars, columns, and clifftops. Stylites believed they could achieve spiritual clarity by living apart from the world without distractions. Their critics said they were merely avoiding the world's problems. How do you see the cactus-sitters' lifestyle? How do they compare to the Church of Las Vegas?

4. Discuss the relationship between Magdala and her father, Xavier. How does it compare with the other parent-child relationships that we see in the novel? What does it mean to be a good caregiver in the apocalyptic world of the Remainder? How does that compare with your understanding of what it means to be a good caregiver in your world?

5. How did your perspective on Magdala change after seeing her through the eyes of Arturo the heretic? What did his point of view add to your sense of the setting and characters? Were there any other characters whose perspectives you wanted to be included in the story? Why do you think the author chose not to include that character's point of view?

6. Arturo's flashbacks show several moments from his childhood and adolescence in the Remainder. Compare his coming-of-age experiences to Magdala's. How do gender, disability, family, and faith affect each of them differently?

7. Arturo repeatedly quotes a passage from the biblical book of Ezekiel: "Like emery, harder than flint have I made you." (Ezekiel 3:8–9). What is the significance of this quotation for Arturo in particular and the characters of Desert Creatures in general?

8. What stood out to you most about the novel's depiction of Las Vegas? Why do you think the author chose to represent Las Vegas, which has been nicknamed "Sin City," as a religious center akin to the Vatican in this changed world?

9. How do Magdala's feelings about her disability change after she reaches Las Vegas? How does the outcome of her pilgrimage influence her perspective going forward?

10. Why do you think Magdala decides to take Araceli to Mrs. Whitemorning? How do her feelings about Araceli change over the course of the journey, and why? Did your perspective on Magdala change during this section of the book?

11. On page 252, Magdala explains, "How the desert is now, dead-looking things aren't dead and living things aren't always alive." What other examples of this confusion between death and life in the novel, either symbolic or literal, did you notice as you read? How does the confusion of death with life create horror—and hope—for people in the Remainder?

12. If you had to join one of the many settlements that Magdala encounters on her travels through the Remainder, which one would you choose and why?

13. Compare Magdala's three journeys across the Remainder. How does her relationship to the desert landscape change with each journey, and how does she herself change? If you were to frame your own personal development through three major undertakings from your life so far, what would you choose? How did the locations of those experiences impact your journey?

More from Erewhon Books